THE QUETZAL SUMMER

Katie Hickman

Hodder & Stoughton

LONDON SYDNEY AUCKLAND

The publisher and author would like to thank Faber & Faber Ltd for their kind permission to quote from 'Church Going' by Philip Larkin from his *Collected Poems*.

British Library Cataloguing in Publication Data

Hickman, Katie
    The quetzal summer.
    I. Title
    823[F]

    ISBN 0-340-56842-9

First published by Hodder & Stoughton 1992

Published by Hodder and Stoughton, a division of Hodder and Stoughton Ltd, Mill Road, Dunton Green, Sevenoaks, Kent TN13 2YA. Editorial Office: 47 Bedford Square, London WC1B 3DP.

Photoset by Rowland Phototypesetting Ltd, Bury St Edmunds, Suffolk.

Printed in Great Britain by St Edmundsbury Press Ltd, Bury St Edmunds, Suffolk.

This book is for my grandmother
Granny Kay
from her loving and only granddaughter

Acknowledgements

No book is ever written in a vacuum, and this was no exception. My thanks as always go to William Sieghart, Sarah Sackville-West, and particularly to Beatrice, James, Phoebe and Lara Hollond for their limitless support and hospitality during its writing (indeed, by the end, I was almost part of the furniture). Thanks also to my parents, John and Jenny Hickman, to Libby and Alexander Russell, Margaret Nairne, Felicity Bryan and my editor Carole Welch.

Last but by no means least, my love and thanks to Tom, my husband, for his special support and for being, as usual, my best critic and my best friend.

A serious house on serious earth it is,
In whose blent air all our compulsions meet,
Are recognised, and robed as destinies . . .

Philip Larkin

ONE

I know you will laugh when I write this, but from the first day I always loved Connie's house.

It is not like the others in the crescent, all white stucco and English diffidence behind a clipped box hedge. Connie's house is exactly as you always described it, and pleases no one but herself: a maverick grey tooth in this complacent white smile of buildings.

Not a house, but a museum piece, is what you always said; a mausoleum, with its ticking clocks and old lady smell of peppermints and starch. You would enjoy the white stucco, I think. In certain lights the sweep of houses is not unbeautiful, but to me they seem like passionless places, too uniform to have any powers of their own. They offer no enchantments, the way that some houses do, to set their occupants down on a particular path, to give them a sense of permanence or of belonging. It is strange to think that the sense of the past within these rooms should have so oppressed you, when for me it has become a kind of liberation.

It is late summer here now, and dusty roses grow at random across the front of the house. At night I can hear their delicate heads knocking against my window.

Connie has been very kind to me. Of all the aunts, I remember you saying, she always was your favourite, the odd

9

one out, the rebel. She is not like an old person at all. She has a directness about her, a gift for intimacy, which I find fascinating; a way of leaning forward when she talks to you, twisting the rings on her fingers, as though you are the only person in the world who can understand her. Her hands are still beautiful, artist's hands, even at her age. When she speaks they dart around her like little flashing fishes. She is a good listener, too. I do not find her in the least English.

She has given me the room which you used to sleep in when you lived here, all those years ago. "You remind me so much of your mother," she is always saying, which pleases me.

Do you remember the room? It's the one right up at the top of the house, on the third floor. When I first arrived it was quite bare – now that Connie lives here alone, that part of the house is all shut up – but for some reason, I don't know why, the empty space is more resonant of you than anywhere else in the house. I can imagine you sitting at the window looking out over the rooftops of the white houses, and beyond them to the green blur of Kensington Gardens. The wallpaper is the one you chose, although a little peeling now, its pattern faded from the sun.

"How strange, your mother always liked that room too," Connie said when I first asked her about it.

I was sitting with her in the little drawing room, the one she calls the morning room. We were looking at photographs. She has piles of them stuck into books, their pages mottled, tinged with the frail smell of the past.

"I can't think why she liked it. All those stairs to climb and no bathroom nearby. By far the most inconvenient room in the whole house, but she liked it. Your mother always knew what she wanted. The sloping roof and the view, she said. She felt freer up there, I expect."

"Freer?"

"From us. The Aunts." She spoke without rancour, as if it was something she assumed I would know. "Even when she was older, she never would sleep anywhere else. I still think of it as 'Bettina's room'."

There are many photographs of you in her collection,

tiny old-fashioned black and white prints of you when you were a child, riding on her back or slung against her hip; and then, later, sitting on a shingled beach, your eyes dark against the glare of the sun. Further on there are ones of you as a young woman in a long dress: glamorous, gay pictures. You must have been about my age, and I found myself wondering what it would have been like to know you then, as Connie did.

"Bettina was always laughing," she said. "You can't imagine how much I missed her when she went away."

'We are connected now,' I kept thinking. 'It is not so much by family blood – how can I feel affection for a family I have never known? – as by a pool of memories across which you are the only stepping stone.'

*   *   *

Being in a city again makes me restless. In the afternoons I go walking. Sometimes Connie comes with me, but these days she cannot walk too far, so usually I go on my own. I find I can think better that way.

At first I used to go to the park, but lately I have taken to walking around the streets. As I walk I often wonder how much of this London you would recognise, and whether you would still feel at home here. Connie says it has changed a good deal. The church in the crescent gardens, St Mary's, has been closed now. Weeds have grown up under the doors; the Holy Ghost boarded up in darkness and the cobweb smell of mice droppings.

There is an area a few streets away from here where I often find myself, a place of hotels and cheap lodging houses. Sometimes when I am walking there it feels as if I have entered a ghetto, a place populated only by itinerant people, by exiles and the dispossessed. When the evenings are warm people sit out on the steps leading down to the street: Arabs, and African people turbaned in heavy silks. From the open windows I hear their music floating out across the lines of washing into the night.

I feel as though I am trying to find something, although I am still not entirely sure what it could be. A familiar face, perhaps, or a landmark; something I can recognise, something which will pull me into the slipstream of this new life. But when I look around me it is all so alien still. It's as though all my life I have been carrying round a crystallised image of England – a land of lace curtains and five o'clock tea, and cricket matches – an England which no longer exists, but which has been imprisoned for ever in the fickle amber of your memory.

Almost all the shops around here are run by Indians. They stay open until late at night. Most of them are grocery stalls, but there is one on a corner which I pass which is a kind of curio shop. It reminds me a little of the *papelerias* that we have at home, those dim slips of shops, hardly bigger than a passageway, which sell trinket jewellery and cheap plastic toys, pencils and exercise books. The doorway is hung with bunches of scarves, as bright as birds' feathers. The first time I passed by I stopped to look at them. They were so beautiful. I picked one up and put it to my face. Immediately I smelt a faint trace of incense which seemed to have been woven into the silk, like another deeper pattern, redolent of other lands. For a moment I could believe that it was not India which I was holding in my hands, but the sweet dark essence of home. The smell of Santa Luz.

Is this what you felt when you left here for ever for my father's country? And what did you do to fill the void?

They say that I am like you, a survivor.

I do not mind the nights here. At night I know I will dream about Santa Luz again. It is in the mornings when I wake up to the sound of London, and to the dusty scent of roses through my window, it is then that I feel something very like despair.

Two

There were no roads to Santa Luz in those days.

They had spent their honeymoon on the boat, six weeks across the Atlantic, through the Panama Canal, and then down the Pacific Coast to the capital, Veracruz; from there the train to the nearest town, Altamirada, and then two wearying, jolting hours along the mountain tracks in Jack's old jeep to the house itself.

What had her first impressions been? Thinking back, Bettina always remembered the boat and the train journeys best. The boat she remembered through an erotic haze of excitement and fear: the white breasts of the seagulls flashing against the horizon, the smell of the hot oily deck and the sea spray; the long nights drifting under the stars towards an unknown land.

She was the only woman on board. A young bride and queen of all she surveyed for those long blue weeks at sea. In the evenings they sat at dinner with the Captain who flirted with her in the mild, courteous way of his race, and called Jack a lucky devil. She could sense the rest of the crew watching her, covertly, whenever she passed by.

But Bettina did not care about any of that. She cared only about Jack, blue-eyed, laughing Jack Hallett, who in two short months had stolen her heart away.

They had arrived in Veracruz after nightfall, the darkness intensifying the alien scent of the place. She remembered the rush of air against her face, with its flavouring of rotted fruit, almond blossom and urine; the way the heat had bandaged itself around her like the coils of a snake. On the quayside there had been a press of Indian porters, a squat, dark-skinned people whose faces, in the darkness, were watchful copper masks. She remembered her elation at the strangeness of it all, and the faint, disturbing flutter of nausea which followed.

"I have a surprise for you," Jack said when they arrived at the station, "but you must promise not to look until I say."

He tied a scarf around her eyes and led her, laughing and stumbling in her high heels along the platform, seeing nothing, but hearing all around her the tones of an unfamiliar language.

Still blindfolded, he handed her up some steps into the train. "Here we are, you can look now."

"Oh!"

"Do you like it?" He sounded anxious.

"Oh, but it's *beautiful*."

The carriage was like an inlaid box: mahogany walls with delicate ebony tracery; a table laid with a white cloth; antimacassars on fat, horsehair armchairs; polished brass fittings and a porcelain basin decorated with flowers in the bathroom. A cool, composed world, far removed from the hot squalor of the quayside and railway platform.

"It belonged to the Peron y Imbaburras, the previous owners of the Hacienda Santa Luz, my farm," Jack told her. "They let me have it when I bought the land, part of the job-lot as it were."

"You mean you own it? That all this is just for us?"

"Just for us," Jack said, delighted by her rapture. "At Santa Luz everything was always done in this style. You'll see for yourself soon enough."

And so they had travelled all through the long night, insulated in their private dream. Bettina was too restless to sleep much. She left Jack's bed and sat by the window, her cheek against the horsehair, listening to the hiss of the steam, straining her eyes into the darkness.

South America. The land of the tango.

Dislocated, luminous images – of conquistadors and cattle ranches, of exquisite horsemanship, and dark-eyed women in lace mantillas – lingered at the edges of her mind.

A brilliant, savage, romantic land. Jack's land.

She watched her husband sleeping, one long arm thrown up over his face; sleeping away the space of time which separated him from Santa Luz. Even now her whole body seemed to liquefy when she looked at him, cancelling out all other thought or need.

* * *

There were those who would always think Jack Hallett an unlikely inheritor of Santa Luz. His parents, conspicuous only by their Englishness, had come in the early part of the century to Maldonado, the flat desert town of the south, where his father had been a manager in a railway construction company. Despite the intransigence of the land, the family thrived there and even conceived an unexpected affection for the place, which was filled with like-minded Britons shipped over in the prosperous wake of the railways, as miners and missionaries.

Those were the days of a certain kind of pioneer, of people who built Empires gladly. They did not think of themselves as tough. As soon as they realised that they were there to stay, the women planted gardens for themselves in their back yards. When watered, the dust-ground would break itself, unasked, into exotic blooms. Poinsettias grew wantonly; banks of erotic-scented jasmine and oleanders proliferated, and had to be cut back like a weed. Strangely, the chillier English roots and flowers which they planted, the carrot, the cabbage and the rose, showed no such resilience.

15

The harder they were to come by, the greater they were prized above all the more delicate fruits of the land.

Self-sufficient, upright, they learnt to speak imperfect Spanish with aplomb.

Jack Hallett, an intense, restless boy always outgrowing his strength, was not contained for long by Maldonado. His energy took him in bouts of wanderlust to all four corners of the untamed continent, from Brazil and Uruguay to the Orinoco River and the brittle wastes of Patagonia. And when he finally came home it was not to Maldonado, but to the north of the country where he bought the farm Santa Luz.

It was an unlikely ending. Like many outsiders he connected truly with the land, although it was said that this putting down of roots had knocked some of the adventuring out of him. There were rumours that there had been a woman there, an Indian girl, so it was no wonder the subject was rarely talked about by the British.

Bettina neither knew nor cared. Love had come swiftly on the summer ballroom balcony. Mad, bad, intoxicating love. Stronger than both of them: stronger than reason; stronger, even, than the Aunts.

"I'm going to carry you away," he had said, "to my kingdom, to Santa Luz. For ever." So they were married in St Mary's church, she in an old white mini skirt, he in a borrowed morning coat.

Except for Connie, none of the Aunts came, and the house across the road stood silently, veiled with their disapproval and rage.

"You are mine, all mine, my brave girl," he had said, taking her in his arms. "There's no going back now."

Dawn came at last, sliding a soft finger of light along the horizon, between the mountains and the sky.

*   *   *

So what had she thought, the first time she set eyes on Santa Luz? Once a place has become familiar, imbued with one's own memories, it is impossible to recall it in any other light. But Jack had talked about it so often that she must have held a picture of it in her mind. Had it been as she imagined?

He had been nervous, almost irritable with her in the jeep, in his impatience for her to see it. She had felt tired and travel-stained (no water had been forthcoming from the shining brass taps), and the jolting of the car was beginning to give her a stitch.

"Nearly there," he kept saying, "just one more corner. Not this one, the next one."

They were driving along an avenue of eucalyptus trees. Their leaves gave off a faint astringent smell. The tyres of the car kicked up little pools of powdery white earth.

"Nearly there." Jack picked up her hand and squeezed it. "Wait for it! Just round this corner . . . look, look . . . Now!"

And there, in the dying light, Santa Luz rising up like a shimmering white phoenix from the lap of the mountainside. Santa Luz with its twenty-four courtyards, its fountains, patios and sudden rose gardens; its endless verandahs and colonnades; the chapel; stables; secret underground wells. An immense, lunatic fastness of stone and earth and mountain rock. And behind it, like an echo, the snow-capped peak of the mountain.

"My God, Jack." The jeep clattered through the gateway into a vast sweep of courtyard. "My God." She cast him a quick, sideways glance.

"Well, what do you think?"

"It's . . . it's extraordinary," Bettina said, a little breathless still. Aware that she must, at all costs, seek out the right response.

She looked around her. In the centre of the courtyard a cross, crudely hewn from grey stone. At its base, grass and weeds beneath the cobbles. A little way off lying against a wall in the last rays of sun, a broken white column.

"Why are you laughing?"

"Darling, darling, no!" She held out her arms to him. "Here, help me down." They stood silently, side by side, in the Great Court.

"Don't you see," she said at last, "I'm so excited. Here I am at Santa Luz at last." She paused, looking up at him. "It's beautiful. Really it is." And it was. A vast, beautiful ruin.

*　　*　　*

At the beginning, of course, Bettina had seen Santa Luz through Jack's eyes. Through his focus and his energy the ravaged shell was transformed into a palace of marvels.

"What you must try to do," she would always remember him saying as he led her through the decaying labyrinth for the first time, "is imagine Santa Luz as it used to be. It was a famous hacienda once; one of the greatest in the whole country, perhaps even the whole continent."

Jack knew Santa Luz's every crack and stone like a catechism. As he talked, he guided her through the eastern courtyards where the rot had first set in; where paint like leprous flesh flaked from delicate balustrades; where the cracked and fallen masonry was now possessed by a vegetable madness of hibiscus and bougainvillaea grown to the size and strength of jungle creepers.

"I was quite young the first time I came here, when the Peron y Imbaburras still owned the place. The old *patron*, Pedro Peron y Imbaburra's eldest grandson, Patricio, was a friend of mine. I can't really describe what it was like, but I felt almost as if I had been bewitched. I probably had," he laughed. "Anyway I knew then that someone, someday, was going to have to rescue this place after the old man had gone, and that that person was going to be me."

18

"You mean you are going to repair it?" Jack's excitement caught at her, until she too had seemed bewitched. "All of it?"

"In time. Yes, all of it."

They had come to an enclosed courtyard. A quietness filled the space, and the smell of old cold stone. At its centre a once-ornamental avocado tree, now grown to monstrous size, thrust blasphemous fingers in through the walls and windows, and the soft adobe roofs broke open to the sky like frail brown eggshells. Through the canopy of the branches, the mountain light filtered into pale green, aqueous shadows.

Bettina watched Jack as he moved through the archway ahead of her and across the flagged stone, his tall, thin form moving with assurance. Santa Luz seemed to have recharged him with energy. But it was not directed at her.

He was wearing a blue shirt that day, and a pale straw panama which he wore pulled down over his eyes. He had stood with his back to her looking up at the tree, absorbed and unaware of her absence. For the first time his concentration on her seemed dissipated, as though he had become detached from her, apart.

"Who is this man?" she thought as she watched him move away. He was absolutely strange to her. It was the briefest insight, a moment of unease lasting no longer than the trace of a shadow under the avocado tree.

"You really love it, don't you?" she had said, coming up behind him.

"Yes." Jack turned back to her at last, the old Jack who loved her, and nothing, after all, had changed. "Someone has to love it." He reached up over her head and picked one of the flowers which hung in a scarlet pediment over the archway. Young tendrils were already racing out across the flagstones like green fire, prising their way between the stones with surprising, insidious strength. Tenderly Jack placed the flower between two locks of her hair. "A house like this is like a woman, it will die without love."

Ahead of them beyond the avocado tree was a stone

19

façade, and in the centre of it a gateway, crudely embellished with carvings. On one side of the gateway stood the figure of a bearded man clad in armour and helmeted like a conquistador. In one hand he held a sword, and in the other a long-handled axe. His body was compressed into a stone niche, an elongated, fluid form, despite the heavy armour. Under his foot was the head of an Indian, his tongue lolling grotesquely under the pressure of the conquistador's boot.

"Manuel Imbaburra," Jack said.

They stood looking up at the stone man. The conquistador's eyes stared straight ahead, fixed on some invisible, private horizon.

"It was Manuel Imbaburra and his sons who built the original part of Santa Luz," Jack said. "This is the entrance to it, through here."

He led her through the gateway into another courtyard, smaller and darker than the rest, flanked with squat stone pillars. "There's something here I want you to see."

On the far side of the courtyard, the pillars ended in a blank wall. On the wall was a second sculpture. It was not a whole figure this time, but a solitary, gargoyle-like head. The figure strained forward giving the momentary impression that the rest of the creature, although unseen, was also there imprisoned behind the bricks and mortar.

"What is it, an animal of some kind?"

Bettina gazed at the figure, trying to make out the unfamiliar form: a snarling jaw, curved teeth, curious, flaring stone nostrils.

"It is very old," Jack said, "almost certainly older than the house. No one knows what it is for sure, or even how it got here, but there's a theory that it's a representation of Quetzalcoatl."

"Quetzal-what?"

"Quetzalcoatl. The Plumed Serpent. Look," he reached up and traced along the stone with his finger. "This is the snake's jaw. The eyes. These petal shapes are the plumes, the feathers of the quetzal, framing the back of its head."

20

"It looks sinister."

"No, not at all. Rather the opposite, in fact. Quetzalcoatl was a peace-loving god. He is supposed to have outlawed human sacrifice, which was the usual fare of gods in those days. Instead the Indians worshipped him with butterflies."

"Butterflies! What a wonderful idea."

"It's a wonderful legend. Quetzalcoatl is supposed to have been a civilising god, the inventor of agriculture, of writing, and even the calendar. Of all the arts in fact. He was also the patron of priests and priestly knowledge. His reign was a time of great happiness and abundance, but because he outlawed human sacrifice he also made many enemies. According to one version of the legend, when Quetzalcoatl's enemies finally defeated him, he built his own funeral pyre, immolated himself, and then rose up into the sky to become the morning star. In another version he is supposed to have put out to sea in a raft made of snakes, promising to return one day and restore his dynasty."

"They don't make stories like that any more, do they?" Bettina smiled.

"The most curious thing is how it came to be here at all. Quetzalcoatl was originally the god of the Toltecs, in ancient Mexico, thousands of miles north of here. Eventually the cult did spread to other parts of Central America – the Aztecs adopted him, and later the Maya – but there is no record, as far as we know, that it was ever practised down here in the south."

Bettina stared up at the serpent's head, carved sinuously into the stone. The god's eyes stared blankly back at her.

"That's Santa Luz for you." Jack put his arms around her shoulders, drawing her to him. "You've seen it all now, my darling. Do you think you can learn to love this crazy place?"

"I love *you*."

'He is obsessed with it,' she thought with sudden clarity. 'Shouldn't he have told me; shouldn't he have explained? He told me nothing. Do I mind?'

21

"That's not the same thing."

"Ah, but I rather think it might be," Bettina laughed, turning away from the statue's gaze. 'He loves me, she thought, and I love him. That is enough. Isn't it?'

That night she dreamt that she was running down an endless corridor, pursued by swarms of butterflies, thousands upon thousands of them, red and gold and emerald butterflies, hissing and spitting at her like snakes.

*   *   *

In time Bettina forgot her dream. In those days she wrote often to Connie. They were unusually long letters, full of the conviction that she was as beguiled by Santa Luz as Jack would have her be.

To really understand Santa Luz you have to be able to imagine the landscape which surrounds it. We are high up in the very heart of the mountains here. The valley, lined with cart tracks and fields and avenues of eucalyptus trees, is cupped by them on both sides. The peak of the largest one, Cotacotani, is covered in snow all the year round.

It is very wild, and very beautiful: an immense, primitive landscape, the colour of old gold . . . although once you've seen it for yourself, the term "landscape" becomes too small, too insignificant, to do it justice.

Everything is on such a vast scale. The first time Jack took me out with him I found myself thinking that a landscape like this was not meant to be lived in by human beings at all. I have this odd notion that the Peron y Imbaburras built Santa Luz to the size it is because they felt impelled to do something to make their mark on the land, to stop themselves simply disappearing, vanishing back into the earth and rock, as if they were plants or lichens or animal bones.

Even the air here is extraordinary, and the light . . . I can't begin to describe what it's like. On clear days it's as though not only the sun and the sky, but the mountains themselves are shedding light, an absolutely pure translucence, but so thick that you get the feeling you could scoop it up in your hands and drink it. I feel as though I am drowning sometimes, drowning in the light.

Jack says that the only ones who have ever really felt at ease with the land are the Indians, because they have never felt the need to possess it in the way that we do.

They believe that spirits called apus *live on the peaks of the mountains, in the river and rocks, and in every natural thing. They still worship them, too, much to the priests' fury because they're all supposed to be good Catholics these days just like everyone else.*

Jack says that these people are different; that they have always gone their own way, and that no one has ever been able to change the way that they think. And I can believe it, although personally I despair of ever being able to tell exactly what they're thinking either way. I would never admit this to anyone else, but I find them rather daunting still, although they do look magnificent, all dressed in red and gold, the colours of Santa Luz.

As a matter of fact we have two Indians living here at the house. One is a man, Martin, who is known to everyone as Martin the Eye, because one of his eyes was scratched out by an eagle when he was a boy. He is a dark, rather sombre man, with watchful, pointed features which give him the air of a melancholy fox. Like all the men on the estate he wears a trilby hat, in all weathers, both in and outside the house, and keeps his hair tied back in a pigtail. I don't have much to do with him, because he is really Jack's man and I feel I shouldn't interfere too much, especially at the beginning.

Instead, I have Maria-Magdalena. Mary Magdalene. I wonder how I can describe her to you? Mary Magdalene is as delightful as she sounds: she is rather serious and very young, just fifteen and already as beautiful as her namesake. She started working for Jack two years ago (they start them young here, poor things) and was, I think, a little suspicious of me when I first arrived, although she always seems very anxious to please.

Her whole family worked here under the old patron, and her grandparents before that. A great Santa Luz tradition. I discovered

23

the other day that her father, who is known by everyone as Tio, or Uncle, is the local "curandero" or witchdoctor. I am assured that he is only allowed to perform good spells!

So, you see, my life here is nothing if not romantic.

She wrote, too, about Jack. She said how much she loved him, how happy they were at last, and how free.

She did not tell Connie about her dream.

*   *   *

"Jack, Jack! Where are you? They've arrived. Come quickly, Jack!"

Jack, discovered at last in the stables with Martin the Eye, came out to greet her.

"So this is where you've been hiding. This house! Really, it's impossible – I feel as if I've been looking for you for *days*."

"Then I'll have to get a whistle for you. Or a bell. Then you can summon me whenever you like."

"Come on, quickly!" Impatient, laughing, pulling him along the cobbles.

"What's the big fuss?"

"My boxes, my trunks. They've arrived. Oh, these damn cobbles. Such hell on my heels. At last. I can't believe it. The railway people arrived with them just now. In a horse and cart, can you believe."

"Ah-ha. I see. The heirlooms." A voice of mock doom. "The books. The Waterford glass. The portrait of Great Uncle somebody or other. You'll have Magdalena wearing a frilly apron next."

"And Martin in white gloves. Ha! fat chance. Don't tease your poor neglected wife."

"And why not? I like to tease her. I always tease, you should know that by now."

"Good grief. What on earth have you got in here." Jack stared at the pile of boxes.

"Oh, just a few things I left behind. We left in such a hurry, remember, I hardly had time to pack a thing."

"Five trunk loads of 'little things'?"

"Oh look, look. The ivory elephants . . . my little enamel boxes. I'd almost forgotten them," she tore impatiently at the tissue paper, "and what's this . . . oh, my mink coat. Connie, you genius."

Bettina, kneeling, pulled the coat from the bottom of the trunk, and drew it protectingly around her shoulders.

"So useful."

"Oh, Jack, you're impossible. Anyway, you said it gets quite cold here sometimes, in the winter."

"Yes, but maybe not quite that cold. Still, we might go to Siberia on a second honeymoon. Who knows?"

"Beast!"

"No, never that. I am delighted that you have your things at last, really I am."

As Jack watched her, he thought that he would always remember her as she appeared to him just then – a flame-haired Pandora among her boxes, knee-deep in whispering tissue paper. For him they were full of such insignificant things: but for her they were like treasure chests, crammed with memories like golden doubloons.

"A-ha, what's that? A camera. A Leica, too. Wherever did you come by this? Now that's more like it, something useful for a change. Look this way. Here, smile."

"I am smiling, can't you see?"

"Not good enough. Here, look at me. Say you love me."

"I love you, beast."

Click. A moment, a fragment of life, ensnared for ever.

"I love you too, my Bettina."

*   *   *

Bettina wanted a room of her own at Santa Luz, just one room which she could make entirely her own. Then, and only then, she would begin on the rest.

For several days she searched the house with thoroughness. It did not dismay her then, as it came to later, with its smell of decay and her own sense of powerlessness against it. For a time she was even filled, if not with Jack's rapture, then at least with a sense of new-found possession.

The two of them lived in the west quarter of Santa Luz, the only habitable part of the house, a series of plain whitewashed rooms stretching through a succession of courtyards to a long verandah overlooking the mountains.

Compared to the rest of the house these rooms seemed as chaste as convent cells, and curiously untouched by Jack, as though in this house so haunted by the memories of other men's lives, it was he who was the insubstantial shade, the ghost.

Now, with her new task in mind, Bettina started to explore the uninhabited wings of the house once again. It seemed to her that in spirit it was to the age of Manuel Imbaburra that Santa Luz belonged most closely. The long galleries, cloisters, and great echoing salons kept the faith, with their heavy furniture, the portraits filmy with mildew, and ceilings fretted with candle soot. In the *sala mayor*, the largest of the formal rooms, she found the curtains and damask hangings so shredded by moth and mice that she felt they would dissolve if she so much as put her hand to them. Other rooms were no more than empty spaces, partitioned with a Chantilly lace of spiders' webs. The whole house was imbued with an inconsolable spirit of the past, at once brutal and visionary: the steely breath of conquistadors.

After some days she found the room. It gave off on to a tiny courtyard, added on almost as an afterthought at the far end of a gallery which they occasionally used as a drawing room. The windows overlooked the mountain on one side, and on the other a small patio with a fountain at its centre. The fountain was in the shape of a pair of curved fishes, their stony scales flecked with lichen.

Bettina led Jack there unerringly. "Look, it's perfect for me. Not too big, but big enough for me to fit all my things." She drew her finger down one of the walls, the white-wash shedding at her touch like dust. "Magdalena and I can have it cleaned up in no time." She turned to Jack, winding her arms around his neck. "You have your study: and this shall be my place. Oh, I want it so much. Please?"

"Then you shall have it," Jack said, stooping to kiss her neck. "How can I refuse, when you look at me like that?"

But somehow the room never quite worked. It was the wrong shape, she decided, too long and thin. Her objects seemed too small, too insignificant to fill the space. Bettina, who had always prided herself on having some taste in these matters, could not understand her failure. It was as though the house, with its hidden symmetries, had some quality which would always elude her.

South America, the land of the tango. What is it that gives our private images of a place such potency? And why do we go on seeking them out long after reality has come creeping in, forever altering the way we dream? Years later the phrase would still come back to her, repeating itself in her mind like a half-remembered phrase of music, and she would wonder why such a delicate image should seem imbued with such sadness.

THREE

Yesterday Connie took me to meet Aunt Lucille. She lives in Kensington, and so we walked there together across the park.

Lucille lives in what Connie describes as a mews house.

"Too small for them really," she said in that dry voice she sometimes uses, "but the right address, don't you know."

They do not see much of each other these days, I gather, despite living so close.

"Your mother and Lucille always looked very much alike," Connie said as we walked along, "especially as children. All that wonderful hair. But inside they were always quite different. Different souls, I used to think."

It was a hot, dense afternoon. Connie walked slowly, very upright despite her cane. We passed the Round Pond, where lovers lay entwined together on the grass like sculptures.

"I used to bring them here, you know, to feed the ducks, when they were little girls," she said. "Bettina fell in once, I remember, and came out covered in weed. But it was Lucille who cried. Bettina had been wearing one of her dresses, and there it was covered in all this green slime, completely ruined."

We sat down for a moment on one of the benches overlooking the pond. The water was very still, full of clouds and blue smudges of London sky. The sound of the traffic was muffled behind the enclosure of trees.

"These young people, really!" She looked with amusement at the lovers, scattered with abandon over the grass. "Making love everywhere. In public. In the middle of Kensington Gardens! They have such freedom these days. In my day . . . sex was *much* more exciting in my day. Everyone seems to get what they want so quickly now. There's no romance to it any more. And no risk. Apart from that dreary AIDS disease. It must get so very dull after a while, I've always thought." Connie tapped with her cane against the pathway. "Bettina, your mother, now she was romantic."

"It's funny, but I never thought of her like that before I came here. Now I realise that she must have been. She took risks."

"Yes, she certainly did that." Connie stood up to go, smoothing her skirts. Two men walking by turned to look at her, approval, even admiration, in their eyes. "She had this tremendous energy always, this greater longing for life," she paused, as though reflecting, "which is why she had to get away. Well, I daresay you know what she's like, much better than I do these days." She gazed across the water. "It was your mother I was always closest to. I was closer to her than to any of my sisters, except possibly your grandmother before she died. It was I who encouraged her to get away, you know," she said, looking at me. "It was I who told her to go. My sisters never forgave me."

We walked on in silence for a while.

"What about Aunt Lucille. How did she feel?"

"Oh, Lucille. I always found it hard to know what Lucille was thinking. As I said, they are very different. They were never close, even as children. I don't think Lucille knows the meaning of the word love. Let alone sex."

"But she married, didn't she?"

"Oh yes, she married all right. Jeremy Bowyer. A perfect fool, I always thought. A rich fool, of course, which I suppose is something. You'll meet him presently. He was

29

Bettina's young man, you know, before she met your father – it seems incredible now – so I dare say Lucille thought she did rather well when Bettina went off, leaving the field open for her, as it were."

"Oh, Connie!"

"Don't laugh, darling, it's absolutely true. I know Lucille better than anyone, much to her displeasure. She doesn't approve of me at all."

"So this Uncle Jeremy could have been my father?"

"No, darling," Connie said with some emphasis, "not in a million years. Nor Lucille your mother. She and Bettina were so very different, although they did always look very much alike, deceptively so," she repeated as we entered the mews. "Oh, and Layla," at the door, Connie took my arm and linked it in hers.

"Yes?"

"Just one thing. Lucille wants very much to see you, I know she does, but she is not . . . an emotional person. Well, well," she pressed her cane against the doorbell, "you'll find out what they're all like for yourself, I dare say. Just bear it in mind, and don't be surprised by her."

A girl in an overall opened the door and took us up to a sitting room on the first floor. It was a long, narrow room, with a row of sash windows on one side overlooking the mews. The effect was like being inside a railway carriage, crammed with furniture and rather airless. The covers on the chairs and sofas were all in shades of pale-coloured biscuit, a little stiff perhaps, but very elegant. I had the feeling, just at first, that I would hardly dare to sit down for fear of disturbing their perfect plumpness and their symmetry.

"Aunt Connie?" A woman rose slowly to her feet. I looked up and for a moment it was you there, waiting for me, at the far end of the room.

"And this must be Layla."

Lucille came towards me, and kissed me lightly on the cheek. Her face was cool against mine, and had the dry powdery smell of expensive women; at once heavy and yet impersonal, like the perfume counter at a large department store, a smell quite unconnected with skin or blood.

"Come in, please, sit down. Susan will bring us some tea."

She nodded to the girl, and then sat down again in the same place from which she had arisen, a neat, precise movement, as though she did not want the room to suffer any unnecessary disturbance.

With the three of us sitting there, the room became like a tight little bandbox, shiny and new and claustrophobic.

"So . . ." Lucille's breath, exhaling softly outwards, was like a sigh. We looked at one another in silence. I wondered what you would have done, and said, if you had been there with us.

Lucille has the same pale skin as you, freckled lightly along the arms and legs, and the same Titian coloured hair, although she wears hers differently, swept back from her forehead in a smooth bob. That day she had pinned it in a tortoiseshell clip, although this was more for decoration than to secure her hairdo which had been so perfectly lacquered into place that it seemed to sit on, rather than fall from her head, like a beautiful, bronzed helmet.

Looking at her I found myself thinking, for the first time, that perhaps Santa Luz had not been kind to you over the years, that the sun and the mountain wind had ruined your skin. But your beauty is of another kind, and is still visible in the sculpture of your bones, and in your fine, delicate hands; in the way you hold yourself when you walk. Aunt Lucille, so plucked, pummelled and coiffed was, by contrast, like an expensively polished nut.

There was an odd, dislocated focus to that moment. The woman who was sitting there was you, and yet not you. She was a person to whom I was related – a blood relation, I kept telling myself – and yet she was a stranger, someone of whom I had absolutely no knowledge, and no connection other than the accident of my birth. Where were we supposed to begin?

"And how is . . . and how are you getting on?" Lucille said.

"Very well, thank you."

"And you, Aunt Connie, are you well?"

"Quite well, thank you. As you can see."

Connie did not seem to feel any such awkwardness. She was wearing a blue dress with peacocks embroidered on to it. In the pale room her azure figure was outrageously bright.

"My God, it's hot in here, Lucille. You don't mind if I open a window, do you? Poor Layla looks as if she is about to pass out."

Connie went to one of the windows and opened it. When she came back she sat down, irreverently, on another part of the sofa. The cushions subsided under her with a shocked sigh. She began to dig around in her bag, and brought out a packet of cigarettes.

"Still smoking? Really, Aunt Connie," Lucille smiled indulgently.

"At my age?" With deft, jewelled fingers, Connie fitted a cigarette rolled in dark paper into her cigarette holder, lit it, and inhaled deeply. "At my age, darling Lucille, I have discovered that I can do anything I please. It is most pleasurable, I find."

Delicately Lucille waved her hand across her face, as though to dispel a subversive fragment of smoke, a movement which contrived to be both placid and disapproving at the same time.

"Turkish," Connie said, regarding her without apology. "Delicious." She drew on her cigarette again. "Layla and I were just talking about Bettina."

We talked about you, of course. Lucille's questions were kind, but there was a certain detachment about them which made me feel as though we were all aiming at something, but kept missing the mark.

After a while the girl came in with a tea tray.

"So you are living with Aunt Connie in Bayswater."

32

It was half question, half statement; expertly deflecting us on to neutral ground.

"Yes. She has been very good to me."

"Nonsense, darling. It's your home here for as long as you want it, you know that." She turned to Lucille. *"Pas devant les domestiques?"* Connie gave a delighted chuckle. "I had almost forgotten. How delightfully middle-class," she said, quite loudly, to herself.

"Bayswater." Lucille, who appeared not to have heard Connie's aside, mused in my direction. "We have some great friends, the Elmhursts, who have just moved to Bayswater. Clarewell Road. Perhaps you know them, Aunt Connie? Johnnie and Mary Elmhurst?"

The way she said this seemed to imply that Bayswater was several light years away, instead of a relatively short walk across the park.

Then I thought: 'Perhaps she is right. Places nurture people, form and shape them, give meaning to their lives. How could the place which had nurtured Connie, so generous, so vibrant, so sudden and uncomplicated in her love, have also given birth to this person, sipping perfumed tea, as cool and detached as alabaster.'

I felt suddenly, and quite unreasonably, angry. How could I ever have mistaken her for you? Everything about her seemed contrived to match that immaculate, bloodless room. She had placed herself in it like an *objet*, perfect, covetable, devoid of human meaning. When I looked at her, I saw the fall of her camel coloured skirt, the slippery oyster silk shirt, the pearls. I saw only externals. Something essential was missing. There was none of your challenge in her, none of your spirit. And was I imagining it, or was there something pitiless in those pale eyes?

In the stillness of the room, china cups, as thin and transparent as tissue paper, rasped with the utmost gentleness against china saucers. I have not finished, I thought. I wanted to talk to her about you, and about Santa Luz. I wanted to make her understand. I had been afraid in my nervousness that I would talk too much, expose too much of myself and of her, in my un-English way. But English is a language in which it is not easy to talk about love. I felt the moment wither.

Outside the sun had begun to dip. It slanted in through the windows, catching at the tender blue tendrils of cigarette smoke. Lucille was talking about Debbie and Charles, her daughter and son. My cousins. First cousins. What did it all mean? The words glanced through my mind, spinning them out until their meaning dissolved; threshing them down to no more than two highly-charged husks.

Next to the window was a glass bowl filled with lilies, their white petals veined with green. Pollen had fallen to the floor in little pools of gold dust. It struck me that this was a strange choice of flower for a sitting room, too charged with meanings to be purely decorative. Perhaps, I thought, someone she knows has died. Even through the smoke I could smell their sweet, solemn scent.

When I was a child I can remember Magdalena once telling me that this was the smell of the Holy Ghost. And when I thought about this I was suddenly overwhelmed with longing for Santa Luz, a longing so strong it was like a physical sickness. I was winded by it, made breathless by this sudden, dazzling pain.

"They will be back soon," Aunt Lucille was saying. "I know how much they are longing to meet you."

I wanted to reply, but the words would not come. I had that curious sensation, as if in a dream, that I was trying to move, to speak, but that I could not. I was paralysed, weighted down with unbearable longing. I stood up and moved towards the window.

"Layla?" Connie looked up.

"Well, really!" I heard Aunt Lucille's voice behind me. "What does she think she's doing?"

"Are you all right, my darling?" Connie's voice was filled with terrible tenderness. "We can go home, if you would prefer."

"No. No, I'll be fine. Really."

How English it all was, this denial of pain. When I looked

down, I saw that my arms were filled with the lilies, crushed against my breast.

*   *   *

Somewhere in the empty house beneath us came the sound of a door slamming, then feet across the hall. I had the sensation that my heart was drumming in my ears. Which one of them was it: Debbie? Charles? I felt Connie remove the lilies from my arms, arrange the bruised buds back in the vase.

"Never mind," her hands were deft, assuaging, "stop squealing, Lucille, there's no harm done."

'Not now,' I remember thinking, 'not like this, I am not prepared.'

Outside I heard the sound of someone beginning to walk quietly up the stairs, so quietly that the footsteps were inaudible. The only sound came from the occasional uncertain creaking of floorboards up the stairwell.

"Debbie, is that you?" Lucille's gaze was fixed on the door. There was no reply. "I told her you were coming." A look of irritation passed over the placid mask. "Excuse me a moment."

As she opened the door, I caught a glimpse of a girl on the landing, a flash of red, a blonde head. From the passageway outside came the murmur of voices. After a few minutes the door opened again and Lucille re-entered. Behind her came two people, a girl and a boy.

"Layla, this is your cousin Debbie."

Standing in front of me I saw a very blonde, very pretty girl wearing a short red dress. She had large, protuberant blue eyes, which gave her a vaguely piscine look, like a startled fish.

"Debbie, this is Layla."

"Hello," Debbie held out her hand. She gave me an appraising up-and-down look. Her hand, despite the heat,

35

was cool and dry. "Aunt Constance, you too." Her tone was polite, but there was nothing in it to suggest whether she was either pleased or displeased. "How nice,' she added, as though it were an afterthought. Then, turning towards the boy, who was still standing in the doorway, "This is Luke."

Throwing herself down on the sofa, Debbie fixed her large blue eyes on her mother, "I've asked Luke to stay for tea." Her voice was breathy, curiously high-pitched, like a little girl's. Although her tone was as neutral as before, the challenge in this statement was unmistakable.

"Of course. Do come in, Luke." Lucille spoke silkily, but her face looked as if some unidentifiable but distasteful smell had permeated the room. "You had better go and fetch some more cups," she said to Debbie. For the first time there was an edge to her voice. I could see Connie regarding the visitor with amusement.

The boy, who was very tall and thin, folded himself into a chair opposite me. He was dressed in black; large, ungainly feet clad in a pair of resonant leather boots. The boots had strangely feminine pointed toes and buckles up the sides which jingled together as he walked. His hair, which was of an indeterminate brown, stuck up from the top of his head in tufts, as though he had been pulling it violently upwards between his fingers.

"It's very kind of you," he said, smiling at Lucille, apparently unaware of her disapproval. "I mean, I hope I'm not disturbing anything."

He sat back, resting one booted foot heavily against his knee.

"You say your name is Luke?" Connie, sitting very upright, was looking at him with interest. "You know you look very like an old friend of mine. You're not a Howard are you, by any chance?"

"Yes, as a matter of fact."

"What kind?" Connie quizzed him.

"Grandson."

He seemed unsurprised by these questions, as though they were ones which were often asked him.

"Oh, my God," he sat up, struck by a sudden thought, "of course!" He clapped his hand to his forehead. "*You* must be Connie Percival." He seized her hand and shook it. "I remember Debbie telling me about her eccentr . . . er, about her aunt."

"Eccentric, ha?" Connie narrowed her eyes, but I could see that she was not displeased. "Well, I have heard worse."

"Oh, I'm sorry . . . I didn't mean . . ." Luke floundered. "Oh dear, I'm not putting this very well. But it seemed so unlikely somehow. I mean, you being Debbie's aunt. Such a fantastic coincidence. My grandfather has told me all about you."

"All about me? Are you sure?" Connie raised one perfectly pencilled eyebrow. Her hands were folded in her lap, but I could see that she was twisting her rings between her fingers.

"Well, no, not *all* about you . . ." the boy gesticulated, ". . . of course not. I mean nothing personal. Well, not very."

"I am delighted to hear it." Connie smiled. "Well, well," she said to Lucille, "apparently, this is James Howard's grandson."

"James Howard." Lucille, who had been listening to this exchange with some surprise, brightened. "James Howard? Do I know him?"

"No, darling," Connie said firmly, fitting another cigarette in her holder. "James Howard is a painter. A very great painter. He was a very dear friend of mine, once, about a hundred years ago."

"So you are Debbie's cousin," Luke said, looking at me. "What an extraordinary family this is turning out to be."

"Oh, arc we?"

He did not reply immediately, but continued to study me, quite unselfconsciously, as a painter might scrutinise his latest model. In anyone else, I remember thinking, it would have been downright rude. But with Luke, somehow, it was not. "You take after her, don't you," he said after a while, glancing towards Connie. "My grandfather was besotted by her for years. It was a famous affair." He looked back at her, fascinated. "I can see why. She's amazing, isn't she?"

"Yes, she is."

"You're not a bit like Debbie, you know." Luke was looking at me again. His eyes were very tired, ringed with grey shadows. He had nice eyes.

"No."

"But you are Connie's niece. Definitely." He ran his hands distractedly through his hair.

"Yes."

"You are laughing at me."

"No!"

"Don't stop. You have a beautiful laugh." As he spoke Debbie reappeared bearing an extra cup and saucer. Smiling, their eyes met, like accomplices, across the room.

FOUR

I dreamt about Santa Luz again last night.

Despite everything, despite everything that has happened, until now it has always appeared to me as a place of innocence, as though my mind has preserved it, not in any later guise, but as the enchanted place of childhood.

But last night I dreamt a different dream. I was seven years old again, and sitting with you on the verandah. I was filled with excitement for something that was going to happen, although I did not know what it would be. You had dressed me in a special dress. It was white, with floating gauzy skirts, smocked across the breast with red flowers. You were sitting with your back to me, and you held a baby in your arms. I could not see its face.

There was a long table in front of us laid out for tea with cups and saucers and plates in a strange pattern I had never seen before. As I looked down the table it seemed to get longer, until it was stretched out as far as I could see, laid out with hundreds and hundreds of place settings in the same pattern, dark blue, pink and gold. I wanted to touch one of the cups, wanted to feel it, hold it to my lips, but each one was so beautiful and frail that I was afraid to pick it up in case it broke apart in my hands.

I saw waiting, full of importance, with you and the baby

39

on one of the old rattan chairs. The chair was creaking and green with age. I swung my feet, trying to drum them on the floor, only I was too small and my legs would not reach the ground. Spiky pieces of cane caught and snagged at the back of my legs. It grew late. In my dream I can remember the way the sun filtered shadows through the trees at the edge of the garden, and how their leaves fell in silvery drifts as their feet. We had been sitting there, just waiting, for a long time. But no one ever came, and we were left alone, the three of us, on the creaking chairs, in the silent afternoon shade.

Afterwards I lay awake on my bed, listening to the sounds of London and wondering if I will ever find a reason for the things that happened. Can a house be held responsible?

Through the darkness I could hear the sound of footsteps on the pavement outside. At times, when I lie awake like this, I am seized with the notion that one day the footsteps will stop outside this door and that it will be Finn or Baltazar, or perhaps even you, coming to find me. The footsteps approach, draw closer, then fade away into the night. Sometimes I think that it must be the loneliest sound in the world.

I remember myself as a quiet child, very dark and delicate boned. As a child I was unaware of my foreignness. I have pictures of myself when I was a baby, wrapped up in a length of woven cotton like an Indian girl, a cap of dark hair and sleepy, half-focused eyes protruding from the tight cocoon. The pictures must all have been taken at much the same time, for in these pictures it is always Magdalena who carries me.

My first memories are of the texture of the land, of the hot cracked earth in the courtyards of Santa Luz, and the coolness of their dipping terracotta tiles. I remember flagstones under archways, sticky to my bare feet with pollen and crushed petals. I remember the wooden pillars in the chapel, stroked over the centuries to the softness of silk. Outside the gates of the Great Court was the path which led away from Santa Luz to Altamirada, lined with dazzling dust and eucalyptus trees as tall as mountains. Under the trees the dust was laced with a sweet-smelling humus of leaves. When I ran they crunched up between my toes, mingling with the dust, as soft and white as talcum powder.

And yet there is something missing in all this. The end is clear in my mind, but what of the beginning? Why is it that when I think back, you are somehow unconnected with this tranquil, twilight place? When I think of you there it is in a kind of interlude, a flash of colour within those silent walls. The glamour of another land lingered on your clothes and on your skin, as piercing and yet insubstantial as woodsmoke.

If I am truthful I realise that, in those early days, it is not you that I remember most clearly at all.

Five

"Take me up the mountain, Magdalena."

"Mountains are no places for little girls, *niña* Layla."

Magdalena was sitting sewing Layla's new dress, cross-legged on the kitchen porch. The material was pale against her hands as she pierced it with her needle. Every now and then she paused to bite off the end of the thread with her teeth. When she did this, Layla could see her teeth, very white and small, and her tongue, as delicate and pink as a cat's.

"Take me up the mountain," Layla wheedled. "You promised."

"No-o, *niñita*. Not yet. It's too far for you to go."

Magdalena leaned forward to inspect her work, holding it up to the light. As she did so her skirt rustled over coloured petticoats which billowed out, stiff as a Christmas fairy, from her little waist.

Layla watched her as she went on sewing. She had once heard her mother say – or had it been her father? – that Magdalena was as beautiful as a witch. 'But she does not look like a witch,' Layla thought, looking at Magdalena's black head lowered gracefully over her work. Her complexion was smooth, her eyes heavy lidded. Her face was as serene as the statue of the Madonna in the chapel, except that instead of being white her skin was the burnished colour of old gold. Around her neck she wore a collar of beads, coiled tightly together into a golden pyramid. When she moved the beads chinked together with a tiny glassy sound.

"How old are you now?"

"Nearly seven. You know *that*."

For a while Magdalena went on sewing in silence. There was no longer any point in pressing her, Layla knew. She would decide things in her own time. That was her way.

The dress was nearly finished. From her pocket Magdalena took a tiny green feather and sewed it neatly into the hem, concealing it inside the material.

"For good luck, for protection when you wear the English dress, *niñita*," she said, smiling. "You can try it on now." She slipped the dress over Layla's head. "When you are seven, then maybe you will be old enough," she stood back to look over her creation, "but I'm not promising anything. You must be patient."

*   *   *

They set off early. The valley was still and cold, shadowed in the blue light of the moon. At first, even in the half dark, the path leading from Santa Luz was familiar, but before long they came to a band of trees at the foot of the mountain and the path turned sharply to the left, leading them into the unknown wood. Soon the white silhouette of the house behind them had passed from sight. The path zig-zagged upwards higher and higher. Although she was not cold, Layla shivered. She drew the folds of the woollen poncho she had been given to wear more closely around her, enjoying the feel of it against her skin and the pungent goaty smell of the wool.

Inside the wood it was very dark. Ahead of them the path

43

was like a moonlit tunnel through the trees. Layla could see Magdalena gliding upwards in front of her. Her footfall made no sound. Her body was of a piece with the land she moved through; incorporeal and pale, as though the moonlight had sucked all the colour from her.

By the time dawn came they were above the treeline. The silver light was now tinged, as though by an alchemist's hand, with a faint tracing of gold.

"Here, *niñita*, I have a surprise for you," Magdalena said.

"What is it?"

"Come to me, up here." She was standing above the path on a flat outcrop of rock. "Close your eyes first, and don't open them until I tell you. Are they closed?" She reached down her hand and pulled Layla up.

"Can I open my eyes now?"

"No. Not until I say." She led Layla along the rock. "Are you ready now? All right, open your eyes."

"Oh!" Layla sat down suddenly on the rock. "Oh!"

Beneath them, cupped by the mountains, lay the valley latticed with cart tracks and fields. In the stillness of the early morning, woodsmoke rose in thin plumes from the houses. A herd of sheep, their bells ringing with a far-away hollow sound, made their way out to pasture in a slow-moving spiral of dust. And at the very centre of the valley, laid out like a map, lay the square, secret vastness of Santa Luz.

"But it's so *big!*"

"Of course," Magdalena laughed. "It's Santa Luz. Do you like it?"

"It's *beautiful*."

Layla picked out details: the cross on the chapel roof, the stables, and the green canopy of the avocado tree just visible over the Quetzal Court.

A tiny figure, no bigger than a pinprick, moved across the flagstones of the Great Court.

"It looks so different from up here," Layla said. "It looks like . . . I can't explain it, it looks like somewhere else. And it's not white any more, it's red. The roofs are all red."

44

"But this is how it's always looked, *niñita*, from the mountain," Magdalena said as she stood up to go, "everything always looks different from up here."

"It's as though I have never been there," Layla stared down, fascinated.

"*Vamos, niña*," Magdalena said, pulling Layla to her feet, "we must keep going. You don't want to miss your birthday celebrations, do you?" Leading Layla by the hand, she turned to face the mountain again.

Magdalena did not walk fast but her step was sure, unfaltering. The higher they climbed, the faster her pace seemed to become. Layla's legs and feet ached. The brittle grasses which grew along the side of the path tore and scratched at her, as if they had been sharpened with knives. There were no trees here. The sun beat down. Layla's poncho began to feel as if it were weighted with stones. Her skin beneath the heavy wool pricked with sweat. And still Magdalena climbed.

After several hours they reached a pass between two smooth faces of rock. To one side of the path was a small pyramid of stones. Magdalena searched for a pebble in the undergrowth and placed it on top of the pile. She showed Layla how to do the same. "This way you pass on some of your burden," she told her, "and make the climb easier."

They sat down to rest by the pile of rocks. Layla lay with her chin on her hands, looking down into the secret valley. They were now so high, and the path clung so sheerly to the face of the mountain, that it made her feel almost giddy to look down. The sun warmed her back, and the grass smelt of herbs. Beneath her a flock of small brown songbirds took flight, arching into the dizzying space which separated them from the valley. Santa Luz was now no more than a tiny red and white speck. Up here, Layla thought, it was almost like becoming a bird herself, they were so high and free. It was as though she could see the whole world spread out beneath them.

From beyond the pass came the sound of bells, and a flock of sheep came picking their way down the path.

Behind them walked a man and his daughter guiding them with sticks. The girl was about Layla's age; a slight, impish figure, black eyes just visible beneath a man's battered trilby hat. Over her shoulders she wore a faded red cloth like a cape. Her feet were naked, and the soles of her feet were cracked and raw.

When he saw who it was, the man greeted Magdalena respectfully, shaking her by the hand. While they talked, the girl inspected Layla briefly from beneath the rim of her hat, but when Layla smiled at her she tossed her head and sprang off down the path in pursuit of the sheep. Layla watched as she bounded barefoot over the rocks, prodding the sheep into line with her stick, and calling to them authoritatively – *pshi-shi pshi-shi* – in a high-pitched, sing-song voice. A shock of dusty hair sprouted from beneath the hat, bouncing down her back as she ran.

"*Felicitaciónes*," said the man, nodding to Layla. With a wave of his hand, he walked on down the mountainside.

She watched the man and the wild-eyed girl as they disappeared from view. In the mountain light their colours seemed like the landscape itself, muted, and yet as luminous as leaves in autumn.

"Why did he say *felicitaciónes* like that?" Layla said, puzzled. "My birthday was last week."

"Today will be just as special."

"What do you mean?"

Shaking her head, Magdalena smiled her secret smile.

Beyond the pass the path diverged. Magdalena took the right-hand fork which kept to the side of the mountain along a stretch of flat ground. They had now entered the neck of another unknown valley. A deep, terrifying chasm fell beneath them. The sides of the mountain were so steep here that Layla could no longer see the bottom.

"Look," Magdalena said, pointing, "clouds, can you see them?"

Faint white bracelets of vapour hung in the air, threading their way along the crags of rock.

"Yes, I see them."

46

Unseeing, Layla stumbled along behind her. The path was in shadow now, and the air felt chill against her clammy skin. Through the soles of her sandals she could feel every pebble as though it were a boulder. Her socks, now torn and grimed over with dust, kept slipping down, rubbing against her sore heels.

For the first time Layla found herself wondering what her parents would say if they knew where she was. Instinctively, she knew they would not like it. Would they be angry with her? With Magdalena? Layla felt a little twist of fear. She must not cry, she would not cry. Magdalena would not have brought her if it was not going to be all right. Would she?

"Are we nearly there?" Layla was ashamed of the catch in her voice. She thought of the little sheep girl, leaping to the top of the mountain in her bare feet, and wished she could be more like her.

"Tired already, *niñita*?"

"How far is it?"

"Not far, not far," Magdalena knelt down beside her. "Don't cry, my Layla. Come, take my hand. I'll help you now."

*   *   *

They left her to rest in the cool darkness of Tia's house. The floor, which was of beaten earth, was very clean. The rest of the room was bare of furniture, except for an iron bedstead in one corner piled high with blankets. Old clothes – trousers, shirts and trilby hats – hung like scarecrows from pegs on the wall. Above the bed was a calendar, now several years out of date. It had a picture on it of Father Christmas riding a reindeer across a snowy mountain. The calendar said, 'Seasonal Greetings to all our Customers, from Aurelio and Herminia Fuentes, Papeleria San José, Altamirada'.

Through the door, Layla looked out on to the porch. A

47

collection of ancient tin cans, which had once contained kerosene, cooking oil and powdered milk, now sprouted with gangling geraniums, scarlet and pink. Beyond it was a cobbled pathway, and the brown adobe walls of the village. Chickens picked softly in the dirt. There was no one about.

Layla could not sleep. Where were Tia and Magdalena? Why had they left her here on her own? She found a stick and started to trace patterns with it on the earth floor. A cockerel, flamboyant with quivering red and white plumes, stretched his head around the door. She could hear his claws scratching on the ground. He looked around, an enquiring croak bubbling up from deep within his throat. Ignoring Layla, the cockerel hopped in through the door. *Pshiii–pshiii*, she waved him away with her stick.

Outside the afternoon sun burnt down on to the silent street, making her eyes ache. Layla wriggled uncomfortably. Why had Magdalena made her put on the English dress? It was already too small for her. She could feel the material pulling uncomfortably under her armpits. Something must have happened to keep them away for so long – but what? She picked up the stick again and started to draw, it would not be patterns this time, but a proper picture. Layla looked around her, thinking hard, then carefully scratched the outline of the cockerel into the pressed earth.

From outside came the sound of voices at last. Magdalena and Tia smiled at her as they came in, but offered no explanation as to where they had been.

Tia sat down, pulling Layla into her lap, cradling her like a baby between her fat breasts, raining rough kisses down on to her as if she were her own child.

"My, how pretty you are today."

"Tia!" Laughing, Layla pulled at her long black plaits, tried to squirm out of her arms, which pinned her in a vice-like grip. "I'm not a baby any more." Vainly, she tried to push Tia away.

"What do you mean? You'll always be my baby." Tia pinched Layla's cheek with her strong old fingers. Like all the Santa Luz women she wore a woven red tunic, and

48

heavy layers of gold beads around her neck. A sweet distinctive odour of milk and mountain air and animal dung clung to her clothes and skin. Layla adored her.

"Ow! But I'm seven now. It was my birthday last week."

"Mmm. Your birthday, ah?" Tia looked at her slyly, and then at Magdalena. "Then we'll have to celebrate, won't we?"

Slowly, to Layla's surprise, the room was filling up with people. First came Tio, and then a number of other men and women, most of whom Layla knew from the farm. They smiled at her, and the women came over and kissed her on the cheeks. There was something about the way they looked at her which made Layla feel special.

Some of the men had brought bottles with them; others carried bags from which they took fruit, biscuits and small bags of sweets. They handed them to Magdalena who laid them out in front of her on the floor.

"Are we going to have a party?" she asked Tio, who had come to sit on the other side of her. Tio laughed, showing the gold stoppings in his teeth. "Afterwards, yes."

"After what?"

"I see you have been drawing," Tio said, not hearing her, peering with myopic interest at the ground. "What is it? A bird? That's good." Layla looked at her cockerel, the long feathers on its rump tailed away lopsidedly into the dust.

"Yes, a kind of a bird."

"Have I ever shown you my bird?"

"Oh, no, please show me."

Layla had seen Tio's bird hundreds of times, but he was old and always forgot. Tio reached behind him, and grasped a long staff which he had propped up against the wall.

At the top end the wood had been chiselled into the form of a bird's head. Its eyes were studded with two green stones. Long tail feathers, glissading to nearly halfway down the staff, were also speckled with tiny chips of malachite. Even in the darkness of the room, the staff glowed with a dull green fire as Tio turned it in his hands. Layla stroked the bird's head, touching it gently with her fingers.

49

"It's beautiful, Tio."

"Yes," he nodded. "It's the quetzal. The most beautiful bird in the world. And the most powerful. I will hold it for you during the ceremony."

"What ceremony?" Layla tugged at his arm, suddenly anxious. "What ceremony, Tio?" she said again, louder this time, into his ear. But before he could answer her Magdalena stood up and drew Layla towards her. "Don't be frightened," she said, pulling her gently into the middle of the room. From the corner of her eye, Layla could see that something hard, metallic, was glinting in her hand.

Layla began to feel a strange, creeping feeling in the pit of her stomach. Why had they brought her here? What had she done? She felt very hot suddenly. Magdalena was saying something to her, explaining something that Layla could not quite hear. She looked down at the bright metal in Magdalena's hand, and then at the press of faces all around her. In the darkness their skin, faintly beaded with perspiration, was the colour of tarnished gold.

Still speaking, Magdalena started to stroke Layla's head, only she was not stroking it, but separating out a long strand of hair. On the wall over the bed she could see Father Christmas gliding down the snowy mountain, his legs thrust out, jauntily spreadeagled, on either side of the reindeer's narrow flanks.

Close to her ear there was a dull-sounding metallic crunch. Father Christmas grinned down at her with a wave, his cheeks bulging like two fat red apples. Another dull metallic sound. And something fluttered down, soft as a butterfly kiss, past her cheek.

*   *   *

"Mummy, Mummy, here I am!"

Layla raced and skidded across the Little Court, skirting

50

the broken fish fountain, its base now dry and scolloped with ivy, into the Middle Court, darting between the stone colonnades where the terracotta container jars as big as Ali Baba's lay drunkenly on their sides, until she finally reached the verandahed porch where Bettina's bedroom lay, its shutters pulled in familiar midday darkness.

Although Bettina was always in a good mood when she returned from one of her shopping expeditions in Veracruz, at the doorway Layla hesitated, feeling suddenly shy. The running had made her hot. Magdalena now made her wear a sun hat in the middle of the day, a floppy white cap which fell down low over her forehead. A slow trickle of perspiration ran down the back of her neck. Layla put her hand up to wipe it away, aware again of her strange new nakedness.

After the dizzying white sunlight outside, it was dark in Bettina's bedroom. At first all Layla could see were boxes – hat boxes and dress boxes, parcels wrapped up with brown paper and carrier bags all spilling out with tissue paper – and there behind them all was her mother kneeling on the floor, smiling up at her, beautiful, cool white arms plunged up to the elbows in the foaming mounds of paper.

"Hello, my darling," with a clatter of gold bracelets, Bettina held out her hands, "come and give me a kiss." Then, seeing Layla still hesitating in the doorway, she let out a little crow of laughter. "Goodness, what a peculiar hat! What has Magdalena been doing to you?"

Although her tone was light, cajoling even, Layla was stricken with a sudden doubt. The symbol of her pride on the mountain now seemed shameful, an ugly thing compared with the vibrant, eau de cologne-scented aura of her mother, and the objects with which she surrounded herself.

"Funny girl, why don't you come in? Haven't you missed me?" Layla saw that Bettina was wearing a new lipstick. Her lips, as she spoke, were like two vermilion arcs. She patted the bed beside her invitingly. "Come on, come and tell me what you've been up to."

Still standing in the doorway Layla felt very small all of a sudden; small and ugly. Bettina gathered herself to her

51

feet. As she did so the tissue paper seemed to whisper around her ankles like dead leaves. She was still smiling, but her manner was brisker now. She took Layla's arm and led her into the room. Layla could feel cool fingers pinching her skin.

"Come on, darling, what's the matter with you?" From an enormous height she bent down towards her daughter, "You can tell me, you know. Are you ill or something?"

Layla shook her head slowly, but said nothing. Her tongue seemed to have withered up inside her mouth.

"Well, what on earth is it then? Why are you always so secretive?"

Bettina shook her arm impatiently. Layla shut her eyes. All she heard was the tiniest rustling sound as the hat slipped from her head into the folds of tissue paper on the floor.

They had cropped Layla's long hair to within half an inch of her head. The hidden sculpture of her skull now stood out, like a huge pale egg, abnormally white against the fine skin of her face, tanned by the Santa Luz sun. Until long into the afternoon they had cut and sheared, perfecting their work of love, but Magdalena's giant scissors were clumsy and the hair which remained was a criss-crossed stubble of uneven tufts.

For a long time Bettina said nothing. She did not scream and she did not shout, as Layla half expected she might. There was only a hissing sound, like a sharp intake of breath, and then a silence, a silence more terrible than any sound Layla had ever heard. When she opened her eyes she saw that Bettina's face was white, bleached like the parched animal bones, picked over by condors, which they had seen scattered along the mountain path. Layla had the notion that the rage written across her mother's face was a white thing, too: a white, hot, speechless rage. Bettina gripped Layla's arm so hard it hurt.

"Who did this to you?" When she spoke at last, her voice was very low. *"Who was it? Who?"*

"Look what they've done to her," Bettina screamed at Jack, her face terrible with rage. "You must do something

52

... these people ... these animals ... look at the child!"

"That's enough. You're frightening her." Jack's voice was quiet. Through a glaze of tears and painful swollen eyelids, Layla saw that he seemed hardly to notice Bettina, but was studying her with calm detachment.

"Come here, Layla."

Layla ran to him. The gentleness in his voice only served to increase her remorse. She wept anew all over his shirt.

"I'm sorry, Daddy. I didn't mean it," she wailed. "It's my fault, it's my fault. I made them do it."

"Stop that now. It's not your fault. There, there, your old hair will soon grow again," Jack patted her head, teasingly pulled one of the offending tufts.

"This is no laughing matter, Jack!" Bettina was outraged. "I want to know who did it . . ."

"Shut up."

"No, I bloody well won't shut up. I'm telling you, this is the last straw . . . How can you just sit there, it's an insult . . ." Bettina was incoherent with rage.

"I said shut up," Jack said coldly. He pulled Layla between his knees. "Besides, this is very far from being an insult. Layla knows that, don't you, Layla?"

"Mmmm-nn."

"Who was it? Martin the Eye?"

"Nnnn." Layla shook her head.

"No, I thought not." Jack stared down at her, impassive. "Magdalena, then?" Layla nodded despairingly into the crook of his arm, felt his arms tightening momentarily around her, his "My God" only the faintest murmur under his breath.

"Magdalena!" Bettina sounded as if she had just tasted something sour. "I might have known."

"And Tio. And Tia. Lots of people." Hiccuping, Layla came up for air. "I couldn't count how many exactly. There was a Father Christmas up on the wall."

"Didn't count how many!" With a golden clatter, Bettina

53

sat down heavily on the sofa opposite them, but Jack no longer appeared to notice that she was there.

"You weren't frightened, were you?" His arms were still around her. "Did they tell you why they did it? Did they explain?" Layla nodded, puzzled by his vehemence. "Do you understand what this means?" Layla nodded again.

"What it means?" Bettina's voice was shrill. "Well, I don't understand. Perhaps you'd like to tell me what it *means*."

"All right," Jack said slowly, not meeting her eyes. He shifted Layla on to the divan beside him, and pulled out a handkerchief from his pocket. "Have a good blow, that's it. Now mop up, like a good girl."

"All right," he turned to Bettina, "if you let me, I'll explain. There's nothing malicious about this, as you seem to think. It's a ceremony known as First Haircutting." He paused, as though wondering how to go on. "It's a way of saying that a child has left babyhood, and is ready to take on an adult role in life. A rite of passage, if you like. If Layla was an Indian child," he paused again, looking thoughtful, "if she were an Indian child she would now start wearing her first set of adult clothes, help her mother about the house, that sort of thing. I'm surprised, because I would have thought she was rather old for it. It usually takes place when a child is no more than three or four."

"Well, I think it's a deplorable thing to do." Bettina pressed her hands to her face. "Look at her, poor child. All her beautiful hair!"

"Bettina, Bettina, her hair will grow again." Jack reached for her hand, but she snatched it away, still angry. Jack sighed, fell silent.

Through the window of her father's study Layla could see the midday sun dwindle slowly into afternoon until the room was divided into slanting, mote-filled cylinders of light. She had always liked this room, with its tattered damask divans and sofas, the patterns and colours of the covers faded long ago into inconclusive old age. Yellowing bundles of *The Times* and old magazines, back copies of

Country Life, the *Illustrated London News* and various agricultural journals precariously tied up in green string, invaded almost every corner of the room. Unlike Bettina's rooms, restlessly metamorphosed every few years, this room had looked the same ever since she could remember. Now, looking round her, Layla noticed how dusty it had become, and how the shredded damask smelt sourly of mice.

"You really don't understand, do you?" Jack was saying.

Layla, who had wriggled her way deep into the corner of the divan, thought that her father looked funny all of a sudden; his face sagged, like an old brown paper bag.

"It's . . . how can I explain it to you? It's like a sign of acceptance." Jack stood up and walked towards the window. Looking upwards, beyond the crumbling white walls, he could see the mountain, its quilting of straw-gold fields luminous in the afternoon sun, as bewitching to him now as it had been the day he had first set eyes on it. He thought of Magdalena, with her witch's eyes, her skin smelling tenderly of oranges.

"What the people are saying is that they have accepted Layla as part of Santa Luz, in a way that I never could be. I was not born here, you see."

"That's such rubbish, Jack. You own the bloody place."

He has aged, she thought, looking at Jack's tall form – thinner, a little stooped now – silhouetted against the window. He is letting himself go. His trousers already hang from him like an old man's. His nails are chipped, never quite clean. This house is like a malign growth, sooner or later it will suck us all dry.

"Yes. Yes and no." Jack sighed. "I own a piece of paper which says I have material possession of Santa Luz. But spiritually the land belongs to them, always has done. They are inseparable from it, in a way that I am not. And now Layla is inseparable from them."

"Oh, for God's sake!" Bettina almost spat the words out. "You're so damn sentimental. It's always your daughter,

55

isn't it? Your daughter and your land? Well, what about me? She's my daughter, too, or had you forgotten?''

'What has happened to me? What is happening to us?' she thought in sudden terror. 'Why can't I stop this?'

"Inseparable from them!" she heard herself go on. "That's just about the last thing I want for my daughter. Inseparable from a bunch of dirty, stubborn, superstitious peasants. Layla spends far too much time with them as it is."

"Well, if you showed more interest in her, perhaps she wouldn't have to."

"And if we left this godforsaken place she wouldn't be able to," Bettina, reckless now, raged on.

Slipping deep into the hideaway folds of the old sofa, Layla thought that they must have forgotten she was there. The argument, in some obscure way, no longer seemed to be about her. Her shameful, mutilated head was forgotten. She found a tiny hole in the old damask and started picking at it with her fingers, pulling out tufts of ancient, greyish stuffing. The smell of it prickled at her nose. Her parents' voices, sometimes low, sometimes high and angry, went on and on. She picked on assiduously, blocking out the sound, pulling out bigger and bigger handfuls from the fraying hole.

When she next looked up, the sun had shifted across the room, and was lying in tigerish stripes across Jack's desk, across the wilderness of estate papers, files and unpaid bills, at the far end of the room. The voices were no longer angry. They sounded closer, softer now.

"So you'll do it then? You'll make her go?" Bettina was saying. "Will you really, Jack?"

"If it makes you happier, I'll try. Yes."

"Try?"

"I'll do it."

"Who will tell her?"

"I will tell her."

"Today?"

"Yes."

"Do you promise?"

"Yes." Jack's voice was barely audible. "I promise."

*　　*　　*

Magdalena opened her eyes very wide.

"Dismiss? What does this mean?"

"Dismiss. You know, make you go away." The thought was unbearable. In anguish, Layla rubbed her hands over her naked head.

"Away? Why?"

In the old stone kitchen, Magdalena picked over a bowl of rice. Bending her head closer to her task, her fingers moved languidly, almost sensuously, through the grain, sifting it with both hands, seizing on a speck of chaff, or a blackened husk, with a predator's sudden accuracy. When she spoke it was in the lazy, dreamy way of someone absorbed in her work, someone who was not really listening. Layla could not seem to make her understand.

"Make you go away from here. Away from Santa Luz."

Magdalena laughed, showing her small white teeth.

"*Niñita*, you have been sitting in the sun too long."

She slid Layla a teasing, sideways glance. In the lamplight, her lips were as red as the darkest cherries. Layla, who had arrived in the kitchen panting and fearful, stamped her foot in frustration, "They will, they will. I heard them."

"Who?" Magdalena continued to pick over the rice, but she sounded more interested now.

"Mama and Papa."

"Ah, Don Jack will say anything to make the *Señora* happy. But she is not happy here. If I leave, will that make her any more happy?" Magdalena shrugged her shoulders, flicking aside her long plait. It fell to her waist, a black Rapunzel's tress, as thick as Layla's arm.

57

Layla could not believe that Magdalena could be so calm, so tranquil, in the face of this disaster.

"Do you think I'm making it up?" she challenged.

Magdalena pushed the bowl to one side, and pulled Layla to her.

"*Niña* Layla, no one can make me go away from here," she said, stroking her cheek, serious at last.

"But . . . but Papa could, if he wanted to. He is the *patrón*."

Magdalena's smooth lips curled up into a fleeting smile, but she said nothing.

"But Papa could," Layla insisted, "couldn't he?"

"He could," she agreed at last, looking quizzically at Layla, "but I have to be here to look after you, don't I? How could he send me away from you?" She smiled. "You must not worry. In the end I think – no, I am sure – he will find that he does not really want to send me away after all."

Six

The summer seems never-ending here. It is two weeks since I last wrote, and yet still the heat continues. The papers are full of the greenhouse effect, and of how we are destroying the world, and its delicate balances, with our aerosol sprays and exhaust fumes and our western greed. In the park the leaves on the trees are jaded, dusty with fatigue, as though they too now long for the cool oblivion of autumn.

I always thought that London would be a good place in which to forget. I imagined it as somewhere grey and gentle, somewhere where the senses would be dulled, or at least transposed, deflected on to other things. But there is something about the blue skies over the rooftops each morning, the scent of the pale roses at my window, which reminds me of that last summer, the summer when Baltazar came back to Santa Luz.

Yesterday, when I could not sleep, I got up early and walked through the park, the same way that I walked that day with Connie, when we had talked about love. There is a freshness about the early morning, even in the streets of London which, if you can capture it, is unlike any other time. The sky was spun with a fine gold fleecing of clouds; the air still cool and new. I walked past the Albert Hall, and then down Exhibition Road as far as the museums. It was Saturday so there was little traffic, only the distant sound of dust carts, and men in shirtsleeves sweeping the streets.

In the King's Road I found a café open. I ordered coffee and drank it sitting at a table on the pavement outside.

"*Italiana?*" the waiter asked when he brought me the coffee. He was small and very dark, with a gold ring in one ear.

"*No.*"

"Ah," he smiled, regretfully.

I wondered if perhaps he was homesick, too.

Behind me, I could hear the other waiters talking to one another as they cleared the tables of the night's débris. A group of them were having breakfast together. Their voices had that quick, thick lilt, undulating, and unmistakably Latin.

There were more people in the street now; people hurrying to work, young women pushing prams. A girl with long blonde hair walked slowly towards me arm in arm with a man, his hair brilliantined back from his forehead, 1920s style. Clearly neither of them had been to bed, for both were still in evening clothes, the girl in a short black and white dress, the man in a dinner jacket, a turquoise bow tie hanging, untied, around his neck. When they saw the café still open they stopped to look at the menu which hung in a frame by the door and then, on impulse, sat down at one of the tables opposite me. The man leant over, whispered something in a low voice. I saw the girl laugh, tilting back her head, pushing a strand of long hair away from her face. I wondered where they had been and where they would go home to after their breakfast in the café, whether they were in love.

"Layla?"

A tall, thin figure was standing by my table. I had been so engrossed in these thoughts that I had not seen him walk up.

"Yes?"

60

"You remember me?" The boy ran his hands through his hair, "I met you with Debbie, the other day, when you were at your aunt's house." He looked at me anxiously, one hand still plucking at his hair.

"Oh yes. I remember, of course. Luke, isn't it?"

"Yes. Do you mind?" He indicated the chair next to me.

"No, please do."

"Are you sure . . . I mean, I'll go away, if you'd like to be on your own."

"Please. I'd be glad of the company."

Luke folded himself into the seat beside me. He too was dressed as though for the evening. He was wearing black trousers and white shirt beneath an extraordinary black jacket, several sizes too large for him. The collar was frayed into a ragged fringe. Moths had nibbled a waltz of tiny holes all the way across the front and down the lapels.

We looked at one another. Seeing my eyes dropping, involuntarily, to the pointillist pattern of moth holes, Luke patted the arm of his jacket.

"It's an antique, my grandfather's," he grinned. "Do you like it?"

"It's very fine."

We looked at each other again. As before his eyes looked tired, the fine skin beneath them pressed with dark shadows. Despite his nervous manner, his gaze was direct. I noticed that the lines of his face were strong, almost classical in their regularity.

Luke ordered two double espressos, and drank the first in silence, long legs stretched out beneath the table. I could see the girl on the opposite table looking at us curiously over the lip of her cup.

"Have you ever thought," Luke said suddenly, "that if my grandfather was your great aunt's lover, that makes us almost related?"

"I hadn't thought of it like that. But yes, I suppose it does. At least, in other circumstances we might have been."

"You don't sound surprised."

"No." Somehow the thought was not as extraordinary as

it sounded. "I seem to be related to lots of people I know hardly anything about."

Luke smiled. "Like Debbie, you mean?"

"Yes. Like Debbie." I remembered the way he had looked at her across the room, and her returning, accomplice's smile. "Is she a good friend of yours?"

"No, not exactly," Luke said. "She's not that kind of girl, if you know what I mean."

He took another mouthful of coffee, staring down into his cup.

"You're in love with her?"

"Yes, I think so. I don't know." He shrugged his shoulders. "I don't know her very well. Used to see her at parties sometimes, that kind of thing. I used to admire her from afar," Luke smiled, a sudden, illuminating flash, as though he were smiling at himself, "I'm old-fashioned like that. She was so glamorous, you see, so aloof, never giggled in corners like the other girls. So when she came on to me at a party, I thought, well you can imagine what I thought. Couldn't believe my luck. She was so sweet to me the other day at your aunt's house, but since then, I don't know, she always seems to be busy, never returns my calls, you know the sort of thing. It's as though now she's quite sure she's got me, she's not really interested any more." He finished his coffee, clattering the cup clumsily down on to the saucer. "I thought it was us brutish men who were supposed to behave like that." He gave another self-mocking smile. "I thought perhaps you might be able to give me a few clues?"

"Poor Luke. I'm sorry," I shook my head, "Debbie's my cousin," I savoured the still unfamiliar word with renewed delicacy, "but I really don't know her."

He looked at me quizzically. "You'd never met before the other day, had you?"

"No." I remembered the close, pale room; the girl in the red dress; and the sweet stench of the lilies. "Perhaps . . . perhaps she thought she needed an ally."

"Perhaps." Luke sipped his second cup of coffee, non-committal. "I think it's far more likely," he added with perception, "that she wanted to shock your aunt, and then found that I was rather more respectable than she had bargained."

"Poor Luke."

"You're laughing at me again."

"No, really."

"Yes you are." Luke looked severe, but I could tell that he did not really mind.

Behind us I could hear the rattle of plates and cups. From the kitchens came the smell of hot bread and garlic. The sun was gaining in strength, falling in warm fingers across my shoulders. If I closed my eyes, I could almost have imagined that I was sitting at a café somewhere in Veracruz, or in the plaza in Altamirada. But I was not in either Altamirada, or in Veracruz. Even so, sitting there talking to Luke, a lightness, a sudden sense of well-being, began to steal over me.

"Why did you leave so suddenly?" Luke examined one of the holes in his jacket, prodding at it with his finger.

"Leave where?"

"Your aunt's house, of course, when I met you the other day."

"Oh, yes, then. I'm sorry, I was thinking about something else."

"I can see that."

For a moment I was tempted. Why is it that it can be so much easier sometimes to unburden yourself to strangers? There was something about him, something more than *simpatía*; something I can only describe as a tenderness. Perhaps he really did feel that through Connie we were, in some obscure way, connected.

For a moment, for just a fraction of a second, I felt that I could have told him everything.

"You can look very sad sometimes, you know."

"It is good, sometimes, to have something to be sad about." I felt the moment slip from my grasp. But when I looked up, I found myself smiling at him. "Besides, I am not sad. Not today."

*   *   *

Luke ran his fingers inquiringly under the window casement. He took a penknife out of his pocket, opened one of the blades, and gently ran it between the two sashes. There was a faint click.

"Great, that's it." He curled his fingers under the top of the lower window pane, pushing it gently upwards. "Here we go." The window creaked, and then sighed smoothly open.

"You'd make a brilliant burglar."

"I should do, I've had enough practice. It's my brother, he doesn't mean to lock me out, not on purpose anyway. He's rather vague sometimes, that's all."

Head first, Luke squeezed the top half of his body through the narrow gap, followed by the long, gangling black legs, lowering himself on his hands into the space below. "Just wait there a sec," he called, "I'll open the front door. Don't go away, will you?"

I watched him run towards the door. Through the glass I could see a large room, lit on two sides by tall, sash windows. A decorator's trestle table stood against the opposite wall. In the centre were two chairs covered in dust sheets. Apart from this the room was empty. The walls and ceiling were very white, a soft, matt whiteness, as though they had been recently painted.

"Layla?" Luke appeared around the corner, stumbling on the gravel. "Oh good," he said rather breathlessly, "you are still here." He seemed to half-expect that I might suddenly vanish, like a genie, the moment his back was turned. "Come on in, this way."

Luke's house, or rather his grandfather's, is remarkable:

64

a country house (as indeed it once was) in the middle of London. The house, with its rather grimy façade, is set back from the road behind a shield of trees, so that you could walk past it many times without noticing that it was there. We stepped through the front door into a circular hall, perfectly proportioned, tiled in black and white. A double staircase led upwards from the hall to the first and second floors.

There was no carpet, either on the stairs or in any of the rooms or corridors. On the first floor Luke led me into a series of high-ceilinged rooms, each one interconnecting with the next through a set of panelled doors. He said nothing, but walked in front of me throwing open each set of doors as we came to it. As we walked along our footsteps echoed against naked floorboards.

There were no pictures in any of the rooms, and very little furniture. Instead, a number of full-length mirrors, framed in ormolu, hung from the walls. The remaining spaces were white-washed, as the downstairs room had been, and smelt of new paint. The impression was one of light and space and proportion, as if the house had been pared down to its purest, most beautiful bones.

In the last room a chaise-longue, the only piece of furniture, had been pulled up to the window and was evidently being used as a bed. It was littered with pillows and a crumpled sheet. The gilded frame was now faded and chipped; one of the legs was broken, and the bed was held up at one end by a pile of books. Beside it on the floor, a pair of men's underpants lay curled; a toothbrush; a twisted tube of toothpaste.

I went over and stood by the window, looking down over the trees and the street beyond. I pressed my forehead against the window pane, the glass cool against my skin.

"It's marvellous," I said, turning to Luke, "it must be like living inside a sculpture." I looked round at the high bare walls all around us, dancing with light. "It's perfect, absolutely perfect like this."

"I knew you'd like it." Luke was sitting on the bare

scrubbed boards, his head tilted back against the wall, long arms loosely folded around his bony knees. "I don't know why, but I just knew."

He seemed relaxed here, as though the nervous cogs inside him had suddenly found an equilibrium, soothed by the calm spaces around him.

"I've always loved this house. It used to be quite different, very dark and cluttered, William Morris red flock wallpaper everywhere, you know the kind of thing. Then my brother moved in."

"The one who's always locking you out?"

"Yes. He's a painter too, like my grandfather. Just before he moved in here, he went to Mexico, and got really into the Mexican muralists, you know Diego Rivera, Siqueiros, and Orozco, all those guys. In those days he also took a lot of drugs. When he came back he stripped all the wallpaper off and painted murals all over the walls. Every inch of them. You know, enormous clenched fists leaping out at you, and naked women with enormous bosoms and machine guns between their thighs. Hideous, really, but some of them were very good."

"What did your grandfather say?"

"Oh, he was delighted. It's just the sort of thing he would have done. Said he never could stand William Morris anyway. The Victorian Society was very annoyed. Most of the wallpaper was original."

"So what happened to the murals?"

"Paul got bored with them. And I must say they were rather oppressive to live with. I much prefer it like this."

"What about your grandfather?" I was intrigued by the sound of James Howard, just as Luke had been so fascinated by Connie.

"He doesn't come up to London very much these days, says he prefers the country, but I imagine he'd like it like this, too."

I walked over and stood in the centre of the room, looking up at the shimmering ceiling.

"Do you paint, as well?"

"No way. Two in the family is quite enough," Luke said. "And you? My grandfather still has some of Connie's sculptures. She's very good."

"No, I don't paint. Not any more." I sat down on the edge of the chaise-longue. "When I was a child I used to draw birds. I used to paint them over and over again. Always the same bird, a quetzal, a kind of bird of paradise with a long tail. I don't know why. Perhaps it was the shape, or the colours, amazingly iridescent blues and greens, which mesmerised me in some way. I must have painted it thousands of times. My mother thought I was obsessive. She was so worried about it at one point that she almost sent me to a psychiatrist, can you believe. And then one day I just stopped."

The room seemed airless suddenly. I could feel the back of my neck pricking with sweat where the sun struck in from the window behind me. I pressed my fingers to my temples. "I'm sorry, but do you have an aspirin by any chance?"

*   *   *

"It's a picnic," Luke explained.

"I thought you were going to buy aspirin."

"Don't laugh. I was and I did. Then I realised that there's no food in the house. And I can't let you go without some lunch first. The aspirin are in here somewhere." Luke, creature of impulse, dropped two bulging carrier bags on the floor.

"I thought we could eat in here." He looked round the room, "Can you help me move this rug? That's it – can you manage? – over here towards the fireplace."

"What a beautiful thing," I rubbed my fingers over the glowing pink cloth.

"It's Persian. Silk. A prayer mat actually." Luke

67

scratched his head, "I'm afraid I've been using it as a blanket. It got quite cold last night, and I couldn't seem to find anything else."

The fireplace, which took up nearly half the wall, was a length of carved white marble. A telephone bill and some old brown envelopes lay crumpled in the grate.

"I'll just go and get some plates," Luke ran off, nearly tripping over the carrier bags. I heard his feet clattering hollowly through the empty rooms and down the stairs.

Inside the carrier bags I found a side of smoked salmon, a paper bag full of bagels and some cream cheese; a jar of olives, two lemons, and a packet of digestive biscuits. Suddenly, I found that I was very hungry.

When Luke came back he was carrying a bottle of wine under each arm, their labels nibbled into lacy, sepia-coloured fragments.

"Olives! My favourite food, how did you guess? Clever Luke, I haven't eaten an olive for, oh, as long as I can remember."

"Good, I thought you'd like them. Have some wine to go with them." Luke struggled with the corkscrew. "I found these in the cellar; they look as if they should have been drunk years ago."

He sniffed the top of the first bottle cautiously, and then poured the wine into two long-stemmed glasses, their bowls chased faintly with gold. "It looks all right. Luckily its always cold in that cellar, even during a heat wave."

The wine was the colour of topaz and smelt of apricots.

"I'm afraid we'll have to share the knife." He laid out the bagels and the cream cheese on a chipped kitchen plate. "In this house you never quite know what you're going to find, or not find, as the case may be. Here, put some smoked salmon on top, like this. It's delicious."

Sitting cross-legged on the floor, we ate greedily with our fingers. The late summer sun came pouring into the beautiful barren room like water into a bowl. In the absence of furniture or any other ornament to absorb or deflect it, the light seemed to have an almost tangible quality, filling out the empty walls around us with a delicate architectural counterpoint of shadows, spilling upwards into the highest cornices, dipping and swimming across the pale domed forehead of the ceiling.

Luke licked soft white crumbs of bagel from his fingers, and picked up his glass.

"Do you know what day it is today?"

"No. Should I?"

"It's the twenty-first of September. The last day of summer."

"Should we drink to that?"

"Yes. I think we should."

"Well, then, here's to the last day of summer."

We drank.

Luke lay out on his side, cupping his head in one hand. "Tell me about you."

"You seem to know quite a bit about me already." I poured some more wine into our glasses. "You knew I'd like this house. This room. You seem to know practically all my relations. You even knew that I'd like olives."

"No, I'm serious." He stretched his hands over his head, stared up at the ceiling. "When I first met you I remember thinking how unlike Debbie you were, even though you were her cousin. She so pale, and you so very dark. But now I'm not so sure. With Debbie, it's like living with the Mona Lisa. You can never really tell what's behind that half smile of hers, never guess what she's going to do or say next. You have something of that in you too. Something secretive."

I was so struck by his comparison that I did not answer immediately.

"Tell me about you," he went on, "I want to hear you speak. I love your voice. I love the way you speak with your hands." He turned his head to look at me. For a moment he looked quite serious. "Where did you learn to speak like that, mystery girl?"

A silence fell between us, a soft, insistent little silence.

"It's so . . . un-English, somehow," he went on. "Very

69

unphlegmatic. Is that the word? Have you some foreign blood, perhaps?"

A bee droned at the window, bumping its body gently up against the glass.

"Now you are the one that's teasing."

"Ha! I see I'm getting warmer." His tone was light, almost bantering again. "OK then, I'll guess. You're a white Russian princess. Yes, perfect. I can see you now, swathed in rich and imperial-looking furs. Most appropriate. Not very sound conservation-wise, but they make very decent fake fur these days, so I'm told."

"Please! Not in this weather, surely?"

"No, no," Luke went on, ignoring me, "you couldn't possibly be English. All English women look such tarts in fur . . . unless they are very old and very Jewish. What else, let's see. I know. You are the daughter of an impoverished, but extremely aristocratic Italian contessa, perhaps? Who wants to marry you off to a rich industrialist (and use the dowry to pay off her impossible gambling debts). But you hate him of course, because he is old and fat. And in any case you have a brilliant career ahead of you as a trapeze artist in a circus, so you have run away to England to find one. And in time you will fall in love with the lion tamer, marry him, and find everlasting happiness."

Luke paused, shading his eyes against the sun so that I could not see the expression in his eyes. When he spoke again, it was in a different voice.

"You don't have to tell me anything, you know. If you don't want to."

Outside, the sky thinned into the colourless arc of midday. The bee, blundering its way in through the open window, hovered above us.

"Have you always lived here?"

My own voice sounded lazy, distant.

"No. I was brought up in Suffolk, when I was a child. Then I went to school in Wiltshire. But I've known this house all my life, it's always been here."

I thought of Santa Luz, and of the impossibility of ever

explaining it to anyone, even Luke, who had never seen it, and probably never would. I did not have the words to create it for him, not even in his mind's eye. And yet – perhaps it was the wine, perhaps it was the idea that this was the last day of summer, and with it the possibility, unlocking somewhere deep within my mind, that after this there could be a new beginning – suddenly I found that I was talking.

I heard myself describing Santa Luz, in all its isolation and its beauty. I heard myself telling him how it had been built by the sons of the great conquistador Manuel Peron y Imbaburra, and their sons after them; how each generation had added to the house, building on rings of courtyards of stone and whitewashed adobe, each ring greater than the last, as an oyster throws out its layers of pearl. I explained, as my father must once have explained to you, how on the back of their vast wealth the Peron y Imbaburras enriched and embellished Santa Luz with furniture and pictures, tapestries and silver and musical instruments from Europe, brocades and silks from the east, each piece carried on foot over the mountains by Indian porters.

Then I told him how the house had overreached itself, grown too big, too expensive to run. How it was raped and disbanded by the same family who had once loved it. How small earth tremors had caused cracks in the walls which none of them thought to have repaired. And how, eventually, the house had been left empty, abandoned like a demanding mistress, until my father bought the land.

Last of all I found myself describing my own private world: the decaying courtyards at the heart of Santa Luz, that secret place which as a child was my house within the house gone wild. I told him about the hiding places I used to build in the Quetzal Court, in the branches of the avocado tree; the places where I hid my treasures in the dry, green-marbled depths of the fountains; the darkened, mousy galleries and echoing rooms. As I spoke I saw myself for the first time from the outside, as others must have done.

As perhaps you did? I saw myself for what I had really been: a child playing in a dying house.

"Why did you leave?"

All the time that I had been speaking, Luke had listened silently, not moving. Now his voice seemed to come from somewhere immediate and very close beside me.

"Why did you leave?"

"I left because . . . because I had to leave."

Luke thought for a while, then said quickly, "My God, you're not one of those exiles, are you? A political one, I mean."

"Heavens, no!" I could not help laughing, "nothing like that. Although sometimes I feel as if my being here is a kind of exile. No, I am here . . . how shall I say it? *De mi cuenta*. For my own sake."

"I have the feeling, I don't know why," he hesitated, "I had the feeling when I met you the other week, and then again today, that you are looking for something. Are you?"

"Yes, I think I am." My body felt light, as though something which had been pressing on me had been lifted. "I am looking for answers," I turned to him, "although the problem of course with finding answers, is knowing what questions to ask."

* * *

So what questions should I be asking? Can you tell me?

The answer waits like a familiar face, just there, around the corner. As yet I cannot imagine this unseen face, but I know that I will recognise it instantly when it is revealed to me at last. We are separated now by only a tiny space, a gap no wider than this page. Why is it that I hesitate to turn the corner?

I wish that I could talk to you now.

Downstairs Connie is waiting for me. The windows of

her drawing room are open, leading out on to the garden. As dusk falls she will go out to look at her plants. It is a daily ritual with her. She pinches off the dead heads between her fingers, waters the sweet peas, the night-scented stock and tobacco plants which flood the house with desire.

Luke was right. Today is the last day of summer. Already the evenings are drawing in and for the first time, now that the sun has set, there is a chill in the air. It will be too cool to sit in Connie's garden tonight.

Instead we will spend the evening in her drawing room, so English with its deep chintz sofas, their covers traced with flowers and twisting leaves and butterflies the size of cabbages.

When she is there, she seems to draw the room around her like a second skin. She will not close the curtains, even when it grows dark. She likes the night, with the scent of the summer still on its breath. On the sideboard and the small table at her elbow she has placed silver bowls filled with dried rose petals and lavender, on which the dust has settled, like a layer of nostalgia, over the essence of other long-ago gardens.

I should go down to her now. We will sit and drink a glass of wine, read the papers, and I will tell her about my day with Luke. And yet I am still sitting here, looking out across the rooftops as I write to you. My mind hovers between two worlds.

I take a fresh sheet of paper and start to draw, a bird of paradise with a long tail.

Seven

It was in the summer, the summer of the great drought, that Baltazar Peron y Imbaburra came back to Santa Luz.

In Veracruz the tarmac in the streets melted like molasses in the sun. On the coastal plains whole lakes disappeared and the water birds suffocated in the mud as though it were quicksand. In the villages, even the vultures seemed faint with the heat.

It was the summer of Layla's graduation and her twenty-first birthday; the summer that Finn bought the quetzal.

A week after her return from the *Universidad Católica* in Veracruz, Layla drove into Altamirada, down along the tortuous mountain road which dropped for three thousand feet from the Santa Luz plateau to the town.

Altamirada, already suspended in the familiar torpor of midday, was absolutely quiet; a town of siesta-sleeping ghosts where nothing stirred, not even a hot breath of wind.

Along the covered arcades which enclosed the square on three sides, the shops – the *papelería* San José, the ironmongers, Francisco's tailor shop, the *comedor* Alemania, the same shops that Layla had known all her life – retreated silently, shuttered against the heat. In the centre of the plaza, beneath a frowning plaster statue of Simon Bolivar, the Great Liberator, his head dandruffed with guano, the two shoe-shine boys, Vinicio and Settimo, lay sleeping along a wooden bench.

On the fourth side of the square, its back to the cloudy mountain forest, stood the church. Thirty years ago the church had been all but destroyed in an earthquake, and of its once glorious baroque extravagance now only the crumbling bones remained. Layla had always known it this way. From the outside, the façade shimmered and spiralled in golden stone. It was so familiar to her that she did not notice the way tufts of grass grew in the cracks across its pockmarked face, or the weeds and creepers which sprouted from the saints' niches, the roof tiles, the belfries, like hair from an old man's ears.

On impulse, Layla crossed the plaza and entered. She walked down the aisles feeling the cool air, tinged with incense, against her face. Sparrows flew in and out through a broken window; a pigeon strutted high up along the altar-piece. Inside, unlike the dark sanctum of the chapel at Santa Luz, the restructured church was curiously modern, quite plain and full of light.

Instead of the familiar Indian shrines and offerings – fruit, heads of maize, fresh rose petals drifting between the columns like confetti – images of the Madonna, crammed into every available space, were honoured garishly with bunches of plastic flowers. Layla walked slowly, stopping in front of each image: the *Virgen Milagrosa*, the *Virgen de Dolores*, the Immaculate Conception, the Queen of Heaven. Small plaques had been fixed into the walls beneath each niche: "Thank you, Holy Mother, for curing my son", "Thank you, Mother of God, for a successful operation", "Thank you, little Virgin, for answering our prayers".

Each statue was made from identical pink-cheeked plaster.

"Marvellous, marvellous Roman Catholic kitsch," Finn had once said, rubbing his hands. "I should think every one of them came from the same factory. Knowing Padre

75

Pio, he probably managed to get them cheap, in a kind of job lot."

Finn. She must go and see Finn. Layla felt in her pocket and put some coins into the Queen of Heaven's collection box. The doll-like face, eyes turned heavenwards beneath a nimbus of gold stars, stared out from stiff folds of glistening, baby blue tulle. From the sidechapel, to her left, came the sound of a woman's voice.

An old Indian woman sat huddled on the floor in a ragged dress. Her hair was tied into plaits, two sad, wispy grey ribbons which hung limply down the sides of her face. At her feet was a child of two or three playing with a pair of candles, her tiny face blackened with grime. Beside the woman and the child, halfway down the aisle, was a figure of the martyred Christ on his hands and knees.

Unlike the others, this was an old image, one of the few to have been salvaged intact after the earthquake – a miracle, many local people said, who visited it with particular devotion in times of disaster or family crisis. The Christ was a startling, life-like figure, naked except for a loincloth and a circlet of thorns. The bones of the shoulder blades, the sinews along the outstretched fingers, the arms and calves, were sculptured with an anatomist's accuracy beneath yellowing skin.

Despite herself Layla found that she was staring at the woman and child, grouped around the Christ figure in their sad parody of the Holy Family. The sidechapel had always been darker than the main body of the church, and the woman had lit a circle of candles around her. She was murmuring in a low voice, imploring, crying. As Layla watched, she started to kiss the Christ's hands and face, stroking her hands over his flayed back, whispering to him in her passion as if she knew him, as if he were her lover. For a moment, in the dying light of the candles, the blood on the Christ's body glinted, running down the neck and shoulders, coursing from the stigmata which gaped like butcher's meat on the hands and feet, as if the figure were actually bleeding.

From the corner of her eye Layla saw a movement in the shadows. Apart from the old woman and the child, she had thought herself alone in the church. Now she became aware of a man standing in the darkness at the far end of the chapel. The man's face was obscured by a dusty trilby and so she could not see his eyes. At first she thought he too was looking down at the woman. But something about his stance, his stillness, made her aware that he was staring straight ahead, staring at her. And she felt sure, suddenly, that he had moved deliberately so that she would see him. She felt a hostility coming from him, an anger that she should intrude upon this old woman's grief. Ashamed, Layla moved on, walking quickly out into the hot, silent plaza.

By day Finn's bar, El Fin del Mundo, was an unexceptional place: bare wooden floors and tables encrusted with candle wax. By day, when it was possible to see the cobwebs hanging from the rafters, and the sticky black rims of the bottles ranged behind the bar, there were usually few customers. But by night, in the softened focus of evening, it took on a kind of seedy glamour; the glamour of salsa and cigarette smoke and occasional drunkenness which often misled the few travellers who penetrated this far into the slow, precipitous backwater between the sierra and the eastern jungles into thinking that they might, at last, have found the "real" South America.

Except on Sundays (market day) and the occasional Saint's day, when the small town was flooded with Indians from the surrounding mountains, the people of Altamirada did not much frequent El Fin del Mundo, which was known, without rancour, as a *gringo* bar. They preferred instead the fluorescent strip-lighting of Pacos on the opposite side of town, which showed football matches and *telenovelas* on a huge 20-inch television set, and sold Coca-Cola in disposable cans.

Apart from one man slumped over a table in the corner hugging a bottle of warm beer to his chest, Layla found the place empty. The débris of the previous night, half-empty

77

bottles and cigarette stubs, still lay about on the tables. A doorway behind the bar led to private apartments, and to the balcony overlooking the Altamirada gorge where Layla knew that she would find Finn. She pushed the door open and made her way down a flight of steps, open to the sky, which led round to a second door. On the door was a sign saying "Private" in careful psychedelic lettering.

Layla paused with her ear to the door. From the other side came the faint, familiar sound: the sound of the voices of birds whispering together.

Layla opened the door. As she stepped through it on to the covered balcony, the soft murmurings erupted into a cacophony of alarmed cries. All around her, birds rose up in a vibrating maelstrom of feathers and beating wings, wheeling and dipping and humming through the air.

Finn's birds were legend. No one, not even Finn or his sister Meredith, seemed to know exactly how many he possessed. On the covered balcony, suspended like a vast aviary over the Altamirada gorge, flew parrots, parakeets and cockatoos, fruit-suckers, barbets and bulbuls; golden orioles and mannikins from India; sunbirds, sibias; starlings and finches; sleek, strutting mynahs who could wolf-whistle like a man; tiny humming birds no bigger than a thumbnail. Some of the birds flew freely around the room, hovering among the plants and creepers which twisted up the walls and cascaded from the railings like green water. The rest hung from the ceiling in cages and painted wicker aviaries, in the domed and gilded palaces of wire of Finn's own designing, made up for him by hand in Veracruz.

In the calm eye of the spinning, dizzying vortex, sat Finn in an old cane chair.

"Hello, Finn."

"Hello, my sweet." Finn's long, beautiful-ugly face looked up at her and smiled. He did not get up. As the other birds subsided from their flurryings, Layla saw that balancing on his shoulder sat a tiny, bright pink cockatoo. "I'm sorry I can't move. We're still a little shy," he explained. "Come and say hello to Myrtle."

From behind Finn's ear the bird peered steadily out at Layla, a beady prehistoric look. Its eyes were black, the eyelids scaly, like dragon's skin.

"She's beautiful!"

As the bird emerged, taking careful sideways footholds along Finn's arm, Layla saw that it was only the face which was pink, an astonished flush which began at the base of the beak and then spread outwards, slowly dissolving into the barest watercolour blush at the nape of its neck. The breast and back were a bright pea green; on the rump, unexpectedly, a brilliant flash of blue.

"Finn! Where did you get her?" Layla was entranced.

From the table at Finn's elbow she took some sunflower seeds which she held out in the palm of her hand. The bird bent towards her, blinking gravely, and took one in its beak.

"She's so tame! Cock-a-too, cock-a-too," Layla crooned at the bird. "Will she let me stroke her, do you think?"

"*Agapornis roseicollisa.*"

"What did you say?"

"*Agapornis roseicollisa*, ignorant girl," Finn repeated. "Please, my Myrtle is *not* a cockatoo. She's a Rosy-faced Lovebird, and a very expensive one at that. She has travelled all the way up from the Amazon to be with me. I've found this marvellous little man who seems to be able to get me almost anything." Finn looked down his long nose at the bird with satisfaction. "Myrtle likes you," he said approvingly, "I thought she would. She doesn't take to everyone you know. She bit Meredith the other day."

"Naughty Myrtle." Layla offered the bird another sunflower seed.

"Unfortunate," Finn said drily, "to bite the hand that feeds you quite so literally. But I have explained to Myrtle . . .' he made a soft *krrkrr* sound into the bird's ear ". . . and she will not be so rash next time."

He coaxed the bird from his arm on to a nearby perch.

"Now, enough about birds," Finn said, standing up. "You have arrived, with impeccable timing, just as I was about to have some lunch."

He led Layla on to an outer balcony which was separated from the birds' aviary by a wall of wire mesh. "Now I want to hear all about you. What's the news from the wicked city. However have you survived?"

When people asked Finn why he had called his bar El Fin del Mundo, he would pause, rubbing his chin with an appearance of thinking hard. In fact he already possessed several replies, one or other of which he would select depending on a number of variables: the mood he happened to be in that day – elegiac, buoyant, or discursive – and, Bettina always said, how much he fancied whoever had asked him. If the person bored him, he would reply shortly that it was merely a joke, a pun on his name, Finn, and leave it at that.

At other times he would wave his hand out towards the Altamirada gorge, which plunged for a thousand foaming feet or more below his balcony, and say, "Because this godforsaken place *is* the end of the world, of course. Can't you see? Here you stand, at the very lip of it. Go further at your peril."

"Of course," he had once said to Layla, "they hardly ever do. It's too strong a diet for most palates, but not necessarily in the way that people expect. That's the beauty of it. This place is what some people think they want: a mixture of back-to-nature innocence, and a García Márquez fantasy made flesh. Which of course it is – why else do they think I put up with it all? – only very few of them have the eyes to see it. In any case, these things don't just reveal themselves overnight."

He raised his glass towards the travellers in the upstairs bar. "Altamirada disguises itself behind its extraordinary ordinariness. Most of this lot come here to live out some half-baked idea, to escape the reality of their boring little lives in Rochdale or Heidelberg or wherever, and then, when Melquiades the gypsy and Remedios the Beauty aren't sitting waiting for them with open arms, they stop looking and sit around picking their toes, complaining that the beer is warm and that there isn't another truck out of here for a week." Finn grinned. "Reality, so to speak, with knobs on."

On the balcony, Layla watched as he tossed tomatoes and avocado into a salad.

Finn had lived in Altamirada ever since she could remember. He had come there by chance during a long vacation from Cambridge, another student traveller on the hippy trail, in those heady days when thousands of them flooded to the remoter regions of the earth, Kathmandu, Kashmir and Cuzco, their minds drugged with the strange cults, mountain light and hashish. Finn's bus, heading east towards the rainforests of the Amazon, had broken down in the mountains near Altamirada. When he stepped down he had spotted a handsome Indian boy – his own Remedios the Beauty, Layla would later guess – fallen in love, and had somehow never brought himself to leave.

His sister Meredith had followed him out a year later, and when their money ran out they had started up the bar, El Fin del Mundo, renting out their spare rooms to other travellers who passed through.

Business was sporadic, which suited Finn, whose brilliant mind was more attuned to poetry and books than rank commerce, although of late, with his Irish wit and white suits, his pony tail and his quixotic taste in birds, he had gained a certain notoriety amongst the travelling fraternity – a marvel in his own right.

He was Layla's best friend and, despite his reclusive nature, the source of all her knowledge of the world.

Finn helped Layla to more salad.

"So tell me now, how is Jack? How are the great repairs?"

"Fine, I think. You know how it is."

"Two steps forward, one step back?"

"That kind of thing. A great crack appeared in the kitchens the other day. Magdalena was in there when it happened, said it nearly frightened her to death. She thought we were about to have another earthquake."

Layla cut herself a piece of cheese, eating it with her fingers. "But you know Santa Luz, nothing ever seems to

81

change there however hard Dad tries. It just goes on, the same as always."

"He should have realised that years ago."

"You know, sometimes I think that in his heart of hearts he doesn't really want it to change. He's furious about this new road they're building."

"The new one from here to Veracruz?"

"No, no, haven't you heard? They're planning to tarmac the track all the way to Santa Luz apparently."

"Well, well. The twentieth century arrives at last," Finn raised his eyebrows and smiled, "no wonder Jack's annoyed."

"Dad says it's just vote-catching. He says the government have to be seen to be doing something for the area; but that after the election they'll simply forget they've ever started it, and leave him to clear up the mess."

"Sounds only too probable. Still, this Veracruz road is on everyone's lips at the moment. The mayor, my friend Virgilio, is thrilled. Seems to think its going to put Altamirada on the map at last. His head is already filled with commemorative plaques, a new statue for the plaza, all manner of civil junketings – all at our expense, I might add. I can just imagine it, can't you? The whole place positively swaddled in bunting from top to toe. I only hope we all live long enough to see it through. I don't think the dear man can have even the faintest idea how long *any* road, let alone a mountain road, takes to get built in this country."

Finn sat back in his chair and lit a cigarette.

"Have you heard the other news?" Layla licked her fingers carefully.

"Ah, yes. I wondered when we were coming to that." Finn inhaled, blowing out the smoke in little rings. The rings floated out across the balcony over the green throat of the gorge below. "Baltazar Peron." Layla watched as the rings hung tremulously, eliding together, dissolving into the warm air. "Baltazar Peron y Imbaburra. Well, what do you think of him?"

"I haven't met him yet."

"Oh? Bettina was here the other day, absolutely full of him."

"Yes, I know, she said she'd been down. He's gone away for a few days. Left the day before I came back."

"So you've come to me for the low-down?"

"Yes."

Layla smiled at him, looked away, wondered why she had ever asked. Baltazar Peron y Imbaburra, she turned the name over silently to herself. She would meet him soon enough. Make up her own mind, uncoloured by anything Bettina or Jack or Finn might think of him.

"I met him once or twice. In Veracruz, years ago."

"What was he like?"

"Interesting." Finn thought for a moment. "An artist, rather a good one I thought. Spoke immaculate English. He seemed to have travelled a good deal, even then. And I mean really travelled – not just the ritual shopping expedition to Bloomingdale's once a year. He was different, not at all like the rest of that family, such little provincials for all their supposed blue blood. I got the impression that as a Peron he was accepted everywhere, but that no one seemed quite to know what to make of him."

Behind them, from the aviary, came a vibrant fluttering of feathers. For the second time Finn's birds cried out, although this time the sound was softer, a querulous, domestic flurry rather than the harsh jungle alarm calls which had greeted Layla when she entered.

"Ah, here you are," the wire mesh door was flung open and Meredith came out on to the balcony, "and Layla too, how lovely."

Meredith wore a voluminous, drop-waisted cotton dress, printed over with flowers, and a large, spongy pair of flip-flops, heavily indented with the tread of her feet. Over one shoulder she carried a leather shoulder bag which bulged with keys, notebooks and papers. She kissed them both, and sat down heavily opposite Finn.

"I wasn't expecting you back so soon," Finn regarded his sister coolly. "I thought you'd be another week at least."

"Well, here I am: sorry to disappoint you."

Meredith kicked off her flip-flops and took one of Finn's cigarettes from the pack on the table. "I'm absolutely exhausted. I've been up since four, and we had three punctures on the way up, can you believe it. The jeep will have to go."

Meredith – loud, blowsy Anglo-Irish rose – shared as little of her brother's particular brand of urbane eccentricity as it was humanly possible to do. She had the same tall, heavy-boned figure, an open face, and indeterminate brown hair which curled around the back of her neck and ears. She was cheerful, thick-skinned, endlessly energetic. She bossed Finn, and organised him relentlessly: their feuds were nearly as legendary as Finn's birds.

Without her, it was commonly held, El Fin del Mundo would have gone bankrupt years ago.

Finn turned to Layla: "Did I tell you, Meredith has been down in the jungle, looking at caimans," there was a barely discernible note of disapproval in his precise voice. "She's going to take the travellers there, poor things, on night hunting expeditions . . ."

". . . just to look at them. Not shoot, or anything like that. Jungle Safaris, that's what I'm going to call them," Meredith interrupted. She selected a tomato from the bowl and sucked at it hungrily.

Finn went on, "Someone told her that they're doing it very successfully in Peru these days."

"Must you always talk about me as if I'm not here," Meredith said without rancour.

"Well, where will it all end, I ask you." Finn pulled a melancholy face. "She'll be after Jack next, persuading him to turn Santa Luz into a theme park, like Longleat or something. Monstrous!"

"Actually, that's not such a bad idea," Meredith laughed. "Well, come on you two, aren't you going to ask me how it went?" She looked round at them.

"Meredith, of course," Layla said, feeling guilty at their lack of enthusiasm. "How did it go?"

"Extremely well, as a matter of fact. Thank you, Layla." Meredith turned to her brother, "I've had another idea, Finn."

"What's that?"

"The ruins at Tumbez. I stopped off there on my way back. They're perfect, a bit overgrown, but people don't mind that, they'll just think they're getting the real thing. I can't think why I haven't thought of it before." Meredith leaned forward, pulsing with enthusiasm. "The best thing is that they're almost exactly halfway between here and the caimans. We could camp there overnight, break up the journey a bit."

"Aren't they haunted, the ruins at Tumbez?" Layla said.

"Tumbez? Whoever told you that?" Finn was surprised.

"I'm not sure," Layla thought for a moment, then shook her head. "Magdalena, perhaps. Or Dad. I really can't remember."

"Have you heard this, Meredith?"

"Oh, that old story," Meredith was dismissive. "Yes, the men were pretty spooked, but only to start off with. At first they didn't want to go in at all, but I shamed them into following me and they soon saw that there was nothing to be frightened of." She turned to Finn, "Quintero is meant to have murdered some Indian woman there."

"Don't tell me. Her soul still comes back to haunt the ruins?"

"Oh, no. Nothing to do with ghosts." Meredith laughed again. "I think they were terrified that Quintero was still waiting there like some kind of bogeyman, ready to pounce on them and cut their throats."

"Quintero?" Layla appealed to Finn.

"Some terrorist leader. He was responsible for a particularly bloody insurrection in the Esperanza province known as *El Mes de Sangre*, which is probably the only reason why anyone still remembers him. But all this was years ago, you're probably too young to remember. He was executed in the end."

85

"I thought it was his own men who turned on him." Meredith said.

"No, no. He was executed in Veracruz, I'm sure of it."

"Oh well, whatever," Meredith shrugged. She put her hand to her mouth suppressing a yawn. "God, I'm exhausted, I'm going to have a siesta." She stood up, "Oh, Finn. I nearly forgot. The dreadful Fuentes is here again. He's upstairs, waiting in the bar."

"My bird man? How extraordinary, I didn't expect him here again for months."

"So you always say," Meredith said. "I tried to send him away, but he wouldn't go. Insists on seeing you."

"You should have told me before." Finn stood up. "Come up with me, Layla, you'll enjoy this."

"Don't encourage him," Meredith said to Layla. "There are too many birds in this house as it is. Besides, the man's a crook, I'm sure of it."

"Maybe, but he does produce some amazing treasures," Finn said. "You know me: I can resist anything except temptation."

*　　*　　*

Upstairs in the bar the man who Layla had seen earlier, slumped over his bottle of beer, had gone. In his place was a little man in a dark brown trilby.

"Señor Fuentes, so soon!" Finn shook the man by the hand. "How are we today?"

"Señor Feen. Not so bad, not so bad." The man took off his hat and clutched it to his chest. Although he was smiling, he seemed ill at ease. Layla saw his eyes flicker mistrustfully around the room, towards her, towards the door, and then back to Finn again.

"So, what brings you here today, Señor Fuentes?" Finn sat down at one of the corner tables, pulling out the chair opposite him invitingly. "A beer please, Gustavo, for our friend here."

Although he was wearing western clothes, a dirty white singlet pulled tight over his belly and brown trousers, the man had the squat, barrel-chested appearance of the sierra Indians. Without his hat on his head was strangely elongated, like a bullet. Down one side of his face Layla could see a ragged, milky white blemish. The eyelashes of one eye were bleached like an albino's.

When the beer was brought, Fuentes took the bottle and poured half the liquid down his throat. After he had drunk he seemed to relax a little. He wiped his mouth on the filthy singlet, and sat down to face Finn across the table.

"Today I have something very special. Exceptional, I think you will agree." He grinned, revealing a mouthful of discoloured teeth. "I come straight to you, Señor Feen . . ." he paused, leaning towards them across the table, ". . . this bird cost me more than one hundred dollar."

"One hundred dollars?" Intrigued, Finn pulled his chair closer to the table. "Whatever can it be, Señor Fuentes? One hundred dollars is a great deal of money."

"No, no. One hundred dollar, this is what it cost me! It is worth more, much more. For you, Señor Feen, I make a special price. Because you are a good customer, and my friend, to you I will sell it for only . . . two hundred and fifty dollar."

Fuentos slapped his hand on the table. He took another swig of beer, his little glinting eyes never leaving Finn's face.

"Two hundred and fifty dollars." Finn smiled politely. "Whatever have you brought me, Señor Fuentes? The goose that lays the golden eggs? No bird could possibly be worth that amount of money. You are jesting with me, I'm sure."

"Jesting, Señor Feen?" Fuentes looked dignified. "I am telling you, in Veracruz I could sell this bird for two times this amount," he jabbed his finger in Finn's direction, "five hundred, maybe even one thousand dollar!"

Finn smiled politely, saying nothing.

"You are not believing me?" The man threw his hands up in disgust. "Señor Feen, would I lie to you?"

"Good Lord, no, Señor Fuentes. Who could suggest such a thing?" Finn was enjoying himself. "I have an idea. Why don't you show me this marvellous bird? We can discuss the price later. Where is it, anyway?"

"I have it outside. In my truck."

Finn stood up, but the man motioned him to stay seated. "No, no. You stay here. I have it just outside."

He darted through the door, into the somnolent, sun-baked street. When he returned he was carrying a shallow cardboard box, about four feet long, crudely perforated along the sides with holes. Fuentes put the box on the table and slid it gently towards Finn. In silence he opened the lid.

"My God," Finn stared inside. "It's a quetzal. He's caught a quetzal."

The bird lay quite still on its side. Its eyes were open, but seemed filmy and lifeless, as though it had been stunned or drugged. Layla stared with pity at the little panting body. One of its legs was bent backwards, and lay stiffly at an unnatural angle.

"Oh, poor thing," she cried. "But it's so beautiful. It's the most beautiful thing I've ever seen."

"It's the most beautiful bird you are *ever* likely to see," Finn said, adding in English, "and the rarest. And also one of the most illegal." He traced his finger reverently down the train of its tail feathers. "A Resplendent Quetzal. Amazing. Absolutely amazing. Its tail must be at least three feet long. The feathers are in perfect condition."

Finn looked down at the bird.

"Did you know that for something like two hundred years, until the mid-nineteenth century, there were many naturalists who did not believe that the quetzal existed. They thought that a bird of such beauty could not be part of the real world at all, but could only ever have existed as a myth, in the minds of men."

The fabulous bird shimmered helplessly in the box.

Beneath Finn's fingers its plumage quivered, as though light had been trapped between the feathers: deep, iridescent emerald green along the head, neck and upper plumage, golden green along the tail feathers, merging to blue, to sapphire, to violet, and ending in a crimson smudge, like a bleeding heart, across the frail breast.

"The mystery is how he ever got hold of it at all. Quetzals are a Central American bird, they have never been found this far south. Where on earth could he have got it from?"

Fuentes, who had been standing watching them through his slitty, peasant eyes, sensed that his prey had been tempted, was almost hooked. He could keep silent no longer.

"The bird is priceless!" he croaked, triumphant. "The feathers alone! But for you . . . just two hundred and fifty dollar. OK?"

"Did you know, Señor Fuentes," said Finn smoothly, not looking up, "that quetzals are an endangered species? And that selling it to me – or to anyone else, for that matter – is illegal."

"Illegal?" Fuentes shrugged his shoulders disdainfully. "It's a bird, that's all. From the jungles. How should I know if it's illegal or not?" His gaze flickered nervously between Finn and the bird. "OK. I tell you what. Two hundred dollars. You buy it for the lady, eh?" He leered at Layla. "Yes or no?"

"One hundred and fifty."

"Do you think you should," Layla said, apprehensive, "if it's really so illegal, I mean. Shouldn't we just make him turn it loose again?"

"In our charming friend's hands, this bird won't last another day. It is well known that you can't keep quetzals in captivity. If I don't buy it, it will die. It might die anyway. God knows what he's drugged it with. If I buy it, at least it will have a chance."

"But two hundred dollars, Finn! You're crazy."

Finn turned to the man, suddenly brisk, and placed the lid back on the box.

"Two hundred dollar, Señor Feen," Fuentes wheedled, pushing the box back towards him. "For a man like you, this is nothing!"

"One hundred and fifty. It's my last offer."

"OK, OK," the little man sighed, as though with a huge effort, "one hundred and seventy-five."

"Done."

*   *   *

"He was in a hurry." Layla watched through the window as Fuentes scuttled down the street towards the waiting truck. "He hardly even bothered to count his money."

She gazed after him, shading her eyes against the afternoon glare. Waiting near the truck, in the shade by the side of the road, was a second man. Layla watched as Fuentes approached him; saw him unhitch the wodge of notes from his trouser waistband, place them in his companion's outstretched palm. The second man had his back to her, but there was something about him, the dust on his clothes, the way he stood, a certain stillness about him, which reminded her, for the briefest instant, of someone familiar.

Layla turned away, back to the darkened room, to Finn and the quetzal. Together they gazed down into the box. The bird fluttered feebly, tremulous wings beating against the sides of the box, then fell back, its breast heaving. A little green and white snail of excrement spurted from beneath its rump.

"A hundred and seventy-five dollars, Finn," Layla shook her head, "you must be mad."

"You mean friend Fuentes must be mad. This bird is worth ten times that much, and he knows it."

"You mean he was telling the truth?"

"Amazing, isn't it?" Finn rubbed his chin, perplexed. "Yes. Surprisingly enough, he was. He wanted me to have it very badly, or he'd never have sold it to me for that price."

"Perhaps he stole it."

"I wouldn't put it past him."

"Perhaps, if he knew it was illegal, he just wanted to get rid of it as soon as possible. Before someone caught up with him."

"Who would bother with that miserable little toad? He's just a small-time crook, making a bit of money on the side. If he was dealing in hundreds of endangered birds, then it would be worth someone's while to nick him. A chance for the government to score some long-overdue brownie points with CITES, or whoever. No," Finn shook his head, "even if he was caught, a few dollars under the counter would get him off the hook in no time. You know the system as well as I do. Much less trouble for everyone that way."

Finn thought for a moment. "On the other hand, something certainly seemed to have put the wind up him." He smiled at the recollection. "I've never seen anyone look so shifty."

"What are you going to do with it?" Layla looked sorrowfully at the quetzal. "When its foot's mended, will you let it go free? No one should keep a bird like that in captivity, even if it were possible."

"For once, even I agree with you. But you can't release a bird like this just anywhere."

"Couldn't you let it go round here," Layla said. "You never know, maybe it'll come back and visit you sometimes."

"Funnily enough, the conditions in the Altamirada gorge might be nearly right. We're certainly the right altitude here." Finn considered the idea, then shook his head. "No, it wouldn't work. Even if this was the right terrain, there are no other quetzals around here; and I couldn't do that to my lovely boy, now could I?"

"Oh, but there might be, mightn't there?"

"No, not a chance," Finn said closing the box.

"But there must have been once. What about the Quetzal Court at home?"

"That's named after a myth, not a real bird. And it may be nothing to do with quetzals at all. Believe me, quetzals are a Central American bird. Panama is about as far south as you're ever likely to find one."

"All right then, what about the quetzal feathers that Magdalena used to have. When I was little she used to sew them into my clothes. For luck, she said."

"Oh God, not more of Magdalena's old mumbo jumbo. Layla, she could have got them from anywhere. They were probably parakeet feathers."

"OK then, I'll ask her when I get home."

"Yes, do. Only tell her that she's not to come begging for any of my quetzal's feathers. Voracious old witch, she'd pluck the poor thing bald with her bare hands if she thought she could get away with it."

EIGHT

It was Jack who first suggested that Baltazar should come back to Santa Luz.

"He needed somewhere to paint. Somewhere remote, where he wouldn't be disturbed. He's preparing for an exhibition, so I hear. I've lent him the house up at El Indio. It was the least I could do," he told Layla. "I can't help remembering that if circumstances had been different, Santa Luz might have been his."

Jack tried, and failed, to imagine what it would be like to be Baltazar. Baltazar, the dispossessed. For some reason a recurring image presented itself to him whenever he was reminded of this fact, and he would imagine him gazing, like Beelzebub, through the gates into his lost white world in the mountains. A thought too terrible to contemplate.

"His father Patricio was a great friend of mine," Jack went on, with some difficulty shaking away this picture in his head. "He was the only one who might have held on to Santa Luz, but the old *patrón*, Pedro Peron y Imbaburra, left it in trust to all his children. There was a time when Patricio tried to buy the others out, but by the time the lawyers got round to breaking the trust his heart had gone out of it somehow."

"The twentieth century seduced them all, that's what

you always used to say," Bettina lay back in her chair, resting her head against the cane. "For the very rich, life was always easy in Veracruz. It must have seemed like paradise after this."

The conversation on the verandah, as they sat watching the evening sliding across the mountain, was ostensibly for Layla's benefit but, as usual, silently subtitled by Bettina and Jack, and the old, familiar wounds between them.

"Just think," Bettina said, closing her eyes against the sun, "decent restaurants, theatres, telephones that actually worked. A shop which didn't take two hours to drive to. I know the feeling. Once you're in Veracruz, it's easier to catch a flight to New York, or even to Europe, than it is to get back to Santa Luz again. And usually a lot more desirable."

'Not now.' Layla, who was used to these exchanges, found herself wishing. 'Not this evening. It is too beautiful an evening for that.'

But Jack, thinking of Baltazar, seemed not to hear her.

"It must be strange for him, having us living here now," Layla said to him. "Do you think he minds?"

"Minds? I don't see why."

It was Bettina who answered her. She opened one eye, looked towards her husband. "Who, apart from your father, would want to be saddled with this old pile of rubble anyway?"

It was the usual challenge, but lazily said, sapped of its usual bite. Layla watched her look out across the mountain. 'What is it that keeps her from seeing Santa Luz as we do?' she wondered. 'She sees these mountains as a physical object. They have no spirit for her, no meaning other than the entirely commonplace one of rock and earth, now silhouetted against the evening sky. The fact that it is part of Santa Luz is irrelevant to her. It could be a mountain in the Swiss Alps. It would make no difference.'

And yet, looking at Bettina, Layla could not help admiring her. In her middle forties now, she was still beautiful. Her skin was good; no longer as fine and pale as it had been, but still with that particular quality of Englishness about it, a translucence which made younger women seem old beside her. The same startling Pre-Raphaelite hair shot through with gold. And there was something else: something in the way she walked, a certain vibrancy in her voice, a gracefulness in the fall of her clothes, which made Layla, with her darkness, feel clumsy beside her. Crude earthenware beside the finest porcelain. Layla turned away towards the mountain again.

Bettina watched Layla as she leant up against the balustrade. 'How she has grown up,' she was thinking. 'How sudden it has all been. She is a woman now, like myself.' Bettina smiled inwardly. 'She was always so dark when she was little, so secretive. A changeling I used to think sometimes. No, no, she was not like me at all.'

She remembered how she used to long for another child, a child who would be entirely hers, who would not slip from her, in the way that Layla had done, into the hands of others' keeping.

'It would probably have been the same with any child,' she thought. 'I was not a good mother, always too quick, too impatient. Always longing for her to be something that she was not. She was so composed . . .' Bettina sighed, closed her eyes again. 'I don't know where she got that from. Not from Jack. Not from me, for sure. She seemed to get her composure from the earth. It was strange. It wasn't natural, not in a child.'

She watched as Layla turned to talk to Jack. She watched as he smiled and slipped his hand into hers. Beyond them, the eucalyptus trees glowed silver and gold against the white walls, still warm from the day's sun.

'Perhaps it could be different now,' she thought, watching them together. 'It is never too late. Now that she is grown up we should make a new beginning. Away from here, away from all the old memories. Perhaps I will take her to England.' She was struck by the thought. 'Yes, England. God knows, I've tried often enough in the past. But it was never the right time, what with Jack always sinking our

95

every penny into this bottomless pit.' The thought of the house rose like the memory of a bitter taste, almond or aloe, on her tongue. 'But perhaps this is the right time now, the time to show her her other self, the self she hardly realises is hers at all.'

She looked over to Layla, still leaning against the verandah palings, and surveyed her with new tenderness. She was wearing a cotton skirt, white with pink and green roses printed on to it, and an old white shirt still crumpled from the long drive back from Altamirada. 'Her looks are improving. Maybe I should buy her some new clothes. Yes, a new beginning. With Jack, too. The three of us together. From now on it will be different.'

A week later Bettina and Layla drove into Altamirada together. Dropping Bettina in the plaza, Layla drove around the block and parked outside the back entrance of Chino's, where the Santa Luz supplies were delivered once a month. She went in through a gateway and found herself in a small back patio full of empty soft drinks crates, kerosene cans and potato peelings.

"Vinicio?"

"*Sí?*" A voice answered her from inside one of the *bodegas*.

"It's me, Layla."

"*Momento, señorita.*"

After a few minutes a neat little man with a leathery face emerged, wiping his palms on a chef's apron.

"*Buenos días, beunos días,*" he took Layla's hand warmly. "Ay, you're back from the great city then? How was it?"

"A terrible heat, Vinicio, a terrible heat. You would not be able to imagine it."

"Ay!" The little man shook his head, "But here, too, or haven't they told you? The butter melts even in the *bodegas*, the fruit is all rotten. And the meat goes off no sooner than look at it." He regarded Layla sorrowfully. "My wife says it is enough to finish her off, this heat."

"Vinicio!" Layla laughed, "it's not that bad, surely?"

"Well, if it gets any worse, you know how it is," he raised his shoulders, with the air of one determined not to be convinced. "She never liked the heat, my wife. Anyway," he wiped his hands again in a business-like way on his apron, "I have your stores ready. I'll be loading them into the jeep for you, shall I? You have a seat inside where it's still cool."

Forty years ago, in a moment of extravagant enterprise, Chino's had been built as a *thé dansant*, an extraordinary white elephant in a town so small, and one which had enjoyed only the most fitful vogue amongst the younger inhabitants of Altamirada. As well as a delivery point for the monthly supplies from Veracruz, Vinicio now ran the place as a cheap *comedor*, frequented occasionally by travelling salesmen in shiny suits who ate their *churrascos* and *huevos al pobre* beneath the dust-filled canopies of potted palms. Vinicio had once tried to rename the place, after himself, but unlike the original owner, long since departed and forgotten, the old name had refused to be uprooted.

Inside the room it was shuttered and cool. It was too early for lunch, and although the tables were laid in readiness, swaddled in thick white cloths, the room was still enclosed in darkness. Layla wandered through to the door at the far side of the room. Through the glass, which still bore the logo 'Chino's' in scrolled red paint, she could see down the road to the corner of the plaza. She looked through, wondering if she might catch a glimpse of Bettina waiting for her, but there was no one in sight.

She drew back, and sat down at one of the tables to wait. The walls were the same deep brown colour, like syrupy chocolate, that they had been for forty years. As a child Layla had longed to lick a piece of the wall, convinced that it would taste of chocolate too, and had once tentatively put out her tongue to try it, ending up with a sad, acid-tasting mouthful of dust.

Looking round, she tried to imagine what it must once have been like in the heady few months of the *thé dansant*. Jack could remember going there once with Patricio Peron, in the days when the Peron y Imbaburras still ruled at Santa Luz. They had picked up some of the local tarts and

97

danced there all afternoon, teaching them old-fashioned Viennese waltzes, the samba and the quickstep.

Layla thought of Jack forty years ago, dancing through those long afternoons; and the melancholy women with their tight skirts and muscular calves, gliding across the parquet in cheap, high-heeled shoes. She imagined, too, the other men and women at the tables watching them, their faces sepia-coloured, as in an old photograph, waiting for partners that never came, drinking tea that tasted of tears.

Through the glass the street outside was suspended in a dreamy haze. Beyond it, under the pepper trees in the plaza, with her packages and baskets, Bettina was now clearly in view. She was talking to Baltazar Peron.

"There you are at last," Bettina waved as Layla drove up. "Come and meet our new neighbour."

Awkwardly Layla clambered out of the jeep. With Bettina standing so close to her she felt suddenly, inexplicably, very English: as if she were no longer herself, but in some way enveloped by her mother's presence, grafted on to her like an extra limb. Instead of kissing him, the Latin way, she found herself holding out her hand. He shook it; said something to her which, in her confusion, she did not quite hear.

"I'm sorry?"

"Oh wake up, darling! In a dream as usual," Bettina said, turning to Baltazar again. "Layla has been longing to meet you, you know. Ever since she got back from Veracruz."

Layla felt a small part of herself shrivel up, like a tiny frostbitten bud. 'Not like this,' she thought, 'I did not envisage it to be like *this*.'

"You must come and have dinner with us again soon," Bettina chattered on, drawing her arm around Layla's waist, "we have hardly seen you at all. Layla would love it."

He was not as tall as she had imagined. His hair, which he wore long, almost to his shoulders, was black, so black it seemed to have the Indian sheen of blue in it.

From the way they were talking, it seemed as though they had known each other much longer than the few short weeks Baltazar had been at Santa Luz. He was saying something. Bettina laughed, throwing back her head, so that her neck was exposed, arched and white like a bird's. Layla noticed that they were speaking in English, and that his eyes, narrowed against the sunlight, were blue.

Under the dusty pepper trees Bettina's pale skin seemed finer than ever. Red lips, red hair. She was wearing a faded blue shirt of very thin, almost transparent cotton; and up her arms, as always, the heavy gold bracelets. She is like a cat, Layla thought, always knowing how to arrange herself to her best advantage.

"So, Friday, then?" Bettina was saying.

She put her hands to her hair, smoothing it behind her ears. Layla watched the gold bracelets rising and falling up her arms as she moved, glittering in the sun.

She does not flirt with him, she thought, she simply pulls his attention towards her. His eyes have not left her face.

Beyond Baltazar, behind the ravaged, pockmarked church, stretched the road to Santa Luz, hard and white in the midday sun.

*   *   *

"Well, what do you think?"

Bettina drove, as she always drove, with only one hand on the wheel, taking the corners too fast.

"Think of what?"

Layla felt hot and irritable. The thought of discussing Baltazar with her mother was suddenly more than she could bear. Avoiding Bettina's eye she gazed down into the gorge which fell to one side of the road. A cloud, the size of a man's hand, drifted beneath them, hovering over the canopy of trees and creepers. In the top branches of one tree Layla could see the skeletal figure of a turkey vulture, outlined against the sky.

"Baltazar, of course, who else?"

Bettina's bracelets sang brassily together as the jeep lurched around another bend.

"Oh, yes," Layla was annoyingly vague. "Baltazar." She continued to stare abstractedly out of the window. "He seems very nice."

Bettina's scarlet lips twitched.

"Very nice!" she repeated to herself in amazement. "Darling girl, he's an absolute *dish*. When I was your age I would have died for him." Bettina looked round at her, smiling her bright, accomplice's smile, "But don't go telling your father that, whatever you do."

Layla watched her pull the mirror round so that she could see her own reflection. Saw her gaze critically into the glass. Check her lipstick, her hair. As if it mattered, Layla thought. There would be no one to see her on the journey back to Santa Luz, no one at all.

Around a corner two men wearing yellow construction workers' hats came into view. They were measuring something along the side of the road with poles and pieces of string. Still holding the steering wheel with only one hand, Bettina swerved to avoid them.

"Mummy! Watch out, you'll have an accident."

Impatiently, Layla ran her fingers through her hair. Her head had begun to ache a little in the heat. Her skin was marbled with sweat, on her forehead, her neck, between her breasts.

"Honestly, Layla, I can't believe you don't fancy him just a teeny weeny bit?"

'I hate her,' Layla thought. 'When she is like this, I really think I almost hate her. Why can't she leave me to have my own thoughts, why must she always intrude so on everything.'

She remembered the conversation with Baltazar in the plaza. Remembered Bettina, how affected and English and strident her voice had sounded . . . 'Layla has been so *longing* to meet you . . .'

Layla could not bear the idea of discussing Baltazar, but in this mood it was impossible to deflect Bettina; impossible to remain silent, thinking one's own thoughts. Bettina would simply chip away, chip, chip, chip, until she had wheedled something, anything, out of you.

"Really, Mummy," Layla said, with resignation, "how should I know? I only met him for five minutes. And in any case you did most of the talking."

"All right, all right. Only asking." Bettina was conciliatory. "No need to be so huffy about it, silly girl."

'Poor darling, she thinks I don't know,' Bettina was thinking. 'Of course she fancies him. I can see the signs a mile off. And let's face it, who wouldn't. It's a shame she had to be quite so shy and tongue-tied about it all. It's not going to get her very far. If only she could bring herself to confide in me . . .'

From the corner of her eye, she cast Layla a brief, appraising look.

'Her looks are definitely improving. Amazing long legs. Sexy as hell, I shouldn't wonder, lucky thing. I wonder if she's still a virgin? God, she'd faint with embarrassment if I asked her.' Bettina suppressed a smile. 'She seems so innocent, so young for her age, and yet sometimes there's a look about her . . . I wonder if anyone really knows what goes on inside that funny, dark head. Finn says I tease her too much. I overwhelm the poor girl, he says.' Bettina, glancing at Layla again, still staring silently out of the window, felt suddenly doubtful. 'Maybe he's right. But I can't help wishing, just sometimes, that she would confide in me.'

"Hey, guess what Baltazar told me," Bettina said, remembering suddenly, "I almost forgot, an amazing bit of gossip. Finn has bought himself the most extraordinary new bird, some kind of bird of paradise apparently."

"Yes, I know, a quetzal," Layla said, relieved that Bettina had decided to change the subject – this, too, was so like Bettina, these sudden swooping changes in her conversation – and then could not resist adding, "I was there when he bought it, last week."

"Oh." Bettina, momentarily, was put out, as Layla knew she would be. "You never told me. A quetzal, now that really is extraordinary . . . Anyway," she rushed on, "the thing is this bird, this quetzal, has turned out to be the most incredible crowd-puller."

"Oh?" Bettina was gratified to see that Layla was genuinely surprised. She looked round at last. "What do you mean, crowd-puller?"

"Well, apparently all these people – Indians mainly – have started turning up on his doorstep, demanding to see this miraculous bird. The news about it seems to have spread like wildfire."

"How strange." Layla stared at the road ahead, thinking hard. "Why, do you think?"

"I've no idea. Baltazar didn't say. Some silly superstition I expect. Or maybe they just want to have a look." Bettina shrugged. "Is it very beautiful?"

"Yes. Extraordinarily so." Layla remembered the little panting bird surrounded, like a Chinese emperor's robes, by its impossible, exquisite plumage. "The most beautiful bird I have ever seen, I think."

"Damn, I wish you'd told me. We could have popped in to see the great wonder for ourselves. I didn't think. Oh, well, next time. I wonder how everyone got to hear about it," Bettina mused. "According to Baltazar it's not just locals. Finn's had some of our people down there, too. Santiago Menchu asked him for a lift the other day, especially so he could go and see it."

"Santiago?" Layla thought of the caretaker up at El Indio, an old Indian bent double with rheumatism. "I shouldn't think Santiago's been into Altamirada for years. And I shouldn't think he's *ever* been down there by car."

"I know. Quite a little pilgrimage when you come to think of it. Too far to go just for a peek at a pretty bird." Bettina looked thoughtful. "I wonder what it's all about."

As they took the turning off the road for Santa Luz, Layla took one last look behind her at the gorge. In the midday heat the forest was eerily quiet, pulsing with silent life. She thought of Finn, who loved the view of the gorge from his balcony almost as much as his birds. At times like this, he used to say, you could almost hear the green growing. Bettina eased the jeep over a ditch and then up on to the track which climbed into the mountains.

"You know, when we were first married I got quite interested in quetzals. In the cult of Quetzalcoatl especially, because of the Quetzal Court at home."

"Really?" Layla felt her irritation evaporating. Coming from Bettina this was an extraordinary admission.

"Don't look at me like that. Yes, I did." Bettina smiled back at her. "They used to worship him with butterflies, you know. I always liked that."

"And what else?"

"All sorts of strange things. The quetzal itself has always been a powerful symbol. Because you can't keep them in captivity, they're traditionally thought of as an emblem of liberty. The miraculous appearance of a quetzal – and there are some well-documented cases, even some quite recent ones – is still considered a sanctifying sign. No wonder everyone's so excited, it all makes sense now."

She turned to Layla again, "In Mexico, where the cult first appeared, the chief priest representing Quetzalcoatl used to wear a fabulous cloak made of hundreds of quetzal feathers. They were so highly prized that the penalty, for a commoner, for unlawfully killing a quetzal was death." Bettina fell silent, thinking to herself for a moment, and then laughed, "I wonder if Finn knows that."

"I doubt it."

Layla looked away again. 'But I know someone who does,' she thought, remembering Magdalena's face, the fear and elation in her eyes as Layla had described the quetzal.

"Anyway, that's enough about Finn." Bettina sensed

that the moment was ripe. "Tell me, how would you like to go to England for a few months?"

*   *   *

"So, you've met our friend Baltazar Peron at last."

"Yes, we bumped into him in Altamirada yesterday."

Layla leant down to unlatch the gate. She nudged her horse forward, holding open the gate until Jack had passed through. "Mummy invited him for dinner on Friday. Did she tell you?"

"Yes, she did. Good idea."

It was early in the morning. Behind them Santa Luz lay broodingly in the shadows. As Layla turned to shut the gate, she saw the tops of the trees flare suddenly gold as they caught the first rays of the sun.

Jack, sitting very upright, rode on ahead, his long legs sheathed in an ancient pair of peon's leather leggings. These had belonged to the old *patron*, Don Pedro, and to his father before him, and now, like a badge of seigniory, Jack too had adopted them whenever he went riding around the farm.

Jack was not passionate or even sentimental about horses as, being an Englishman and a farmer, some people expected he might be. He rode well. Not showily, but with a vigour which his tall, increasingly stooped frame no longer allowed him on the ground. On the rare occasions when he visited Veracruz he took no interest in the polo matches or racing at the Club Hippico, but he rode like a true horseman, as though the animal was an extension of his own body.

"So, what did you think of him?" Jack asked Layla as they rode on, and then as though pre-empting her reply, said, "Rather a nice chap, I've always thought. Clever, too."

"Mummy seems very keen on him."

Layla regretted the words as soon as she had spoken them. She still could not think of the conversation in the plaza without a twinge, but she was aware that what she had said sounded spiteful and childish, and she was ashamed.

Jack, if he minded at all, did not show it. "Yes, she does, doesn't she," he said mildly. He held his reigns up high in one hand like a gaucho, looking neither to left or right, but staring straight ahead of him towards the distant snowline of the mountains. After a few minutes he added, "It's nice for her to have a new neighbour. It's nice for all of us, of course, but particularly for your mother, especially now that the Iturraldes have gone back to live in Veracruz again." A ghost of a smile passed over his face, but Layla could not read the mood behind it. "It's one of the reasons I asked Baltazar to come back and live here for a while," he went on. "He makes her laugh. You would have noticed that, I expect. In Altamirada."

All around them, for as far as Layla could see, the fields lay patterned with tigerish, early-morning stripes of light and shade. How like the two of them this was, she thought. If Bettina had been here in her place she would have been full of questions, exclaimings, speculations; wanting to prise every last drop of information from this one comment. But because it was the two of them, Layla and Jack, they rode on side by side in silence. Clearly Jack thought there was nothing more to be said. It did not occur to Layla to ask him for explanations.

'Some people said that Jack was a cold man. He was not. The thing about her father,' Layla reflected, 'was that he never pried. You could tell him things. He would listen, sympathise. Advise only if you asked him to. His advice was always good, practical, succinct. Jack never wasted words. And he never tried to make you say more than you wanted to say; or attributed to you thoughts or feelings or desires which you did not have, but which someone else thought you might, or should have. Your thoughts were your own when you were with Jack.'

Behind them the sun had now risen clear above the trees. Layla pulled off the poncho which she always wore when they went riding together in the mornings, and tucked it behind her saddle. It promised to be another close, cloudless day.

Even at Santa Luz, high up in the cool elbow of the mountains, the weather had continued to be unnaturally hot. Although each afternoon thunder clouds gathered promisingly overhead, they had presaged rains which never fell. Maria-Magdalena said it was an omen, but Layla was not unduly worried. This was always the hottest and driest time of the year, and now, riding along with Jack, she felt no urgency speaking to her out of the land.

The horses moved slowly, thigh-deep through a field of ripening maize. Layla could feel the ground, hard and cracked, beneath their hooves, but the heads of corn were as yellow as butter in their silky, purple-tassled pouches. When she looked up there was still a distant trace of snow on the peaks behind Cotacotani.

They were headed now along the path which led towards El Indio, on the furthermost boundary of the farm lands. Since her return from Veracruz, Layla had spent a good deal of time riding or walking round the farm but until now El Indio, where the farmstead rented by Baltazar lay, had remained unvisited.

At the edge of the field the track diverged into two; one path striking off up the mountain, the other continuing around its skirts to El Indio itself. Layla reined in her horse.

"Do you want to go on?"

"I thought I'd ride on up to El Indio," Jack said.

He had made no further reference to Bettina, or to Baltazar, as Layla knew he would not. "Want to have a word with old Santiago. There's some fencing up there needs seeing to. I thought I'd go and have a look, see what needs to be done before I send Martin up on Monday. Do you want to come?"

106

Layla shook her head. Having held back for so long, she was now filled with curiosity to see El Indio again. But, for some reason, she did not want to do it with anyone else, not even Jack. She wanted to see it alone. "I thought I'd go on up the mountain, maybe go up and see Tia." Layla made her excuses. "I haven't had a chance to see her since I've been back."

"OK. I'll see you later then."

"Yes, later."

Layla watched Jack set off down the path, a strangely solitary figure cantering into the distance. When he was nearly out of sight she turned her horse's head towards the mountain and struck off up the path.

Layla rode slowly up through the cool forest. She remembered the day, years ago, when Magdalena had brought her up the mountain for the first time. Then the path had been an unknown place, half-seen in the moonlight. Hobgoblins waited behind every trunk, ready to pounce. Since then it had become as familiar to her as the rest of Santa Luz, as familiar to her as her own face reflected in a mirror.

Layla reached the treeline and came to the rock where Magdalena had first shown her the view of Santa Luz. She remembered the extraordinary sensation of looking down on the house from this height, how different it had looked from this new perspective, and how vast, spread out like a red and white map below them. She turned now to look at it again, wondering why it was that although certain things, like distances and time, seemed to diminish with age, this view of Santa Luz had always remained the same. It appeared more complete, more of a piece, from here than from anywhere else. It was impossible not to look. The house compelled all eyes, a lodestone fixed for ever in the lap of the mountains.

Layla nudged her horse again, urging it upwards. She took her time, letting the animal find its own way between the rocks and ruts along the track, and soon found herself at the first pass. The pile of stones was still there. Layla dismounted, searched around in the undergrowth for a pebble and placed it on the pile. She then sat down to let the horse rest. She closed her eyes, feeling the sun burn, harder now, on her face. The cool of the morning was over; today it would be hotter than ever.

It was very quiet on the mountainside that morning. Sitting there she remembered how she had sat on this very same spot with Magdalena. She remembered the ache in her legs, the hot, tindery smell of the parched grass over the mountainside, and the feeling that the journey up the mountain would never end. She remembered, too, a faint but persistent feeling of apprehension.

Layla gazed down into the valley beneath her, only half seeing. She thought of the little sheep girl she had seen that day, with her tangle of dusty hair, remembering with a smile how much she had longed to be like her. That day had been special, bridging the gap between the two worlds within Santa Luz. That day she had made a choice. She could have turned back, she could have refused to go on, couldn't she? But she had not. She had made her choice.

Then another thought came, unasked, into her mind's eye: Bettina's rage, and the look of desperation in her eyes when she had seen Layla's sad, cropped head. As she sat there it struck her, quite forcibly, for the first time that Magdalena had been wrong to do what she had done: to have deliberately chosen a time when both Bettina and Jack were away in Veracruz. It struck her too, in a moment of clarity, that this was what Bettina had been so angry about. It was not the ceremony in itself. It was the way in which it was done, on the sly, behind her back; as though she was of no account. There had been some talk of dismissing Magdalena – Layla remembered this only dimly – but it had never come about. Of course not. Santa Luz without Magdalena was unimaginable.

Layla stood up and made her way back to the two smooth rock faces which marked the pass. Instead of making her way onwards up the mountain towards Tia's village, she looked around her and, seeing that there was no one around, made her way quickly through the bushes to the left of the rock.

The undergrowth was thicker than she remembered. Protecting her face with one arm, and feeling for the guiding surface of the rock with the other, Layla pushed her way through. After a while the vegetation petered out into a steep, slippery surface of scrubby grass. At first her progress was slow, but after a few minutes the ground levelled a little and she found herself walking less precariously along a sandy ribbon, once an old sheep track. Layla followed this path, which dipped and sloped downwards along the contours of the mountainside, finally coming to an end at the base of a massive outcrop of stone.

From a distance it looked as if this outcrop was all of a piece, but anyone examining it at close quarters would soon see that the furthermost edge of the outcrop was in fact a vast, freestanding boulder, separated from the mountainside by a narrow corridor. To this corridor Layla made her way, easing herself between its smooth walls. She emerged the other side and, catching her breath, looked down over El Indio.

El Indio, strictly speaking, was not the name of the valley at all, but the name of the rock under which Layla now crouched which was said to resemble the face of a man. But because the rock overlooked the valley, both the valley itself and the farmstead now rented by Baltazar were by inference also known as El Indio. Except for the caretaker, the Indian Santiago Menchu, no one had lived at El Indio for many years until Baltazar's return.

Beneath her the valley, as always, was eerily quiet. Jack used to say that it was the shape of it, a near perfect circle, which played tricks on the ears, a kind of geological joke. But Santiago, who was used to the capriciousness of the land and its tricks of light and sound, said the valley was filled with *apus*, the spirits of the rocks and streams and surrounding mountains.

Layla crouched beneath the rock, her head throbbing from the heat and the exertion of the climb. Her thin shirt clung to her back and her skin felt oily with sweat. Above her, the clear blue of the early morning sky was already becoming overcast. The air was very still, very close. The sun, slanting through the clouds, cast the valley in a strange green light.

From her viewpoint, Layla could see the house perfectly. Apart from an old Toyota parked in the courtyard at the back, there was nothing about the place to indicate any human presence. No sound of voices; no laundry hanging up to dry, no crates of wine, baskets of fruit, or provisions boxes from Chino's in the *bodega*. Nothing to indicate that Baltazar had taken possession of it at all.

The main part of the house, shaded by pepper trees, was constructed around three sides of a rectangle. It was entered either from the courtyard at the back of the house, where *bodegas* and outhouses made up the fourth side of the rectangle, or from the front where a flight of steps led up to a long, balustraded verandah, similar in style to the verandah at Santa Luz. Scarlet bougainvillaea grew across the front of the house. Someone had hung a coloured cotton hammock between two of the pillars. It caught the breeze, moving to and fro.

As she watched, a figure emerged from the shadows at the back of the verandah and came swiftly down the steps. Instinctively, Layla shrank back. She crouched down, hardly daring to breathe, her body tensed, pressed against the hardness of the rock behind her.

Baltazar?

Layla felt both exhilarated and a little foolish. She could feel her heart pounding against her breast. Perhaps it was the dizzying drop beneath her, or perhaps the precariousness of her eyrie-like perch, but looking down she felt suddenly faint. Her limbs became weak, sapped of their strength.

As she moved backwards, she scraped her arm against the abrasive rock. The scratch, while not deep, drew blood. Layla winced, dabbed at the scratch ineffectually with the tail of her shirt. Her whole body felt tender, a fragile thing compared to the massiveness of rock and mountain all around her.

At the foot of the steps the figure paused, put his hand to his forehead as though to shade his eyes from the glare of the sun. Layla followed his gaze, and saw that he was watching a man on horseback – most probably Jack – riding up into the valley. A faint plume of dust heralded their progress. The man – Baltazar, Santiago, she was too far away to see for sure – seemed to recognise the horseman. As the plume of dust drew nearer he put up his hand to wave, and then started to move slowly through the grove of trees, as though to greet him.

From her hiding place, it seemed to Layla, it was like sitting in the gods of an enormous amphitheatre, the figures below her performing like actors in an unrehearsed play. She watched in fascination as the little pin figures inched towards one another. Jack's horse moved smoothly forward. The figure on the ground, by contrast, seemed slow, almost jerky in his movements. He picked his way along in erratic bursts. He kept stopping, bending over, Layla noticed, as though he was looking for something on the ground.

Why had she come to spy on him like this? It was ridiculous, a silly childish game. Layla shifted uncomfortably under the rock. She could have come with Jack, she thought, she could have come on her own. She had the perfect right to go anywhere on the farm whenever she wanted to, even to El Indio.

By now the two figures had almost reached one another. Overhead the black clouds began to grumble. As the first drops of rain started to fall, Layla could bear it no longer. She turned and made her way quickly back up towards the pass.

So, although a few minutes later Layla was to hear the gunshot quite clearly, it was Jack alone who witnessed the murder of Santiago Menchu.

111

NINE

It is strange to think how love and death have always been connected in my life.

Last night I dreamt about Baltazar.

I do not often dream about him these days, just as in the beginning I did not dream about him, although for different reasons. In the beginning he was too much with me, in the forefront of my mind, for him to come to me in dreams.

Even before I knew him – and it was a long time before I really knew him – in my mind's eye I saw him everywhere. His presence was with me wherever I went. He was at my shoulder when I rode around the farm, at my side when I drove into Altamirada; he was in all the shadows and the secret places of Santa Luz. I half feared to look at myself in the mirror, in case I should find his face looking out at me beside my own.

The strangest thing about my dream is that it is the same one I had the night Santiago Menchu was killed.

It is a simple dream. I am in a room at Santa Luz, a room I do not recognise. I am kneeling on the floor facing the wall. As I kneel, I become aware that there are people, perhaps a great deal of people, standing behind me, although I do not know who they are, or what they are doing there. I cannot turn around to see them because my head is caught in a vice-like grip. I am fixed there, looking towards the wall. After a while, I sense that Baltazar is there. He has come forward out of the crowd of people behind me, and kneels down by my side. I am sick with longing for him, but because of the vice pressing around my head, I cannot touch him, or even turn to look at him fully. All I can see is a shadow in the corner of my eye. As we kneel there a ray of sunshine comes shining in through the window above us and strikes me lightly on the breast.

I suppose I believed that with him I would be complete. It was not only the fact that, like me, he had been born at Santa Luz. For me, he *was* Santa Luz. He was the earth and rock and sky made flesh. He was the two worlds, perfectly merged. His blood was the blood of twenty generations, compared with mine, which was but one generation deep.

Santa Luz did not belong to us, it never had. It did not belong to my father, or to me. We were just passing through, custodians of the Quetzal Court for a little while, no more. That summer, with all its uncertainties, I think I believed that he was the link which would bind me to Santa Luz for ever.

Sometimes when I watched you with Baltazar, when you laughed together, I was jealous. I used to imagine what he and I would look like lying together, dark on dark. And I tried to imagine what you would feel if you could see us like that. We would look so beautiful together, with the morning light coming in through the shutters, glancing over us like the blades of a sword. I think I hoped you would be jealous, too.

I had been with men before. Do I shock you? I am telling you now only because I realise how little you ever really knew about my life outside Santa Luz. Perhaps I should say, how little I let you know.

Of course, I met a few men when I was living with Maria-Ines in Veracruz. At first they were mostly the brothers and cousins of my school friends and, later on, fellow students at the *Universidad Católica*. For the most part they were young, and there was little passion in them.

113

We were, I think, no more than decorations to them, like flowers to be worn in their lapels. They had no desire for us, other than that we should sit beside them in their cars, or in the pavement cafés where we went to greet our friends. There they would buy us sodas and milk shakes. Drinks for little girls. Even their kisses were chaste. Love, if it came into it, had the pallor of religious devotion. Girls like us, I came to understand, were their future wives, and the mothers of their children. As such we must be kept pure, immaculate vessels for their later use. Sexuality was a man's preserve. There were other women, of course, who they would go to. Whores from the old town, mainly. They used to do it with them, I'm told, in the back seat of the car, five or six of them, one after the other.

I was walking down the street the other day, and I saw a book in a shop window, *Old Gringo* by Carlos Fuentes, a story about the Mexican revolution. It reminded me of something I had forgotten. It reminded me that in Vera-cruz I was always *la gringa*. Even though it was often Maria-Ines, with her pale skin and hair the colour of lemons, and not me whom people would mistake for a foreigner. I was always *la gringa*. At the university once or twice I was taken out by a boy who thought, mistakenly, that I would be easier than the others. Different.

I found myself wondering the other day if they ever called you *gringa*. I can't imagine that anyone did, but if they had I don't suppose you would have cared. You never minded being different. And that, of course, requires its own kind of courage.

TEN

Baltazar Peron was not a sentimental man. The last time he had entered the fastness of Santa Luz was more than twenty years ago, when he was a boy of nine. Since then, like the rest of his family, he had not given a thought to whether the house lived or died. In fact, until recently, he had rarely thought about it at all except as a curiosity, a distant memory from the past.

Since his return to Santa Luz he had passed the house many times; had seen it rise and fall, like a vast white ship on the horizon, each time he made his way to and from El Indio. On several occasions he had been to visit Jack and Martin the Eye in the estate office, but these were brief, business-like meetings which had taken place in the Stable Court, from which little of the main body of the house was visible. But until now he had no great curiosity to look inside. Now, for the first time in twenty years, Baltazar found himself entering Santa Luz from the Great Court. As he walked through the gates, hanging open on their rusty hinges, and passed into the vast flagstoned courtyard, he knew that the Santa Luz of his childhood was no longer.

Under his feet a creeping carpet of weeds and grasses grew promiscuously between the stones. The crumbling walls were pitted, as though with bullet holes, with the spores of age. The only thing which was familiar was the crucifix, mounted on a stone plinth at the centre of the courtyard. And to its right the squat white outline of the chapel. On the still evening air the scent of the eucalyptus trees and the warm stone, the scent of his childhood, overwhelmed him with an unbearable wave of nostalgia.

It was still early. On impulse Baltazar turned and made his way across the courtyard to the chapel. At the top of the steps, as he remembered, was a semi-circular platform. On it lay the remains of a ritual fire, a charred circle of ashes. Crouching down, he put his hands towards it and felt the embers still warm.

Pushing open the door to the chapel he was surprised to find that it opened smoothly on well-oiled hinges. Inside, except for the altarpiece, the building was quite plain. This, too, was as he remembered it: a monumental, primitive building, as dark and cavernous as the belly of a Noah's ark.

It was years since he had been inside a church, but as soon as he had stepped into the darkness the familiar, sweet stench – incense, lilies, remembered as though it were yesterday – engulfed him. Baltazar felt a bitter taste of bile rising to his mouth and, to his horror, beads of sweat began to prick against his forehead. Leaning against the nearest pillar, he waited for his nausea to pass.

He was still crouching there when he felt the girl behind him. He did not stand up immediately, but listened to the sound of her footsteps moving down the aisle. He wondered how long she had been there, obscured by the shadows.

"Are you all right?"

In the half-light it was difficult to see her face with any clarity.

"Thank you, yes. It's nothing," he straightened up. "It's the smell, the incense. I had forgotten how strong it was in here," he smiled at her apologetically. "I think it's gone to my head."

The girl leaned against the pillar opposite him, hands behind her back. She did not look at him.

"You'll get used to it. If you wait a while."

Baltazar put his handkerchief back into his pocket.

"I hope you don't mind my coming here," he said, rather more formally than he had meant to.

The girl looked surprised. "Mind? No. Why should I mind?" she said. "The chapel is open to anyone who wants to come here. *Estás en tu casa.*"

"Thank you," Baltazar gave a little bow.

'Was she being deliberately ironic?' he wondered. Somehow he thought not.

She had moved away from him and was walking to the front towards the altar. He saw that she was wearing what looked like a very old dress of some faded, flowery material. It had a low, rounded neckline, and a tight waist, a strangely childish design which somehow, Baltazar decided, looked surprisingly well on her. When the light was behind her, he could see the outline of her legs beneath the thin material.

Baltazar followed behind her down the aisle. They stopped together, side by side, in front of the altar. Unlike the rest of the chapel, the altarpiece was a baroque fantasy of pure silver, once extracted from the Peron y Imbaburra's own mines.

"Did you often come here? When you were a boy, I mean?"

When she spoke she did not look at him, but gazed intently up at the altar. Columns of silver, as light and delicate as sticks of liquorice, spiralled into the blackened rafters.

"Yes, often. I used to come here with my Tia Esmeralda every day, twice on Sundays. She was a very religious woman, my aunt. She was my great aunt, actually, my grandfather's sister. She brought me up. We used to call her Aunt Emerald. She always insisted that we spoke to her in English."

"Why?"

"It was a sort of snob thing she had, I think. She never

117

got married – a great stigma for a woman of her generation – and I think it helped her feel special, different in some way. One of your ambassadors here, back in the fifties, I forget his name, once told her she looked like Edith Sitwell. She was a great anglophile."

For the first time she looked at him and smiled. Beneath the sweep of her dark hair, her face was lit up by the smile, a sudden, startling, illumination. 'How unlike her mother she is,' he thought. 'About as unlike as it is possible to be.' There was a serenity about her, he realised, a kind of stillness, which was strangely compelling.

"I think you are fond of this place, no?" he questioned her.

"Yes, it's always been one of my special places here." She paused, as though uncertain whether to go on, and then added, "I like to come here at night."

"At night?"

Baltazar thought of those long, sleepy masses. The inside of the chapel had always been so dark and close, with the murmuring press of Indian bodies kneeling all around him on the floor. The black box which was the confessional had looked like a coffin turned on its side. Padre Ignacio sat inside it, the grille throwing a lattice of shadows across his grim, beaky profile. And that smell. Always that suffocating smell of incense, which blinded all other senses. And somewhere, deep within the recesses of his mind, the Indian boy lying bleeding on the ground.

"Aren't you frightened?"

"Frightened?" She drew on the word blankly. "No, not frightened. Not to come here."

"But it must be so dark in here at night. So . . . ghostly," Baltazar said. His tone was deliberately light. "Most girls I know would be frightened to come here on their own." The girl gazed at him with her dark eyes, saying nothing. "At night, I mean. On their own."

Baltazar felt himself floundering, conscious that he had missed the mark with her. He turned his sights back towards the altar, searching for another approach.

"It's good to see Santa Luz again."

To the left of the altar, an effigy of the saint, stiff as a Christmas-tree doll in her black and gold robes, stared down at them with glassy eyes. He was surprised, after all these years, by how pagan the figure looked.

"Yes."

She fell silent again. She was not helping him at all. Baltazar searched his mind for something, anything, which would force her to respond.

"Santa Luz," he began again, more thoughtfully this time, "Santa Luz, I think she is what you would call the eponymous saint of the hacienda, no?"

"Oh, is that the word?" The girl smiled at him again. "Your English is better than mine, I think."

"They say that the Indians will only bring her out of the chapel at times of great crisis or danger."

"Yes, I have heard that, but I have never seen it done. Have you?"

"Just once," Baltazar said. "A boy was killed, in the Great Court. But that was many years ago."

On either side of the altarpiece were a series of painted wooden panels, which together formed a tableau depicting scenes from the life of the Indian saint. Compared to the extravagance of the altarpiece, with its silver flutings, twists and coils, the painting of the panels was crude, and in parts irretrievably obscured by dirt and candle soot. But there was an energy in their very simplicity which never failed to impel the eye.

"Santa Luz was one of the first saints of the New World to be recognised by the Catholic church. Did you know that?"

"Of course. When I was a child, Magdalena used to tell me stories about her."

"Using the panels?"

"Yes," she said, surprised, "how did you know?"

"In my day we had a priest who lived here, Padre Ignacio. He used to do the same."

"Really?"

119

The girl seemed delighted at the thought. She turned and looked up towards the first panel. This showed a dark-plaited Indian girl wearing the traditional worsted and heavy bead collar of the mountain women.

"Santa Luz was an Indian girl from these parts – it was not called Santa Luz in those days, of course – she was a priestess among the Indians," she recited. "One day she had a vision of the Virgin Mary, and was converted to Christianity."

"Our Lady appeared to her on the mountain, Cota-cotani," Baltazar took up the story, "and urged her to accept the Christian god. If she did this, her people would stop resisting the Christian friars, and there would be peace."

"And as proof of her vision the stigmata appeared on her hands and feet in the form of roses, which grew out of her living flesh."

Silence fell between them again. At their feet, at the base of the altar, the stairs were covered with Indian offerings, candles, rose petals, gnarled heads of maize.

"I've always liked the sound of Santa Luz. An ambiguous kind of saint, and the perfect patron saint for the farm."

"Ambiguous?"

"Well, the fact that she was martyred at the hands of the same people who later canonised her. You remember the rest of the story? After the vision she decided to take Holy Orders and become a nun, a Carmelite. But less than two years afterwards the Inquisition burnt her at the stake as a witch, saying that she had lied to them about the vision, and that it was all a hoax. She was accused of continuing to perform the outlawed rituals of her own people in secret, fire worship and blood sacrifices. And when they questioned her, she did not attempt to deny it."

On the fifth panel Santa Luz stood with her head bowed in front of her inquisitors. She was wearing the robes and veil of a Carmelite novice. One man, dressed in a priest's frock, had been painted larger than the others. He stood facing her, with his finger pointing accusingly. Just visible, peering from behind the skirts of his robes, the artist had painted in a tiny scarlet figure of a demon, complete with horns and a toasting fork.

"But it wasn't true, was it? The priest who had accused her of these things confessed."

"On his death bed. Naturally. It always is, isn't it? Catholics, and priests especially, have always had an impeccable sense of timing," Baltazar said drily. "Santa Luz was reputed to be very beautiful. The priest had tried to have his way with her. She declined his offer, of course. And so, no doubt thinking to himself that she was only a worthless Indian – and in those days even the existence of souls in the Indians was still debated by the church – he forced her. When Santa Luz accused him of raping her, he invented the whole story in order to discredit her. It was his word against hers. No contest, as you say. So the Catholic church first martyred, then canonised her. An extraordinary irony."

In the last tableau the saint was dressed in Indian clothes again, the blood red tunic with the collar of gold at her neck. There was something both beautiful and barbaric about her. She was standing at the stake, the first flames licking up about her skirts to her waist. Instead of being tied to the stake with ropes, she seemed to stand there of her own accord, her hands outstretched.

"My mother says she is like the Mona Lisa," the girl said, still staring upwards at the panels. "It's true. Her eyes, they seem to follow you everywhere."

Unlike the conventional depiction of a martyr, eyes raised submissively to heaven, the artist had painted Santa Luz so that she appeared to be staring straight down into the belly of the chapel beneath her. There was an expression, oddly disconcerting, of triumph in her dark eyes.

They made their way back down the aisle.

"The Indians have always loved her best."

"Of course," Baltazar agreed. "She belongs to them in a way that no other Christian figure possibly can. But why? She was a martyr, undoubtedly. But a Christian martyr or an Indian martyr? It very much depends which side you look at it. She's kosher either way," he laughed. "Oh, yes, I've always thought Santa Luz a very diplomatic saint."

"And which side do you see her from?" Layla asked him.

"Santa Luz was an Indian through and through. No question. No vision could ever change that," Baltazar said without hesitation. At the doorway he stopped to let Layla pass through in front of him.

"You seem very sure," she said.

"Oh I've always been sure of that. You see, my mother was an Indian."

"Yes," Layla said, "I know. Living here, the stories about the saint were not the only ones I grew up with."

Baltazar walked back with Layla across the Great Court and into the house. To his surprise, he found his way through the labyrinth of courtyards and passageways without hesitation. They walked slowly, not speaking. He was aware that there was something disturbing here, something more than the fact of seeing with his own eyes what had been rumoured amongst his family in Veracruz: the colonnades, the sunken terraces and vaulted walks bruised blue with age; the dry fountains in the patios; the famous rose courtyard a wilderness; the cracked white adobe sprouting with grasses and vines.

A bird flying overhead gave a solitary cry. The sound seemed to pierce a certain heaviness in the air. That was it. It was not so much the decrepitude of the ravaged house which disturbed, as the profound, dreaming quietness which enfolded it.

They found Jack sitting on the verandah. The World Service news crackled from a wireless at his elbow. There was no sign of Bettina. When Jack saw Baltazar he switched off the set and came towards him, hand outstretched.

"Dear boy," he said, taking him by the arm, "come on in and sit down. Let me get you a drink. My wife will be along in a minute. I see you have already found Layla along the way."

122

"Yes, Layla has kindly been showing me round. But I'm still a little early, I'm afraid."

"Not at all, not at all. We are delighted to see you."

"The famous *hora inglesa*, as my grandfather used to call it. Even among our countrymen, my family have always been notorious for their extraordinary unpunctuality," Baltazar smiled. "I have just broken with the time-honoured habit of several generations of Perons."

"Not at all." Jack waved him to one of the rattan chairs. "Now, what'll you have?"

"Anything. Whatever you are drinking."

"Beer?"

"That would be fine."

"Something for you, Layla?"

"No, thanks." The girl had not sat down with them. "I must go and change. I promised Mummy" – she exchanged a look with her father – "I'll be back in a moment."

"And tell Magdalena that Baltazar has arrived," Jack called after her. "And your mother, too."

Baltazar watched as Jack prepared the drinks, stooping a little over a wicker table as old as the chairs. He wore a checked shirt, fraying at the collar, a pair of old, dirty denim trousers and soft shoes. Baltazar noticed the way his trousers fell from him, bagging around his thin shanks like a skin which had become too big. His face and hands had a brown, leathery texture, like a piece of old snakeskin. The mountain sun and wind had never been kind to Anglo-Saxon skin.

So this was the man, Baltazar reflected, who had once shot a puma on the mountain. As a boy one of his earliest memories was of seeing Jack ride into the Stable Court with the dead animal slung across his saddle. For many years after that, next to his father, Jack had been a kind of hero to him. He was the same age as Patricio, but looking at Jack now, Baltazar was sure he looked years older than his father would have done had he still been alive. An interesting face, he thought, casting a professional eye over him;

but when he looked closer there was a melancholy there too, something solitary, burnt out.

"Here you are," Jack came back with two glasses of beer. Baltazar took his, noticing that the liquid was slightly tepid, and that the glass, which Jack had only half filled, was not quite clean. Looking around him, he guessed that this was where the Halletts spent most of their time, and yet even this had a makeshift, unkempt feel to it. Baltazar only dimly remembered this particular verandah. It had once been, he suspected, part of the old servants' quarters, in the old days when there had been thirty or more servants living at Santa Luz at any one time.

Behind them against the wall was a dresser on which was ranged an odd assortment of plants and plant cuttings in terracotta pots. Scattered in between them was a collection of old gardening tools, a little rusting now, a riding crop, and a pair of gardening gloves, heavily impregnated with reddish soil; Bettina's, he guessed.

On the table, beneath the glass, lay piles of old books and yellowing magazines and seed catalogues, thick with what looked like years of accumulated dust and grime. A collection of riding boots and walking shoes lay stacked together beside the doorway and next to them, although there was no sign of a dog, an old basket, lined with hairy brown blankets. It was strange, Baltazar thought, that although this was the most lived in part of the house, the sense of decay was stronger here than anywhere.

A figure appeared at the doorway. Expecting to see Bettina, Baltazar half rose to his feet, but it was not her. Instead he saw an Indian woman, the Halletts' servant, coming towards them. She was carrying a tray with clean glasses and a bucket of ice. "Thank you, Magdalena." Jack cleared the drinks table so that she could put the tray down. "You remember Don Baltazar, don't you, Magda?" Jack said to the woman in Spanish. "The son of Don Patricio."

"*Sí, señor.*"

The woman looked up and smiled fleetingly, but she did not greet him directly, or call him by name, as the other

Indians at Santa Luz had always done without hesitation. She must have been only a few years older than he, and yet he did not recognise her, or find her name familiar. Jack saw his look of enquiry.

"Her father was Tio Menchu," he explained.

"The *curandero*? Yes, I remember him, how could I not." He glanced up at the woman again. "Menchu, did you say?"

"Yes," Jack said, in English again. "He died about two years ago. And in case you're wondering," he added, "Santiago Menchu was her father's cousin."

"I see. I'm sorry," he said to the woman, "for your cousin Santiago. A terrible thing."

"*Gracias, señor.*" The woman acknowledged him shortly, without looking up. While Jack and Baltazar talked she busied herself around the table, wiping its grimy surface with a cloth, setting out the glasses and the ice. Her movements were soft, dexterous. Her footsteps silent.

"I believe Bettina has asked Finn and Meredith to come along tonight, too." Baltazar was aware of Jack's eyes following the Indian woman as she moved around the table. "Have the others arrived yet, Magda?"

"*No, señor.*"

"But you'll bring them straight out here when they do?"

"*Sí, señor.*"

"Thank you. *Está bien.* Leave that now, I'll bring the rest of the things with me when I come in."

'These English!' Baltazar thought with amusement. The way he spoke to her was not the way the *patron* would normally speak to a servant. Jack's manner towards her was familiar – he addressed her consistently as 'tu' – but there was something else underlying this, something almost deferential, as though he were trying to coax something from her which she did not want to give.

Baltazar found himself following Jack's eyes, covertly studying the woman's face. This time he had the odd impression that he had seen her somewhere before after all, although he could not think where. For she was startling to look at. Her face was the face of a Greek icon, smooth-skinned and yet angular, her eyes slanting slightly upwards, expressionless as two black stones. 'Was it ever possible,' Baltazar wondered, 'to tell what was passing through that perfect, sculptured head?'

*   *   *

"Hundreds of them every day, it was quite extraordinary." Finn gesticulated with his soup spoon. "They all filed past as if it was Mao Tse-tung's cadaver. I've never seen anything like it."

"What did they want?" Bettina leaned forward, fascinated, her chin cupped in one hand. "Not just to look at it, surely?"

"Well, what else could they do?" Finn shrugged. "If there was some other reason, I certainly wasn't privy to it, put it that way."

Dinner took place not in the refectory as Baltazar remembered from the old days but, oddly, in a small ante-room just off the *sala mayor*. The room bore the signs of extensive repairs, with modern ceiling rafters and newly plastered, white-washed walls – Jack's work, he suspected – but he sensed it was little used. It had a musty smell, and the air temperature here, nearing the heart of the house, felt cold against his skin, as if cooled by the walls of a well. Otherwise the room was sparsely furnished, with bare tiled floors and a few pieces of cumbersome furniture: a large dining table with carved feet, and matching, ecclesiastical-looking chairs with high backs, like cardinal's thrones. Bettina had placed him at the foot of the table. Behind him, through a pair of old curtains, Baltazar was uncomfortably aware of the vast, galleried maw of the *sala mayor* disappearing into darkness.

"They only came because you let them," Meredith,

Finn's sister, was saying. She helped herself to more soup, which was served silently by the Indian woman. "You just have to be tougher with them, how many times do I have to say it. They're all the same, give them an inch and they'll take a mile." She turned to Baltazar and said in an undertone, "Like some people not a million miles away from here, wouldn't you agree?"

Baltazar was not entirely sure what she meant by this last remark. He smiled non-committally.

"Well, we certainly seem to have landed ourselves in a very extraordinary situation."

Meredith was neither loud, nor aggressive in any obvious sense, but there was something overwhelming in her manner which Baltazar recognised as peculiarly English. With her large bosoms and pudgy sandalled feet, there was an earthiness about her which he found faintly repulsive.

"All the chaps I'm employing on my yungas project started out that way. I don't know if I've ever told you about my yungas project?"

"Yes, Meredith, I'm sure Finn's filled him in," Bettina said quickly, trying to deflect her. "Besides, we still haven't heard the whole quetzal story."

"We're taking tourists night-hunting for caimans," Meredith carried on blithely, "not to shoot them, of course, just to observe, like a safari really. I'll take you down there one day, if you like."

Her behaviour towards him, he became aware, was coy, almost flirtatious. He wondered if she did it unconsciously, or consciously to annoy Bettina. At the far end of the table, Baltazar's eyes met the girl's. Without thinking, he gave her the ghost of a wink. The girl looked quickly away, and then down at her plate, but not before he saw that she was smiling.

"I had terrible trouble with them to start off with," he heard Meredith go on, "but I always make it clear what I will put up with, and what I won't. They never try anything on with *me*."

Bettina said nothing, but her eyes were very bright. He

noticed that she had hardly eaten all evening. She had left her soup untouched, and was kneading the bread on her sideplate into little balls between her fingers. He looked down the table again. Jack was sitting silently, barely replying when he was spoken to. The girl, too, had said very little. Now he saw that she was talking to Finn. Her voice was low, so that he could not hear what she was saying, but he noticed that she seemed more expansive and at ease with Finn than with anyone else. He found himself wishing that he was sitting closer to them, instead of being trapped between the conflicting claims of Bettina and Meredith.

"Everyone seems to think that there is some great mystery about the Indians here. I don't agree," Meredith said. "There's no mystery so long as you just treat them like everyone else, like ordinary human beings."

"Come on, Finn," Bettina, following Baltazar's gaze, cut in rather too sharply, "tell us more about the quetzal."

"Well, there's nothing more to tell really," Finn said. "After a few days they all stopped coming. And that was it." He turned to Layla. "Oh, and you'll pleased to know that the leg is better. It healed beautifully, as good as new."

"All the more reason to let it go now," Meredith said. "I looked it up in one of your books. You can't keep quetzals in captivity."

"Yes, I am aware of that, thank you," Finn said tartly. "I do know my birds. And I'll be the judge of when it's ready to go."

"You'd better watch out, Finn," Bettina leaned towards him, her hair falling across her shoulders in the candlelight. "In ancient Mexico, the penalty for a commoner killing a quetzal was death."

"Well, darling, it's a good thing we're not commoners living in ancient Mexico then, isn't it?"

"Do you really think it's a revival of the Quetzalcoatl cult?" Bettina seemed obsessed with the subject.

"God knows. They certainly treated it like some kind of sacred bird. Did I tell you that they kept on bringing it offerings . . ."

". . . by the end the whole house was like a grocer's shop, unbelievable . . ."

". . . but it does seem very unlikely, so far south."

"A nine-days' wonder, that's all. These things always are." Meredith cut through again. "What do you think, Baltazar?"

She smiled at him, revealing two rows of very white, very even teeth.

"Well, you know how it is around here. A marvellous-looking bird like a quetzal, not normally found in the area, might well appear to them in the light of something miraculous. The Indians have always believed that the land is full of spirits, in rocks, streams, mountains . . . so why not in a bird?"

"Quite. It could keep some lucky anthropologist going for years," Finn said.

"But what about the Quetzal Court?" Bettina said. "Surely the cult must have flourished here at some stage, in some form or another."

"But no one has ever known if that's what the sculpting is for sure." Jack spoke out for the first time. "As far as I know it's only ever been the theory of one man – that German archaeologist who came to do some thesis here years ago. He claimed that the figure shared certain characteristics with the Toltec stone carvings at Tula, in Mexico, where the cult is supposed to have originated. I don't know if you remember him, Baltazar?"

"No, I was too young. But I have heard him mentioned. I'm not sure anyone gave him that much credence, did they?"

"What about the pochtecas?" The girl spoke at last.

"Pochtecas?"

"Yes. They were a kind of travelling salesmen who specialised in the trade of quetzal plumes – in those days they were even more valuable than gold – but they also acted as a kind of mystical brotherhood, spreading the cult of Quetzalcoatl wherever they could. It isn't that unlikely that one of them should have managed to get this far south."

"Layla, you didn't tell me that you knew all this," Bettina said, surprised.

"I didn't know, at least not until yesterday," the girl said mildly. "Magdalena told me. Her name for it isn't Quetzalcoatl, by the way, it's Kukulkan, or something like that."

"There you are," Bettina said, looking round with triumph, "Kulkulcan, a well-known derivation. It's too much of a coincidence, surely. The original cult must have died out centuries ago, but it has obviously left behind a kind of residue of superstition. When Layla was little, Magdalena used to sew green bird's feathers into all her clothes, don't you remember, Jack?" Bettina looked thoughtful. "God knows where she got them from. I used to get so furious with her about it" – as she spoke, as if on cue, the Indian woman came into the room again, and started to clear table – "but there was nothing I could do to stop her," she followed the Indian woman with her eyes, "nothing any of us could do."

* * *

They took their coffee on the verandah. The moon rose over the mountains, and from the garden came the scent of jasmine on the night air.

"I don't know if I told you, Jack," Finn said leaning up, legs crossed, against the balustrade, "but Santiago Menchu was one of the people who came to see my quetzal."

"Poor Santiago," Meredith said. "What a terrible business it must have been. We did so feel for you."

"It was," Jack said shortly. He took a mouthful of coffee, but Baltazar saw that his hands were trembling.

"Poor Jack," Bettina put out her hand to him, a sudden

130

tenderness in her voice. "The man dropped dead practically at his feet. They shot him four times before they finally killed him, apparently. A really dreadful business. God knows what would have happened if Baltazar had been there, it doesn't bear thinking about."

"What happened exactly?"

"Thieves." Jack's hand lay passively between Bettina's, not moving, not holding. "They must have heard that someone had moved in. He disturbed them." His voice sounded staccato, as though he were speaking in shorthand. "As simple, and as terrible, as that."

They fell silent. From somewhere outside in the dark, a night bird called. Baltazar took a deep breath.

"And you really still believe it was as simple as that?"

"Don't you?"

"Come on, Jack, we've been through this before."

"Thievery is a violent business. Especially in this part of the world. You know that."

"There is violence," Baltazar chose his words with care, "and there is violence. There was nothing amateur about this. Santiago was not just bumped off in a moment of panic. Someone went there, deliberately, to assassinate him."

"Dear boy," Jack's voice was steady, almost indifferent, "I'm afraid you have been away from here for too long. Why would anyone want to *assassinate* a country peasant?"

"I don't know," Baltazar said, as mildly as he could, "and that's precisely why I think you should call someone in to find out."

"What's this, Jack? You mean you haven't told anyone about Santiago's death?"

At the far end of the verandah, with Layla at his side, Finn stood bandaged in cigarette smoke. With his long legs and beaky nose, he had the air of an anthropomorphised heron just visible through the darkness.

"Are you mad? No, of course not. No one in this country involves the police unless they are absolutely obliged to. You know that as well as I do."

131

"Jack didn't want to upset his family any more than he had to," Bettina defended him. "Bringing in anyone from outside would have been a completely pointless exercise."

"What's your explanation then, Baltazar?" Finn was still curious.

"Quintero."

"Quintero!" Jack gave a snort of disbelief. "Quintero was the invention of a right-wing press. And besides, he's dead, everyone knows that."

"A death without a body? Stop hiding your head in the sand, Jack. There was never any proof."

"Is that the same Quintero you were telling me about the other day?" Layla who had been sitting silently on the balustrade, listening carefully, now spoke.

"That's the one," Finn said, "although I must say, I thought he was dead too. Quintero was part of a group known as the PNRPI, the *Partido Nacional Revolucionario para el Poder Indigeno*," he explained. "It wasn't exactly a political party, as the name suggests, more of a kind of pressure group – if that's not too coy a way of putting it. Loosely speaking, it was an Indian rights group. *Tierra y Libertad*. Up the Indians. All the usual things. They didn't operate for very long, but when they did they made the Sendero Luminoso look like amateurs. Quintero was the founder."

"What exactly are you trying to say?" Bettina, still holding Jack's hand, was mocking. "That he's suddenly risen from the dead? I don't think even Tio Menchu could have managed that, even on a good day."

"It's a rumour, that's all."

"But just supposing it was more than just a rumour?" Baltazar felt his irritation rising. "What is the expression? No smoke without fire. I just think that it's too dangerous a possibility to ignore."

Who was this man, this unkempt, stubborn old Englishman, with garden dirt under his fingernails? He realised that he had never really believed in Jack in this new guise before, Jack as the *patrón*, the usurping king, sitting here like a greying old spider at the centre of his web. Baltazar felt a surge of pity for the ravaged house. He thought of his father. If his father had been alive the house would never have come to this. He passed a hand over his eyes. What was it about this place that inspired such feelings? He had thought to resist it, thought himself immune, but he was not. He felt his nerves on edge, tingling, as if the whole place was bewitched.

ELEVEN

News of the murders of Joaquim Iturbide, Maria-Esmeralda Ponche and Purificacion Menendez, all from the Santa Luz estate, came one evening not long after Bettina's supper party for Baltazar. Their bodies had been found the day before in the Altamirada gorge, scattered within a radius of about a mile in and around the Tumbez ruins. Jack was called from the Alcaldia's radio-telephone by Finn. Meredith had been among the party who had found their bodies.

The next morning Layla went down to Tumbez with Jack. Bettina had not wanted her to go, but she had insisted. Jack arranged to take one person from each of the families of the three dead with him in his jeep: the rest had started the long walk down from the mountains as soon as they heard the news so that they could collect the bodies for burial.

The three people who had been elected to travel with the *patrón* consisted of one old man and two women. Layla recognised them only vaguely by sight. She found them waiting for Jack just outside the Great Court, standing patiently in the shade of the trees. As she approached them, Layla saw how the white dust beneath the trees clung to their tattered plastic shoes, coating the backs of their legs like talcum powder.

All three were strangely composed in their grief. The youngest was a girl no more than ten years old, her dress tattered with age and grime. Like the other two, the expression on her face was blank, uncomprehending.

As the jeep wound its way down the farm track to Altamirada, the heat from the gorge rose up to meet them. Layla sat in the back with the two women. She could feel the press of their bodies against her, and smell the animal scent of their skin and their clothes. At first Jack started to try to talk to them, but they answered his questions despondently, with monosyllables or with silence, and after a few attempts, he too fell silent. Layla took the girl's hand and held it, a small female gesture of solidarity, but the coarse little hand lay lifelessly in hers, like a tiny dead bird.

The ruins which they called Tumbez lay below the town of Altamirada, at the place where the forested throat of the gorge finally ironed out into the upper reaches of the Amazon.

It was midday by the time they arrived. The ruins, which were to be used as a meeting point, were entered by a crude gateway held together with old planks and barbed wire. The gateway led to a track through the forest, and ended in a clearing by the banks of a river. In the clearing they found other jeeps, and a posse of uniformed policemen standing around smoking cigarettes. The four policemen, tall insouciant figures in khaki and svelte, black leather boots, nodded to Jack and Layla, but ignored the three Indians.

To one side of the parked jeeps she could see that a kind of open air office, a table and a few chairs, had been set up under a tree. It was a peaceful scene, as if guests were expected presently to arrive and take tea by the riverbank. On the opposite bank of the river was a massive ceiba tree. It had no leaves, but the bare branches on one side of the tree were luminous with acid pink blossoms.

After they had been waiting about ten minutes, they saw the mayor of Altamirada, Virgilio Paz, appear from one of the footpaths and come hurrying towards them. He shook Jack and Layla formally by the hand, and ushered them over to the table.

Virgilio was a small man buttoned uncomfortably into a blue serge suit. From the bottom of his trousers which, like the jacket, were a little too tight and short, stuck a pair of pointed leather boots, brand new and shiny, made from caiman skin. Layla had always thought there was something faintly ridiculous about Virgilio's appearance, as if he were trying out a not very successful disguise. For only one look at his face gave away his origins – the heavy-lidded eyes and sculptured cheek bones of a sierra Indian. As Jack and he exchanged a few words, Layla found herself staring at his boots. The caiman skin, for some reason, made her think of Meredith. She wondered, inconsequentially, if Virgilio had been involved with any of her projects.

After a time, the mayor excused himself. Layla watched him go over to the three Indians standing silently around the jeep and greet them earnestly. Even in these circumstances, she thought, he had the dignity of a *mayordomo*, composing the proceedings here under the trees by the riverbank with the same formality as any of his municipal functions. She watched him move between the three, shaking each one by the hand, and thought how his gentleness and courteousness compared with the brutal acts of the night before.

At the table under the tree Jack and Layla sat silently, waiting. Jack's shoulders were stooped; his face, like the Indians', was closed, withdrawn, as if he had taken his cue from them. Even in the shade, the air in the gorge was viscous with humidity, as though it had been sealed over with a lid. Despite it, Layla found that she was shivering with nerves.

Apart from the two Indians, she was the only woman here. Perhaps Bettina had been right; perhaps she should not have come. From time to time a burst of laughter came from the group of policemen. She was uncomfortably aware of the way their eyes lingered over her when they looked towards the tree. Surreptitiously she glanced over to them, and then towards Virgilio again. They are all part of it, she thought. Even Virgilio, this gentle formal man whom I have known all my life. In this small world, the killers could very possibly be known to all of us, but they could be related to this man. They could be his *compadres*. Not just shadowy names or shadowy faces, but his friends, his *compadres*.

Layla stood up.

"How much longer are we going to have to wait?"

"I don't know." Jack stared past her into the middle distance. He seemed enervated, whether from the heat or from shock, Layla could not tell.

"They're bringing the bodies up from the *quebrada* now." He pointed across the river, to the right of the ceiba tree where the ground dipped sharply. "This was just the nearest place where it was possible to get the vehicles. It could take some time, I'm afraid."

"I can't sit here any longer. I'm going to have a walk around. Do you mind?"

"No."

"Dad?" Layla put her hand on his shoulder. "Dad, who killed them?"

"I don't know." Jack looked over towards the policemen, and then back into the middle distance. "I doubt if any of us will ever know."

The ruins of Tumbez consisted of a complex of grey stone pyramids, believed to have been an ancient ceremonial centre. At the time of their discovery, some thirty years previously, the government had displayed a brief interest, enough to ensure that the site was partially cleared. But apart from the keeper, whose job was to keep the surrounding jungle at bay, the ruins were in much the same state that they had been in for a thousand years or more. Their isolation meant that the ruins were little known outside the immediate locality. Even Jack had only ever visited the place a handful of times before.

A path, closed over by the canopy of the trees like a tunnel, led through the forest to the ruins themselves. It was further than Layla had remembered. Although she walked fast, it was ten minutes before she found herself at the first of the pyramids.

In the still heat of the afternoon the grey stone shivered before her. Layla walked up to it and, on impulse, started to climb up the ruined masonry. She climbed easily and swiftly. The fantastical structure – choked with orchids and vines, and the smooth, twisting roots of trees, as thick as dragon's coils – had an organic feel to it. As her hands and feet probed for a hold, it was hard to know where the stone structure ended and the rainforest began.

A few minutes later, she found herself balancing on a crumbling, vertiginous platform at the top of the pyramid. A pair of tiny green humming birds, no bigger than her thumb, probed the orchid blossoms at her shoulder. Layla looked around her. On one side the Altamirada gorge rose up steeply towards the distant spine of the mountains. And beneath her on the other side, for as far as she could see, spread the rainforest. Flame-of-the-forest trees and the ruined peaks of the remaining pyramids stuck out like beacons from the foaming green canopy.

"Layla!" A voice called to her from below. The sound reverberated, echoing, between the trees and the stillness of grey stone. She looked down, and found her head swimming from the steep drop beneath.

"What are you doing up there?" It was Baltazar. "You must come down."

His voice sounded faint, as if it were coming from a long way away. She tried to look down at him, but the drop sent her heart racing again.

"I'm coming," she called.

Layla went to climb down again, but the sides of the pyramid looked twice as steep from this angle as they had when she had climbed up. She hesitated, uncertain which way to position herself. She shifted her legs a little to one side and looked down again. From this angle the sides of the pyramid seemed to drop almost vertically beneath her. How had she ever climbed up in the first place? It was impossible. A cold sweat started to prick out on her forehead.

"Are you all right?" Baltazar was still standing at the base of the pyramid looking up at her.

"I . . . I'm not sure . . ." Layla heard her voice quaver with panic.

"Don't look down," Baltazar shouted up to her. "Turn around and try to come down backwards. Whatever you do, don't look down."

Layla turned and positioned herself with her back to Baltazar. But her hands were clammy with sweat, and she could no longer grip safely against the smooth stone.

"What on earth possessed you to climb up here?" He was standing by her side, his hand under her elbow. "Here, hold on to this root with one hand. That's it, now put your toe in this crevice here. No, this one. Further down, that's it." She could feel one of his hands pressing hard into the small of her back, steadying her. "What on earth possessed Jack to bring you here? Now bring your other foot down a little, to this rock here. That's it, good." She could feel his other hand on her ankle, pulling her foot down into the next safe foothold. "He must be out of his mind." He did not speak angrily, but with a kind of weariness. His eyes looked tired and red, as if he had not slept. Although he guided her down gently she could sense an urgency in his manner.

"I wanted to come. It's my fault, not his." Why did she feel the need to defend her father this way? "Thank you," she forced herself to meet his eyes, "I don't think I could have done this on my own." She could feel her palms stinging where the vines burnt through her hands like rope. "I'm sorry."

"That's all right. It always looks much steeper coming down than it does going up," he smiled at her. "Look, we're nearly there." They reached the ground at last. "Are you all right?"

"Yes. Yes, I'm fine."

Layla could feel the tension flooding from her. Her limbs felt weak, sapped of their strength. She could feel her knee joints trembling.

"Here, sit down for a moment," Baltazar guided her to a rock at the base of the pyramid. "Now, put your head between your legs."

"No, no, really I'm all right," Layla protested.

"Please," gently Baltazar pushed her head down, "you'll feel so much better." Layla could feel the skin of his hand, warm and dry, on the back of her neck as he held her there. "Now, how's that?"

"Better. Much better, thank you."

Baltazar moved away, and sat down opposite her on another rock. "Just sit and rest there for a moment; then we must go back."

Despite his apparent composure, Layla could feel a kind of nervous energy emanating from him. He sat, not looking at her, tapping the toe of his boot rhythmically against the ground. He wore a pair of very old jeans, now smeared green with bark and vegetable mould from his climb up the pyramid. His hair was lank and dishevelled. Through the stillness, the jungle reverberated around them with primitive calls. Harsh, tearing sounds like the ripping of a piece of paper; liquid patterings, like honey dripping from a tree. In the distance, howler monkeys roared.

"The birds are so tame here they are practically dropping off the branches," Baltazar said. "Have you seen?" He pointed upwards, to where a pair of parakeets sat preening just overhead.

"Meredith used to call this the Garden of Eden."

"The Garden of Eden," Baltazar shook his head. "Poor, poor Meredith."

They lapsed into silence again.

"Have they brought them back?" Layla asked at last, dreading the answer.

"Yes, they are bringing them now."

Baltazar ran his hands through his hair, pushing it back

from his face. His skin, Layla noticed, was very smooth and dark: an Indian's skin. He turned to her.

"I don't know what possessed your father to bring you here." He spoke matter of factly. "I'm going to take you back to Altamirada."

As Baltazar and Layla came back into the clearing, the Indians from Santa Luz who had walked down from the mountains – a journey the better part of two days – were now beginning to arrive. From a distance they seemed to move slowly, almost languorously; a sinuous single file of men and women snaking through the forest towards the riverbed. Layla saw Jack and Virgilio rise to their feet from their seats under the tree, and walk over to take up their positions on the banks of the river. They did not seem to have noticed the Santa Luz arrivals. When Layla followed their gaze she saw that, emerging slowly from the *quebrada* on the other side of the ceiba tree, was the search party at last.

"Damn," Baltazar swore under his breath. "Layla, I'm taking you back. Come now, please."

She felt his hand on her arm, steering her towards the parked vehicles. But her eyes were still fixed on the two groups on either side of the ceiba tree. The search party seemed to have swelled in size, was like an insect swarm moving towards them. The Santa Luz cortège reached the flat of the riverbanks at last. In a few moments the two would meet.

"Layla." She felt Baltazar's grip tighten.

"Yes . . ."

Layla wanted to look away, but then found that she could not. Something had happened. What were they trying to keep from her?

The men from the search party had almost reached the clearing. Layla could see their sweat, tiny beads of amber standing out on their foreheads. Some of them walked in pairs carrying what looked like rolls of blanket between them. Others were carrying bags in their hands and over their shoulders. Plastic, transparent bags.

"What have they got in those bags? What are they carrying?"

Layla heard her own voice distantly, as if in a dream. Behind her she felt Baltazar put his hands on her shoulders. He was saying something to her, but she did not, could not, listen. All she could hear was the sound of the river, very soft and low.

As though they had been taking part in a processional, the two columns came to a halt in front of one another.

"What are they carrying?"

She could feel the weight of Baltazar's hands, pressing down on her shoulders, holding her back.

"You should not be here. I am taking you home, now," he said again.

"I have to know. You must tell me. I have to know."

With effort she turned to look at him. She felt giddy with the heat. Giddy and sick. His face was shadowed. His eyes were devoid of all expression. It was as if he had withdrawn from her.

"There are more of them than we thought. More dead, I mean."

"More?" Layla forced her lips to move. They felt thin and numb, frozen to her face. "How many more?"

"About twenty, we think. So far."

"*About* twenty?"

"Yes. You see, the way . . . ," he paused, as though searching for the right words to go on, "it has been hard to tell." He took his hands from her shoulders. "I am sorry. You should not have had to witness this."

On the other side of the river the two parties stood facing each other at last. Overhead the sky was a colourless vacuum, leaden with heat. Slowly the search party put down the bags containing their terrible harvest. Layla saw the Santa Luz people go forward, hesitantly at first, until the two groups had merged together, two rivers running into an open sea.

The three Indians who had travelled down from Santa Luz with Jack and Layla had crossed over the river. Layla could see the girl, a small forlorn figure in her ragged dress, picking her way through the press of people.

"My god, the girl."

Before Baltazar could stop her she was running quickly over the stepping stones across the river towards them. Under the ceiba tree, she saw the girl stop in front of two men carrying a rolled up blanket between them. As Layla reached her, she was kneeling down in front of the bundle.

"*No!*"

She heard herself shout out. Too late. The men had pulled back the blanket. Layla heard the girl give a small, startled cry. Over her shoulder, Layla saw the woman's face quite clearly. Her eyes were still open, and she appeared to be staring straight past the girl as though she were still alive. In a strange trick of death their eyes met. Her face had aged. Her cheeks were coarsened and the delicate skin round her eyes and mouth was lined, but even in death she seemed to carry with her the same wild aura of mountains, earth and air as she had done when Layla had first seen her, running after her sheep, shaking her matted hair from her eyes. From somewhere, far, far away, Layla could hear the anguished sound of women weeping. It merged with the sound of the river, and was carried away on the still air, deep into the forest.

*   *   *

Meredith's state of mind shocked Layla almost as much as the fact of the Tumbez massacre itself. Meredith, so loud, so outspoken, so unshakably sure of the rightness of the world and her place in it, seemed to Layla to have been diminished. It was not only her manner: physically, too, she appeared smaller than she had been before, old and somehow shrunken in size.

Layla found her sitting curled up in a chair in her

bedroom, wearing an old cotton wrap. The material was faded, its design touchingly childish, white rabbits with blue bows around their necks. Meredith hugged it to her fiercely.

"You can't imagine," she began when she saw Layla, "you simply can't imagine what it was like. It was not just murder –" she seemed almost to gag over the word, "it was more than that. Something is *going on* down there . . . something evil . . ."

"Don't," Finn put his hand protectively on her shoulder, "don't think about it any more." There was a tenderness between them which Layla had never seen before. "It's over now."

"But that's just it, don't you see," Layla was appalled to see two tears begin to trickle down Meredith's cheeks. "It's not over. It can never be *over*. I shall have to live with the sight of it all my life. Those bodies lying there, scattered." She turned and looked up at Layla, pulling her robe more closely around her. "Did I tell you? I found this boot. There was a woman's foot still inside it." She put her hands up to her face, and pressed her eyes as if to gouge out the thought. "They cut those people up into little bits. All of them. It burns my eyes . . . this place, this people. Who could do such a thing?"

*　　*　　*

It was dusk when Baltazar came to collect Layla. He brought a newspaper with him, and Finn read out the brief commentary printed inside.

Last Tuesday, in the remote, north-eastern province of Esperanza, a group of twenty Indians was found murdered in the area around the site of Tumbez. The chief of police for the district, Capitan J. Buenaventura Valdez, expressed his concern, and said that while no definite

144

leads had been forthcoming, the forces under his command would do their utmost to bring the perpetrators of the crime to justice.

The mayor of the town of Altamirada, Sr V. Paz, also expressed his grave concern over the killings, but denied the suggestion that they had any connection with the outlawed PNRPI, founded by the terrorist leader Diego Quintero.

A land feud is thought to be the cause of the deaths.

"Well, that's the most *La Verdad* has to say." Finn folded the paper carefully, and handed it back to Baltazar. "A paragon of penetrating, investigative journalism."

"I don't expect anyone thinks that the news of the death of a few Indians is worth the paper its printed on,' Baltazar said.

They were sitting on Finn's balcony. The door into the aviary was ajar behind them, and the occasional cry of one of the birds pierced the dusk. Layla noticed that the cage in which Finn had been keeping the quetzal was empty, and wondered if he had had to move it to avoid disturbing the other birds. In the green throat of the gorge beneath them, the cicadas called to one another.

"What puzzles me," Finn said, "is how anxious everyone seems to be to deny that Quintero has anything to do with it."

"Amazing, isn't it." Baltazar shook his head. "They couldn't have called more attention to it if they'd taken out a full page advertisement. What a country this is. What a press."

"What do you think about this land feud theory?"

"Pure invention. At least half of the victims were from the Santa Luz estate – they didn't actually own any land to dispute. Technically, I mean." Layla saw Baltazar glance over to her, as though wondering whether to go on. "No," he said after some consideration, "I would have said this was vintage Quintero."

"But how can you be so *sure*," Finn sounded agonised.

145

"There have been rumours going round for some time. Surely you must have heard them?"

"Yes, but that's just it. Rumours, Baltazar." Finn stood up, his usual languorousness evaporating. "Has it occurred to you that we know next to nothing about this man? We don't even know what he looks like. For years we all thought he was dead, for Christ's sake. Perhaps he *is* dead. Perhaps it's someone entirely different masquerading as him."

"Look, what we've just witnessed appears to us to be an apparently motiveless act – no warnings, no ultimatums, and, as far as we know, no one claiming responsibility. But if it's Quintero you can be sure he knows exactly what he's doing." Baltazar drew out a packet of cigarettes from his pocket and lit one carefully. "I say this because he's done the same thing before, in '74, just before he was supposedly executed. I don't know if you have ever heard people talk of the Quebrada Alta affair? Well, almost exactly the same thing happened then. Twenty people massacred for no apparent reason. After that, when it eventually came to light that Quintero was behind it, the local people were so terrified that they were prepared to agree to almost anything he and his PNRPI wanted. Ruthless, but extremely effective."

"Terror tactics."

"Right. My guess is that he's done this just to let everyone know he's back in business again."

"You mean he would butcher twenty people, just for that?" Layla looked at him with horror.

"Yes," Baltazar said, "I'm afraid so. This is what I've been trying to get through to Jack. If it's Quintero, he means business."

*　　*　　*

146

Baltazar drove Layla back to Santa Luz through the night. She slept late and was only woken by Bettina coming into her room at midday the next morning.

"It's Magdalena," Bettina perched on the end of Layla's bed, "she's gone."

"What? Gone where?"

Bettina shrugged, "I was hoping you could tell me that. Neither Martin the Eye nor I have seen her since yesterday, and her bed hasn't been slept in. So selfish of her," she said, aggrieved, "to leave us in the lurch at a time like this."

"I shouldn't think she'll be gone for long," Layla said. "You know what she's like."

Magdalena had done this too many times before for either Layla or Bettina to be seriously worried.

"Did she tell you she was going off?"

"No, not a word. But we were all in such a hurry yesterday morning. She's probably gone to see Tia, I should think, to tell her the news."

"I should think that's where the news came from in the first place. The bush telegraph never fails," Bettina said crossly. "It's us who always ends up hearing everything last." She stood up. "Oh well, I'll just have to get Emanuela or Lupita to come in and help. And they'll be upset, I know it, and sit around moping all day."

"Oh, Mummy, how can you say that?"

Layla's voice was no more than a whisper. At the doorway Bettina stopped. She turned back to Layla, full of remorse.

"I have no right to say that." She crossed the room again and sat down on Layla's bed. "I'm sorry, sweetheart. Forgive me, please?"

She took Layla's hand and held it. Layla looked up at her. To her surprise she saw that Bettina's eyes were red-rimmed. The skin of her face, usually so fine, looked dull and puckered, as if she had not slept. Even her hair seemed to have been snapped of its fire. Layla picked up her hand and kissed it.

"Of course. You didn't mean it, I know."

"It's just that I've been so worried. You didn't get back until so late. And Jack hasn't been back at all."

"But I asked Finn to call you on the RT. Didn't he get through?"

"Yes, he did. But I thought that Jack . . . that Daddy might try to get through to me himself. I had hoped . . ." Bettina passed her hands over her face, pressing her eyes with her fingers as if she hoped to blot out some thought or image. The gesture reminded Layla painfully of Meredith the day before. "You see, I had hoped –" Bettina seemed about to say something, but then for some reason thought better of it, " – well, never mind that now."

She leant over to kiss Layla and then stood up again briskly. "I must get on. The *carabinieros* are going to be here for a few days while they carry out some enquiries. I've offered to quarter some of their men here. It's too far for them to keep driving backwards and forwards to Altamir-ada every day."

Santa Luz was unnaturally quiet that day. In the fields beyond the house, no one worked the land. Even the higher pastures remained empty; the sheep left locked into their night-time corrals. All day silent streams of people filed in through the Great Court gates to the chapel. A ritual fire burned on the steps from which clouds of incense billowed, thick as spirit matter.

Restlessly Layla wandered through the house. After a time she found herself in the Quetzal Court. Looking round her at the squat pillars, the walls traced with an ancient mosaic of lichen, she was surprised to find how long it was since she had been to this part of the house. She moved across the courtyard to the place where the gargoyle-like figure of the plumed serpent, Quetzalcoatl, fashioned in silent grey stone, strained from the wall. She traced the contours of the blind sockets which were its eyes, its nostrils, and the crumbling ruff of feathers around its neck. Bougain-villaea the colour of a quetzal's breast swept down one wall from the balustrade overhead, its wood as rotted and soft as an old tooth.

As a child she used to come here almost every day. Then she had known every grass and creeper which grew between the flagstones, every new leaf, or so it had seemed, on the great avocado tree. Now the place felt almost strange to her. Not a breath of wind from the mountain reached this central core of Santa Luz.

Layla was about to turn and make her way back when, under the colonnade to her right, she saw a door standing open. The door, she knew, led into a little room, hardly bigger than a vestibule, which had once been used as a chapel before the present chapel was built. The place had been deconsecrated many years ago, and was one of the few rooms at Santa Luz which Jack kept permanently locked. Curiously, Layla walked over and looked inside.

After the blinding light in the courtyard, the interior of the room was as black as night. Then, as she stood in the doorway straining her eyes, she heard a faint rustling sound coming from below her. She looked down. At her feet danced a tiny whirlpool of dust. Mingling with the dust was a handful of scarlet blossoms, windfalls from the bougainvillaea. And amongst them a tiny, luminous green fragment no bigger than a mote of thistledown: a bird's feather.

Layla stepped into the room. Inside she felt the temperature drop, as if she had entered a cellar. She sniffed the air. Over the musty smell of damp stone there was a faint sweet redolence, like incense. The room, which was rectangular in shape, was bare of all adornment. But as her eyes became accustomed to the dark she became aware of a tiny yellow glow, so low it was hardly visible, coming from the far end of the room. Walking towards the light, Layla saw that someone had lit a candle, placing it in the stone niche which had once served as an altar. It was an old-fashioned, thick-based candle, made from expensive yellow tallow, quite unlike the cheap, brightly coloured ones from Chino's which were usually burnt in the chapel. Waxy tears ran down its sides, and it gave off a sweet perfume as it burnt, the scent which she had noticed when she first entered the room.

She drew closer. Around the base of the candle she could now see that fresh flower heads and petals had been arranged, in the manner of a ritual Indian offering. In amongst the petals – unmistakably, she now saw – were birds' feathers. The feathers appeared to be floating in what looked like a pool of water. Layla put her fingers cautiously down into the liquid. When she took her hand away, her fingers were sticky to the touch.

TWELVE

Here in London it is autumn at last. Yesterday we had the
first frost. I went to the park and felt the ground metal-hard
under my feet. Groundsmen were raking leaves of withered
gold into piles, like harvest sheaves. From each pile there
came a delicious, acrid scent entirely new to me – the smell
of an English autumn.

As I walked I watched a group of children in Smartie-
coloured raincoats and boots chase each other round and
round, shrieking and jumping and rolling ecstatically into
the piles, until their clothes and hair were feathered with
the soft, rotting leaves. Their laughter – piercing and pure
– carried a long way on the thinning air.

Except for that one time I told you about, during the
long, never-ending Indian summer, I have not been much
to the park. It seemed to me that there was a pitilessness
about those days with their bright, adamantine skies, which
was exposed most clearly in that green space. Perhaps it
was the lovers lying together; perhaps it was the thought,
the lost memory, of all the English summers you must have
had before you came to Santa Luz. I felt only pain when I
contemplated them, as though my perceptions were in some
way heightened by the warmth, my nerves worn raw by the
endless light.

The autumn, as I knew it would, has brought with it softer, less painful days. In the autumn soft-bellied life retreats into its shell. I can look from my window across the rooftops, breathe the cold air, and – at last – feel memory recede.

Last week Aunt Lucille invited Connie and me to have dinner at her house. It was a Saturday night and so we dressed up for the occasion. Connie said that Lucille would expect it. I had half thought that she would think Lucille pretentious for making so much of a simple dinner party, but she seemed to accept it, even take a sneaking delight in the idea.

"People of my generation used to dress for dinner every night," she told me. "A perfectly ridiculous habit, of course, but I do miss it sometimes. The ritual, you know. Lucille's dinners are not the most thrilling way to spend an evening, but at least we can enjoy wearing something pretty. I hardly ever seem to be out of my gardening clothes these days."

This was quite untrue, of course. I have never met anyone who takes such an avid interest in clothes, or who wears them with such obvious pleasure. On any other woman of her age it would be somehow out of place. But not with Connie. In the attics at the top of the house she even found something for me to wear, too.

When I was ready I went down and sat with her in her bedroom while she finished dressing, something I have taken to doing quite often over these last few weeks. I think Connie's bedroom is one of my favourite rooms in this house. It is not the room which you will remember, on the second floor. Some years ago she moved her bedroom down to the first floor, to the room she says you will remember as the old drawing room. It is still the place where, when she is alone, she spends most of her time.

"Let me look at you." Connie, sitting at her dressing table, turned around when I came in. "Yes, I thought so." She turned back and started rapidly to pin her hair up into its chignon. "So, do you like it?" she asked after a moment's concentration in the mirror, her mouth full of hairpins.

152

I watched her arms, rising and falling, a strangely fluid, youthful movement.

"The dress? It's beautiful." I sat down at the foot of her bed, smoothing my hands down over the skirt so that it would not crease. "It fits like a glove. Thank you."

"Don't thank me, thank Bettina," Connie said. I could hear a tiny crunching sound each time she dug one of the pins into the thick coils of her hair. "After all, it's her dress."

Do you remember it? It is a very simple 1950s style, with a tight boned bodice and fitted skirts. The bodice is cut off-the-shoulder and rather low, the arms and shoulders consisting of nothing more than an over-lay of fine gauze. The material of the dress is quite beautiful; a shot silk, very dark green, so dark it is almost black, but when it captures the light it turns to a most brilliant, luminous emerald. When I first stepped into it, even after all these years, I could almost imagine that it smelt of you.

Connie looked at me in the mirror, her head to one side.

"Perfect. You are taller than Bettina, so even the skirt is the right length now," she said approvingly. "There's just one thing though; come and sit here for a minute."

She stood up and made me sit down in front of her mirror. Then she took her hair brush and started to sweep my hair upwards, gathering it skilfully into her hands. I could feel the soft bristles scraping luxuriously up the back of my neck and across my scalp.

"That feels wonderful."

"I used to do this with your mother," Connie said, still brushing, "she never had any idea of how to dress her own hair."

"Really?" I was surprised. "She's always telling me I don't take enough care of myself. You know, clothes, hair, all that sort of thing."

"Well, when she was younger she had a pretty haphazard approach to it herself, I can tell you. Now, don't talk to me, I'm concentrating."

In the dressing table mirror I watched her as she held

my gathered hair in her hands, parting and coiling in this way and that. She was wearing a high-collared dress of burgundy velvet, with heavy gold clasps, in the shape of shells, in her ears. What must it have been like, I wondered, when you lived here all those years ago. And how you must have missed her, I found myself thinking, when you first came to Santa Luz.

As Connie brushed, I gazed into the mirror at the reflection of the room behind me. It is arranged around such solid dependable things: the Empire bed, and that cavernous cupboard like something out of a fairy tale; an old chintz covered sofa and two armchairs. And yet it is here, among her pictures, her sewing, and her favourite books, the winter bulbs planted in bowls, that she enshrines her most private self.

On the mantelpiece over the old marble fireplace there is a clutter of memorabilia; a curiously distorted pottery vase and a childish picture, a little faded now inside its glass frame, of two stick women, hand in hand. The smaller one, unmistakable with her striking, scribbled nimbus of red hair, has a bubble coming from her mouth: "I love you Connie," it says in large childish writing, "from Bettina".

At the bottom of the dressing table mirror are three little drawers. I pulled each one out in turn. They opened stiffly on tiny ivory handles. In one was an old pin cushion and a set of mother-of-pearl buttons attached to a piece of card. In another a hairnet and two pieces of coloured cotton wool. In the third I found an old-fashioned locket, a delicate thing on a gold chain. Inside was the picture of a man.

"Who's this?"

Connie looked down at the locket, held in the palm of my hand.

"Goodness, wherever did you find that?"

"In here, in this little drawer."

"How extraordinary. That, believe it or not, is James Howard."

"Luke's grandfather?"

"Yes."

"The one who was so in love with you?"

"Yes." In the mirror I saw Connie smile. "The very one."

"You never speak about him."

"No," Connie said shortly, sticking more pins into my hair. I looked down at the picture in the locket again. A rather fierce, bushy-eyebrowed profile stared back at me.

"What was he like?"

"A difficult old bugger, most of the time," Connie said with some feeling. "When I was fifteen, my mother, your great-grandmother, decided that I should have my portrait painted. James Howard, in those days – it must have been sometime round about 1930 – was a completely unknown painter, fresh out of art school, who made his bread and butter money by doing exactly that. Children and dogs were his speciality."

"And?"

"He painted my portrait, but when it was finished he refused to sell it to us. I can't remember what his excuse was: he needed it to hang in an exhibition or something. Some trumped-up excuse. Nothing would persuade him to part with it. That was James all over. Once he had made his mind up about something, that was it."

"Was he in love with you even then?"

"No. I don't think so. He loved all women – almost indiscriminately, I sometimes used to think – but I don't think Lolitas were ever his thing. No, it was more like a premonition of something to come."

Connie stepped back to survey her work.

"And so?"

"I met him again when I was in my twenties, at art school. My parents were terribly against my going there at all. In those days it wasn't at all *comme il faut*, you know. James was my tutor. We fell in love."

She laughed. "It confirmed all my parents' suspicions, of course. There was the most terrible hoo-ha about it all. It all seems quite absurd now."

"Why didn't you marry him?"

155

"He was already married."

"Oh," I felt ashamed for having asked, "I see."

"Don't sound like that." In the mirror, I could see Connie looking at me in amusement. "It was probably a lucky escape. When his poor wife eventually died (he was Catholic, you see, so no divorce), he did kindly ask me to marry him, but I refused."

"But why? Didn't you love him?"

"Oh, yes. I loved him a great deal." For a moment, in the trick light of evening, her face seemed younger, softer than before. "But by then we had Bettina and Lucille – my sisters and me I mean. As you know your grandmother, my youngest sister, was killed in a car accident. Her husband had been killed in the war, even before Bettina was born, and so when she died we adopted their two children. What else could we do?"

"But the other two, the other aunts, couldn't they have looked after them?"

"Yes, they could have," Connie agreed. "Lucille would have been all right. But not Bettina. Lucille was the favourite you see – always so quiet, so pliable. Bettina was too wilful for them. They took her on, but only out of duty. I knew they didn't love her in the way they loved Lucille. You see," Connie added, reaching for another mouthful of hairgrips, "I knew I could never have children of my own. Bettina was like my own child. I couldn't leave her."

"Couldn't you have taken her with you?" I looked at Connie, appalled.

"No," Connie laid down her hairbrush and picked up the locket. "He wouldn't have her. Why should he? He had already brought up one young family. What did he want with someone else's child? He wanted some time off. He wanted to travel, to paint. He wanted me. Bettina did not come into his scheme of things. And he was stubborn. Oh, he was a stubborn man."

She dropped the locket back in the drawer and shut it quickly.

"Of course, I was stubborn too. I thought, I can be just

156

as difficult as you. Love is not conditional, I said. If you
want me, you must take me warts and all, as it were. Of
course, in his eyes, I was the one making conditions. What
a pair we were." Connie laughed, but when she looked at
me her eyes were very bright. "He went off on his travels,
and I never spoke to him again."

I thought of the picture in the locket.

"He looked . . ." I searched for the right word,
". . . *simpático*. I don't think there's a translation for that."

"Ha!" Connie made a dismissive gesture with her hands.
"He was a difficult, stubborn old sod," she said dryly. "But
I'll tell you something," she looked at me, her eyes still
bright, "he was quite the best lover I ever had."

"Connie!"

"Well, it's true. Why is it that young people always seem
to think that they are the ones who invented sex. Bettina's
generation – in the sixties you know, all that flower power
stuff, and talk about 'free love' (love is never, *ever* free; a
terrible, meaningless suggestion if ever there was one) –
they were the worst. They seemed to think that they had
some kind of monopoly on love. They were quite shocked
sometimes when they discovered they hadn't. Anyway,"
she glanced at her wristwatch, "we must get on. Let's have
a look at you."

She had swept my hair up into a smooth chignon, pinning
it to one side so that it emphasised the line of my neck, and
the small, neat shape of my head. She plucked at the hair
at the sides of my face, loosening it until its severity was
softened.

"There. What do you think of that?"

I took her hand mirror and held it so that I could see the
back of my head reflected in her dressing table glass.

"It looks lovely." I was really pleased, "You're so clever,
thank you."

Connie sat down on the bed beside me, regarding her
handiwork.

"You look beautiful," she smiled at me. "Really you do.
And now there's just one more thing."

"Yes?"

"I want you to have this."

From her finger Connie took one of her rings and placed it in the palm of my hand.

"Oh, Connie."

"I was going to leave it to you anyway." Connie was watching my face. "James gave it to me."

The ring was in the shape of two golden dolphins coiled around each other. Each of their eyes was studded with a tiny emerald. I felt the metal, smooth and heavy in my hand.

"Oh, Connie . . . I couldn't. It's exquisite."

"I want you to wear it for me. Will you?"

"But . . ."

"No 'buts'. I want you to wear it. Besides," gathering her things, Connie stood up to go, "James would have wanted it too, I know."

* * *

Aunt Lucille's sitting room was as pale, airless, and twice as crowded as before. When we arrived she was already there waiting for us with her husband Jeremy (it is funny how I cannot somehow think of him as 'Uncle' Jeremy, whereas Lucille could never be anything other than 'Aunt'), a large florid-looking man who wore a gold watch-chain across his waistcoat, Debbie, and Charles. Besides the family there was one other couple called Elmhurst; a fat, rather deaf old man called Geoffrey, a distant Bowyer relation; and last of all, to my surprise, Luke, who had been asked in, as Lucille put it, to make up the numbers.

Luke came over to me.

"Hello, Layla."

"Luke, what a surprise. I never expected to see you here."

I was really pleased to see him. He looked surprisingly neat, in a grey suit. "What's all this, no more moth holes?"

"I told you, I've become respectable." Luke glanced over his shoulder at Lucille, but she was safely down at the other end of the room. "I have been taken, as we say here, into the bosom of the family. Into the bosom of *your* family, I should say. In fact, a Bowyer soirée is no longer complete without me."

"How does it feel?"

"I'm not entirely sure." Luke pulled at his tie, trying to loosen it a little. "Alarming, on balance." He looked across at Debbie. "But it does have its compensations, I suppose. I haven't worn one of these for years," he pulled at his tie again, "if I'm not careful, I think I might choke myself. Oh, to be a girl and wear a nice sensible dress."

"It must be love."

"Love? *Love*," Luke repeated, as if he was considering the word for the first time. "'It must be love, love, love'," he sang, "do you remember that song?" Plunging both hands into his trouser pockets, he started to jangle his change nervously. "Still, she's looking good, isn't she?" He followed Debbie with his eyes. "And so are you, if I may be so bold."

I found that he was concentrating on me with that same intensity that I had noticed the first time I met him. "Has anyone ever told you that you look just like Audrey Hepburn?"

"Hello, Layla." Debbie appeared at Luke's side. She looked me up and down.

"What an extraordinary dress. Did it come out of Aunt Connie's dressing-up box?" Her voice was innocent of all expression.

"Yes." I looked down at the green stuff, smiling. "As a matter of fact it did."

"Oh." Debbie widened her eyes, already so pale, so protuberant, in amazement. "I didn't mean – I mean, it was a joke – I think it's a very nice dress."

She had the same startled look that I remembered from

before; the same extraordinary blondeness. Her hair, so fine and thin that it stood out from her head like spun gossamer, shone as white as a child's in the lamplight. She turned to Luke.

"Luke, angel," she put her hand on his arm, "would you mind fetching my drink. It's on the table over there."

"Yes, of course."

Luke went off obediently, and Debbie turned to me again, fixing me with her unblinking, piscine stare.

"I'm sorry I haven't been in touch. Mummy kept saying that I should ring you. Especially after . . . well, you know." Her gaze, momentarily, flickered away. "She keeps saying that you probably don't know many people in London," she carried on in the same rather breathless monotone, "but I've been so busy, you know how it is."

"That's all right."

"Still, I expect you've got plenty of your own friends by now," she was saying.

"Well – no, not really. Not yet."

"Oh." She paused. "That's a shame."

"Look, it's all right. Just because you're . . . it doesn't mean you have to worry. I mean, I'm perfectly all right with Connie."

"Luke says he saw you the other day." I was fixed again by the huge, pale, eyes; aware now, too, of something hidden – an accusation? – behind their pale gaze.

"Yes, I saw him once. We had a picnic."

Yes. We had a picnic. On the last day of summer, I wanted to say. On the last day of summer we talked, and we laughed, and I was happy. And I found I could tell him things which I have never been able to tell to any of you. Things which none of you have ever bothered to ask me about, because they will always be outside your knowledge, your experience. But without knowing these things, how can you ever fully know me? What you see here is a sham, a mere imitation of the real person, the person I once was.

"I'm sorry, what was that?" Debbie had said something, but I realised that I had not been listening to her.

"I said, Luke and I are so happy together." She was looking at me curiously. "Didn't he tell you?"

"Tell me what?"

"Luke and I are going out together. I mean, why do you think he's here now? Everyone is so pleased for us." For the first time Debbie smiled. Now that there was no one else listening to us there was even a hint of complicity in her voice. She leaned forward, and put her hand on my arm, "Even Mummy." I was surprised to find that when she smiled her face was transformed. Momentarily she looked almost animated. "Look, we really should get together. I'll get Luke to bring a friend, and we'll go somewhere, the four of us. We can go to a film, or out to dinner; or we could even go to a club if you'd like."

"Yes, that'd be great."

In those few minutes she had disarmed me completely.

"I know Luke really likes you. He gave me a long lecture the other day about how I should look after you more. I'm afraid we English just aren't very good at it, that's all."

*   *   *

The Bowyers' dining room, in the basement bowels of the house, was as long and narrow as their drawing room, papered over in red and black flock wallpaper. The table-cloth, too, was a deep crimson damask and the effect, after the extreme paleness of the drawing room, was at once oppressive and womb-like.

At dinner I sat next to Charles. Charles is large and ruddy like his father, and tries hard to be kind.

"You know," he began conversationally, "you're not a bit what I was expecting. Debs told me you'd been here the other day, but her description of you was, well," he contemplated me over the rim of his wine glass, "put it this

161

way, she certainly managed to leave out the best bits," he finished gallantly.

"Well, it was some time ago now." I realised that he was trying to put me at my ease. For something to say, I added, "Perhaps she just forgot 'the best bits', as you so kindly put it," and then immediately wished I hadn't.

"Oh no, not Debbie. She doesn't forget things, not that kind of girl." Charles shook his head, slowly spreading pâté on to a wafer-thin finger of toast. "Debbie's bloody bright – although you wouldn't think it sometimes, the way she goes on. She and my mother, you know, don't always hit it off." Chewing his toast, he contemplated his sister for a moment. She was talking to Geoffrey Bowyer. Or rather, he was talking to her. Debbie nodded occasionally, and I could see that blank expression, thinly veiling her boredom, descend on her again.

"My father's always saying that if she'd been a boy, she should definitely have gone into the City," Charles went on, "says she'd probably have made more money than the two of us put together." He grinned at me, his mouth still full of pâté. "Tell me, do they have an equivalent to the City, down in your neck of the woods, I mean?"

He leant across me for the wine decanter, and poured himself another glass of wine.

"Well, there's the capital, Veracruz," I said, not understanding the question, "but apart from that there's nothing really big enough to be called a city. Only towns, but even they are mostly quite small. Near where we live–'

"No, no, that's not what I meant. I meant The City. You know, capital T, capital C. The square mile. The financial centre of London." In the crimson glow of the dining room Charles's face, already on the florid side, looked like sweaty red cheese. "You have been away from civilisation a long time, haven't you?" he smiled, quite kindly.

Thoughtfully I scooped the remaining pâté from the dish in front of me, and started to eat it from the end of my knife. "Yes, I suppose I have."

"Really, Charles, you idiot," Debbie leaned across the

table towards us, "of course they don't have anything like the City over there. In those sorts of places most people hardly know what money is, let alone a bank. They're still using barter over there, didn't you know? It's all the rage."

"Barter!" Charles wheezed with delight.

"Don't pay any attention to them, Layla." Aunt Lucille had overheard this exchange. "They are just silly, ignorant children," she said reprovingly but I could see that she too was smiling.

"Layla, I was just telling John about Connie's house" – she drew me skilfully into her conversation – "such marvellous, big gardens you can still get in Bayswater. Connie says hers has been particularly good this year. The Elmhursts live just round the corner from her, you know."

They were all trying so hard to be kind. I knew they were. But I kept being left with the impression that there was some joke which everyone had understood and was laughing at, except me. It was as if I had suddenly discovered that the languages we spoke, while outwardly identical, were in fact as strange to each other as if I had been speaking Swahili. I looked down the table to Connie, but she was deep in conversation with Luke and Jeremy. The table was too big for me to talk across to them without shouting.

When Lucille got up to go into the kitchen, it was John Elmhurst who turned to me. He picked up the jug in front of him.

"Would you like some water?"

"Thank you."

He poured me out a glass.

"Lucille was telling me earlier about the troubles you have been having recently. I am so sorry to hear of it."

"Thank you. It has been . . . difficult."

"To put it mildly. Do you mind talking about it? We needn't, if you'd rather not."

Up until now I had thought John Elmhurst quiet and rather reserved. But now he spoke with real concern, and I felt absurdly grateful to him. It occurred to me that none

163

of the Bowyers had ever made any attempt to talk about our "troubles": I wondered if this was from delicacy, or from the potential embarrassment of seeing a stranger's emotions laid bare.

"Of course we read about it in the papers," he went on, "but it is difficult to know what's really going on. They never tell you the whole story, do they? Still, often it's even less clear when you're in the thick of it."

"Yes. For a long time none of us had any idea what was going on, even though it was all coming to a head right under our noses."

"What's the man called? Kant-something?"

"Quintero."

My voice sounded quite steady as I said the name.

"Quintero. Oh, Quintero." Charles, a little louder and redder than before, turned to us. "You're a brave man, John, I thought we weren't supposed to mention him."

John turned to me. "I'm terribly sorry, I didn't realise."

"Please, that's quite all right. Sometimes it helps –"

"Frightful man. A kind of Pol Pot figure, isn't he?" Charles went on, sawing into his plate of roast beef. "Still, if you must choose to live somewhere like that, what can you expect? All you ex-patriots should have thought of that before you went to live there in the first place."

From the corner of my eye I saw John glance at me anxiously.

"Oh, I'm sure Layla agrees with me. Why else has she come to live over here now? A jolly good decision, if you ask me."

"I'm afraid you have no idea of the reasons why I've come –" I started to say, but Charles blundered on.

"Anyway, as far as I can gather, this Quintero seems to have killed mostly Indians, hasn't he? I'm not condoning it, of course, but a few less Indians here or there, in the long run what difference does it make?"

"You're out of order, Charles," John spoke softly.

"No, no, now we've started this conversation I think we ought to finish it." Purposefully, Charles poured himself another glass of wine. I noticed that his hand trembled slightly as he held the bottle. Then he turned to me again, and it was only then that I realised that he was drunk. I saw John turn to Lucille and say something to her, but I did not hear what he said. It was as though I had been hypnotised by Charles. I could not take my eyes off him. I wanted to hear what he would say next.

"I mean, there are far too many of them as it is. Indians, I mean," Charles went on, his voice raised. "People always think I won't know anything about these things, but I'm telling you I know just as much as the next person, and I know that it's the same in all these bloody countries. They can't support themselves as it is, and all their children die of diarrhoea. So the West hands out aid like it was going out of fashion, and for a while things get better, but then what happens? Because they're healthier they breed better, and they won't use contraceptives, even when the government hands them out like sweets. So in a few years they're back in exactly the same boat that they were in before, probably worse, because now they've got even more children to support –" he tailed off vaguely, forgetting the train of his argument, "– etcetera . . . etcetera. What's the matter? Not hungry?"

"No, I'm quite all right." I put down my knife and fork. "It's just this knife and fork. At home, you know, we don't bother much about things like that. Do you mind?" I picked up a slice of roast beef between my fingers. "It's so much easier this way."

I followed up the beef with a roast potato, dipping it into the gravy on the side of my plate. "You should try it sometime, you know." I could see that he was staring at me wide-eyed. "Food tastes so much better when you eat it with your fingers, I always think."

I scooped up a handful of peas and crammed them into my mouth.

"You'd better not let my mother see you eating like that," Charles cast a nervous glance towards his mother's end of the table.

"Oh, I wouldn't worry about that."

I did not care if she saw me or not. I picked up another circle of nearly raw roast beef, and was about to put it into my mouth when I thought better of it.

"On second thoughts," I said, "perhaps you're right." I unwrapped the parcel of meat and held it up between my fingers. "Meat, you know, doesn't agree with me as much as it did. Not after Quintero had –" I waved my hand vaguely in the air, as if searching for the right word "– well, after all that, you know what I mean. You know, it's amazing how much human meat resembles animal meat. When both are dead, there really isn't much difference."

On the opposite side of the table I could see Debbie staring at me. She sat quite still, as if she too had been hypnotised.

"Quintero was a very thorough man," I went on. "When he killed someone, first of all he used to cut out their hearts –"

"For God's sake, Layla," Charles put down his knife and fork.

"– then, quite often, he would dismember the body in other ways too," I started to tear up the piece of meat between my fingers, "you know, cut off hands, ears, noses, that sort of thing. You can see now," I turned to Charles, "how it might put you off eating meat, can't you?"

"Layla, stop it." Charles put his napkin to his mouth.

"Charles, what have you been saying to her?" Lucille's voice was shrill. "What have you done?"

"He's drunk." Debbie was still staring at me, transfixed, like a rabbit caught in the headlights.

In the long, red room, I could sense rather than see with any clarity that not only Debbie and Charles, but everyone had turned towards me. But I had released the horror now. It was too late, I could not stop.

"I have this friend called Meredith," I talked on into the silent room, "an English girl. She told me that when she was down at Tumbez she found this Indian woman's boot.

166

And when she picked it up, she found that there was a foot still inside it."

I looked down at my hands. In the candlelight the meat seemed to have taken on the same colour as the wall, staining my fingers as red as blood. "You know, it's funny," and as I said this a great howl of laughter came welling up inside my throat, until my voice was trembling with the effort of keeping that terrible laughter at bay – "but even though I never actually saw it myself, I can't seem to stop thinking about that boot."

*　　*　　*

Luke found me in the kitchen. I was washing my hands in the sink, scrubbing at my bloodied nails with the washing-up brush. He leant up against the wall, one long leg crossed over the other, watching me as I washed and rinsed, and then washed again.

"You should have told me," he said after a while. "You should have told me what happened."

"It was in the papers, wasn't it? That man, John Elmhurst, he'd read about it."

"A Reuters column inch, at the most. That sort of thing just doesn't make major news over here." Luke waited, but I said nothing. "I thought you could confide in me," he said. "You should not be carrying round that sort of thing on your own. It's too much. That's what friends are for, right? To share the load."

"I don't have any friends here." I spoke the words bitterly into the hard white sink.

"Yes, you do. You know you do."

I dried my hands on a tea towel, but when I sniffed my fingers they still smelt to me of dead flesh. I turned back to the sink and started to wash them all over again. Luke just stood there watching me, saying nothing.

167

"Who told you?" I said at last.

"Connie did."

"I see."

We lapsed into silence again. Under the hot water in the sink, my skin was turning slowly pink and crinkled.

"Have I made a terrible fool of myself?"

"No, of course you haven't." I heard Debbie's voice behind us. Something about the look she gave Luke made me wonder how long she had been standing there, but she came up and – to my surprise – put her arm around me. "It's not your fault. My brother is a fool; a stupid, drunken fool."

"You can say that again," Luke said with disgust.

"It's all right, really. I don't know what came over me; some of the things he said just hit me wrong, that's all." How could I expect any of them to understand?

"Connie's going to take you home."

"Yes, I think that would be a good idea." I felt terribly tired. The thought of having to face all those enquiring faces in the dining room was more than I could bear.

"I'll drive you," Luke offered.

"That's OK. Connie just rang for a taxi," Debbie said. Her arm was still around me. I could feel the weight of it, curiously intimate and female, across my shoulders. "It'll be here in a minute. Come on, Layla, let's find your coat."

We said goodbye at the door.

When Connie was out of earshot she started, "Layla, I just wanted to say –" but then trailed off as if, whatever it was, she was finding it difficult to put into words.

"Yes?"

"You see, I had no idea. What you had been through. I mean, I *knew*, of course. But it's not the same as really knowing, is it? Being made to *see*, through that person's eyes." She kissed me on the cheek. "It wasn't only Charles. I'm sorry, too, for the things I said."

In the orange street light I could see that her eyes, those huge, unblinking pale eyes, were full of tears.

THIRTEEN

Captain Jaime Buenaventura Valdez, a man of cultured tastes and only the mildest corruption, stayed with his men at Santa Luz for the best part of a week. The time was longer than was strictly necessary for his enquiries but, as the chief of police of the province, his sojourn there, he believed, was no more than his due. After all, he told himself, Santa Luz had once been one of the country's most famous haciendas; and in this slow backwater where he now found himself, perks of the job, to a man of his sensibilities, were few and far between.

Jaime Buenaventura Valdez dreamed of a posting in one of the big towns, preferably in the capital, in Veracruz itself. He imagined himself attending the opera, immaculate in top-boots glistening like black molasses, and white gloves. But the truth was that he was not in Veracruz, but here in this savage mountain and jungle province of the north. In Esperanza there was no opera. There was no place which could truthfully even be given the name of town; the roads, such as existed at all, were no more than dirt tracks; and it was too hot to even contemplate the wearing of gloves.

Buenaventura's men had set up their enquiry desk – a simple matter of a wooden table and two chairs – in the shade of an old porch. The porch, more like a kind of raised

169

walkway, led right around the front of the house, and faced on to an immense, overgrown courtyard. Various doorways led off the walkway. The captain had tried some of them, only to find that the rooms behind had long ago crumbled away, and that the doors, as in a film set, opened out into thin air.

During the day the great courtyard at Santa Luz pulsed with the press of bodies. The Indians sat around in groups; the women in their stiff skirts the rich, reddish colours of the earth, their necks fettered barbarously with gold beads; the men in their pony tails and trilby hats. Buenaventura noticed that where possible they positioned themselves with their backs to the house, facing out towards the mountain which rose with such immensity out of the land that he was shocked anew each time he caught sight of it.

If Buenaventura was truthful with himself, he realised that this latest unrest among the Indian population was something which troubled him little. It was not that he despised these people, as some of his countrymen did – for did not he, Jaime Buenaventura Valdez, have Indian blood himself? Not too much, mind you. Just a drop or two, way back, on his mother's side; just enough to make him a true patriot of his country. Enough, in other words, not enough to be any serious inconvenience – it was simply that they had no relevance in his personal scheme of things.

At midday each day the English *patrón* joined the captain in the Great Court to enquire after his progress.

"Everything all right, Captain?"

"*Sí, señor.*" The captain snapped his heels together, an anachronistic German mannerism still practised by the police which Jack found curiously unnerving. "It was a good idea of yours to come here. It would have been too complicated to have brought all these people down to Altamirada, I think."

"Undoubtedly, Captain. They have been through enough over the last week, without uprooting them all again so soon."

Jack examined the bland, handsome *mestizo* face, narrowly rescued from effeminacy by the pockmarks on his cheeks. He took in the immaculate khaki uniform and the boots shone up three times a day; the gold chain, discreet but heavy, around his neck; the faint, odiferous trace of aftershave.

"I imagine that your enquiries must be nearly at an end by now." Jack's gaze flickered past the captain into the milling courtyard. Buenaventura, revealing a row of very white, very even teeth, smiled and nodded non-committally.

"As soon as we do, *señor*, rest assured that you will be the first to know."

"You are too kind," Jack said, as agreeably as he could.

In these daily exchanges both men were formally, scrupulously, polite to one another, but Jack did not enjoy having the police here, as Buenaventura was well aware. In his opinion they had already overstayed their welcome. The chief of police was inclined to snoop – Magdalena had caught him several times wandering around the Quetzal Court, looking, she said, as if he owned the place – and his men were no better, town boys with their insulting eyes, their insouciant, swaggering walk.

"You are so very isolated here." The captain, searching for a new line of conversation, followed Jack's gaze around the crumbling stone courtyard. "My men tell me that the authorities are planning to build a new road. We passed some *obras* on the way up here, I seem to remember. This must be a very welcome change for you all."

"In these parts, Captain, I find that change is very rarely for the better." The Englishman spoke with vehemence. "Roads belong to the twentieth century, and the twentieth century is an invention of the west. It has no meaning in a place like this. As you can see for yourself, these people live in their own way, quite outside our own notions of progress or civilisation."

"But, Señor Hallett," the captain said smoothly, "surely you would not deny them the chance to choose?"

"If it were a question of choice, then of course. But with

171

people like this it never is. Not their choice, anyway. All the medical facilities, the new schools, the improved sanitation," Jack waved his hand towards the huddled groups of Indians, "the things which these people really need, would be all very well, of course, but they will never reach them. The only thing which will reach these people is the dross. An empty Coca-Cola culture which will whittle away at everything, their traditions and their beliefs, even the way they dress, until they have nothing left to call their own. So you see, *mi capitán*, this is why I do not welcome the new road."

Buenaventura watched Jack turn and walk away from him, down the dipping wooden steps into the courtyard. He must have been a good-looking man once, he thought, watching the tall form in his dirty old corduroy trousers and faded cotton shirt. Who was he, this Englishman, this great landowner, who dressed like one of his own peasants and who locked up himself, and his family, in this phantasmagorical ruin of a house? Of what was he so afraid?

"Señor Hallett!"

Buenaventura followed Jack down, and fell into step beside him.

"Captain?"

"Do you mind if I walk with you?"

"Please do."

Jack strode on across the courtyard. As they walked the throng of Indians in the courtyard seemed to dematerialise in front of them, a parting of the waves, instinctive rather than deferential, as the *patrón* passed by.

They said that these people were different from the other Indians of the sierra, a tribe apart, Buenaventura remembered. As he stepped among them he noticed, not for the first time, that they had a particular way of looking at him, or rather not looking at him, as if their eyes were focused on some different dimension. It was not that they looked past him, but *through* him as if, ghost-like, he did not really exist.

"Well, Captain," Jack said, sensing the reason for Buenaventura's presence, "have you something to tell me?"

"Ah, Señor Hallett." Buenaventura raised his shoulders, spread his hands: a mute, eloquent gesture. "The circumstances are difficult. These people are very frightened. There is no positive proof."

"I see."

The name – Quintero – hung between them, unutterable, like an evil incantation.

"Señor Hallett."

"Yes, Captain?"

"Would you take some advice from me?"

"That depends on what you are about to advise."

"Leave this place." Buenaventura paused, waiting for some reaction, but Jack said nothing. "Then at least send your wife and daughter away."

"In a month's time my wife is planning a trip to London with my daughter; she has not visited England before, and my wife is anxious for her to get to know her, our, country. Does that satisfy you?"

"It is precisely the next few weeks which should be of the greatest concern to you. To us all." Buenaventura's voice was soft. "After what has happened, Señor Hallett, this is no place for women. Surely you can see that?"

"But nothing has happened here," Jack turned on the chief of police. "What happened, happened in the Altamirada gorge, at Tumbez, many miles away from here." His eyes, squinting against the sunlight, were a very pale blue, a little watery; the eyes, Buenaventura realised for the first time, of an old man.

Years later, Buenaventura's memories of Santa Luz would always seem encapsulated by that particular moment. The two of them stood facing one another by the stone crucifix. He would remember the dry astringent smell of dust and eucalyptus, the burning midday sun, the blur of Indian bodies, red and antique gold, a scene as old as time.

"You realise then, that while you remain here, I cannot guarantee your protection?"

173

"Believe me, Captain Buenaventura, I have lived here for many, many years," he heard the Englishman say. "These are my people. No harm could possibly come to me, or to my family, while we are at Santa Luz."

"As you please, Señor Hallett," Buenaventura found himself shrugging in reply, relieved to have absolved himself of the responsibility, "as you please."

For the second time, Buenaventura watched Jack walk away from him. As he was about to enter the house again he was joined by the Indian, Maria-Magdalena. Buenaventura watched them standing together: the taciturn old Englishman, so tall and gaunt and desiccated, and the Indian woman, with her soft skin and her extraordinary eyes, black and hooded as an Egyptian queen's. They parted, and as Buenaventura watched the woman walk out into the sunlight, he felt a stirring inside him, a sudden desire for this beautiful creature. She was, he realised, the first Indian to move him in this way. He had never thought of them as objects of desire, or of any other particular emotion. Over these last days, when he might have expected to reach a better understanding of them, they had become for him, increasingly, inhabitants of their own twilight world in which he had no place.

Buenaventura watched Magdalena as she walked across the courtyard. Had the *patrón*, he wondered, ever been tempted this way. He must have an eye for pretty women. After all – Buenaventura thought with a smile of the English wife, kissing his fingers towards her in his mind's eye, sublime woman! – he was married to one. And yet he had the feeling that it was this one, and not the other, who ruled here.

He watched as the people gathered round her, calling her by name. They greeted her – men and women alike – with a respect which they had not even shown to the *patrón* himself. Beauty and power: as a combination, the most dangerous and the most intoxicating of all. In the old days, he thought, women like that were burnt as witches.

On the far side of the courtyard the Indian was joined

by the girl, the *patron*'s daughter. He watched them talking, their heads bowed together. Like the Indian woman, the girl moved among the gathering gracefully, as if she belonged in their element. It was curious, he thought, how much they resembled each other. He looked from the girl to Maria-Magdalena and back again. In this light, he could almost believe there was more than just a passing resemblance. But no, it was an absurd thought. How could there be?

Captain Jaime Buenaventura Valdez made his way back towards the shade of the porch.

*   *   *

That evening, which was to be Buenaventura's last at Santa Luz, there was a gathering in the Great Court such as had not been seen since the time of the old *patrón*. By the time evening fell the crowd who had gathered there during the day seemed to have doubled in size. Jack ordered five sheep to be slaughtered. Martin the Eye and some of his men built a *fire* at the foot of the chapel steps, and the meat was roasted over the flames on spits. Magdalena, Lupita and Emanuela served out *chicha*, fermented maize beer, from vats the size of wine barrels.

"Do you ever remember so many people gathered here before?" Layla asked Magdalena as they stood together watching the fire.

"Only once. When the old *patrón*, Don Baltazar's grandfather, died. I was very young, just a little girl, but I'll never forget it."

"You often used to tell me that story, when I was small." Layla laid her head against Magdalena's shoulder. "Do you remember? I used to come to your room at night sometimes, when I had bad dreams. I would get under the covers

175

with you, and you would tell me stories about the Peron y Imbaburras."

"Of course I remember, *niña*," Magdalena teased her, "how could I forget? You would fall asleep in my bed and snore all night long."

"Magda, I didn't!"

"Oh, yes, you did, *mi chinchita*," Magdalena pinched her cheek. "Snored just like a little black pig."

Layla gazed into the fire, feeling her cheeks sting with the heat. She wondered if Baltazar had been here, the night they buried his grandfather. Had it been like this? With the smell of the singeing fat, rich and oily, mingling with the night scents, jasmine and rose, from the overgrown gardens of Santa Luz.

The story was so well known it was almost legend. For three nights and three days after his death the household held a vigil in the chapel. Then, on the evening of the third day, as night fell they had sealed the coffin and brought him out.

Layla tried to imagine what it must have been like when the funeral party emerged into the Great Court and saw beneath them, in the smoky light of their tapers, that a crowd nearly a thousand strong, every man, woman and child from the estate, was standing silently at the foot of the steps. As the chapel doors opened and the procession came down into the courtyard, the crowd parted. They did not weep and they did not speak. Instead, when the coffin reached the ground, some of the men came forward and took it from the shoulders of the pallbearers. They then passed it in silent homage, from shoulder to shoulder, from hand to hand, across the great press of bodies which filled the courtyard, through the iron gates, and down the avenue of eucalyptus trees.

They carried the coffin in this way for nearly a mile, through the dark night to the little graveyard at the far end of the avenue. And then, when they had set him down and their task was finished, they kissed the ground in which he would lie, turned around silently and went away.

Layla looked at the faces around her. The firelight and the shadows seemed to have ironed out the worklines, the imperfections and the cruelties of day. What she saw was only their beauty exposed, their fine bones and their skin the colour and smoothness of amber.

'Why is it that they only come here to celebrate death?' All around her the children ran barefoot, up and down the chapel steps and along the wooden colonnade. Their faces shone, licked by the crimson shadows. 'Would they do the same for us?'

Layla, turning to ask Magdalena, felt the question die on her lips. "How little we really know them," she thought. "I have known these people all my life. I love them, and yet how much do I really know what goes on inside their minds?"

On the other side of the fire, someone had started to play the pipes, a high-pitched, reedy tune, the melancholy sound of the mountains. Although she did not know why, the sound filled Layla with sadness.

Magdalena put her arm around Layla.

"All right, *chiquita?*"

"Yes." Layla brushed her hand over her eyelids. "It's the smoke, that's all. Magdalena?"

"*Sí, niña?*"

"You know those stories you used to tell me, when I was a little girl? Not the ones about the family, the other ones."

"What stories were those?"

"You know the ones, about the quetzal bird."

"Yes." Magdalena's voice was smooth, like rich brown honey. "I know the ones."

"You know what they are saying, don't you?" Layla looked into Magdalena's eyes, eyes as deep and dark as jungle pools.

"Beautiful fairy stories, Layla. Stories for little children."

"Magdalena, I was *there*," Layla pleaded with her. "The quetzal has gone. Finn's quetzal. Someone has stolen it."

"Did he tell you that?"

"No, he didn't. But I went to look for it, the other day when I came back from Tumbez. It wasn't there any more."

"Does he know that you know?"

"No. I meant to ask him where it was, but I forgot."

"Good." Magdalena nodded.

"Magda –" Layla hesitated, "what's going on, Magda? I went to the Quetzal Court. I saw what was inside the *capilla*."

"You saw nothing!" The black eyes flickered, a moment of unease. "Nothing has happened to the bird. The bird is quite safe."

"But you don't understand, what about *Finn*!" Layla shook Magdalena by the arm. "Finn and Meredith! Sooner or later people are going to find out that the quetzal has gone; they're going to think it has died – and then what will happen to them?"

"*Niñita*," Magdalena smiled at Layla reproachfully, "they will say that they have let it free, that's all. There will be no need for anyone to think that it is dead."

"No, it won't work, you know it won't." Layla was insistent. "You must tell Finn. He's here, I saw him arrive about half an hour ago. You must tell everyone that you have taken it –"

"*No!*" Magdalena hissed, grasping Layla by the arm. "No. No one must know. It will never be safe otherwise. Quintero, he wants the bird. And if he finds it, he will kill it."

"Quintero? What are you talking about?"

"The bird is Kulkulcan, what you call Quetzalcoatl. We believe the bird represents the day, light, all good forces," Magdalena explained. "But Kulkulcan is never alone. He has a brother, Tezcatlipoca. This means Smoking Mirror. Tezcatlipoca is the night, darkness, all things evil. It is he who always wants human sacrifice . . ." she paused, waiting for this last fact to sink in, ". . . don't you see: the sacred bird is the only thing more powerful than he is, the only thing which can protect us against him. That is why we had to take it: to protect it, to protect all of us. I am explaining this to you so that you will understand why you must never tell anyone. Promise me." Magdalena's fingers bit into Layla's arm. "Promise me you will never tell?"

"All right."

"You must say it, Layla."

Magdalena gave her arm a little shake.

"All right, I promise."

"There, you see," Magdalena released her arm, "a big fuss for nothing. You must not worry so much. Nothing will happen to them, I promise you. There," she smoothed her hand down over Layla's hair, a soothing gesture she had used since Layla's childhood, "you have my promise too, see."

"Don't do that," Layla shook her away impatiently, "I'm not a little girl any more."

"No, you certainly are not." Magdalena, serene again, laughed at her. "And I know someone else who does not think you are a child any more, either." Magdalena looked at Layla slyly. She was teasing again now, almost playful, as though their conversation had never taken place. Layla knew, with absolute certainty, that the subject was now closed. It would be impossible to get Magdalena to refer to the stolen quetzal again.

"OK," Layla gave a small sigh of resignation, "who do you mean?"

"Over there." Magdalena pointed towards the gate.

"Baltazar?" Layla's pulse leapt. "What is he doing here?"

"Don't you know?"

"No, why should I?"

"Ay, Layla," Magdalena exclaimed, "you are blind, or something? I can see it, *niñita*, even if you cannot."

"See what?" Layla wished she could gather up the darkness and fold herself up in it like a cloak.

"He likes you."

"Oh, no, don't say things like that."

"He does, I can tell."

179

Despite herself, Layla felt her whole being blossoming. "Magdalena, how can you possibly tell!"

"The way he looks at you."

"He doesn't look at me."

"Yes, he does. He's looking at you now."

Before she could stop herself, Layla glanced over towards Baltazar. Across the courtyard, across the burning rim of flames, their eyes met. Layla looked away.

"Magda, stop it!"

Magdalena laughed with delight. She took hold of Layla's arm again, gently this time. "What a thing it would be," she whispered softly into her ear, "what a thing it would be if you were to marry a Peron y Imbaburra." She laughed again, arching her neck. In the smoky light of the bonfire, her black eyes were huge; her skin suffused with a deep golden red glow. "Ay, Layla, imagine that!"

*   *   *

"It's turning into quite a party, isn't it? You wouldn't think we had buried more than twenty people over the last week," Bettina said to Finn. They were leaning together over the balustrade a little apart from the crowd, near the squat, baroque stone entranceway to the house. "How on earth do they do it? It's like a scene from purgatory down there." She looked down into the courtyard. The music was playing louder now, flutes and drums swelling the sad refrain of the pipes. Two men and a woman stumbled past, blearily clutching at each other for support.

"God, look at them all, drunk as lords." Bettina drained her glass of wine. "Actually, I quite feel like getting drunk myself. Lupita!" She hailed the Indian woman going back into the house, "*Más vino, por favor.*"

"*Sí, señora.*"

The woman took the empty bottle and glided away into the house behind them.

"Well, sweetie, you know what they say: 'Let us eat and drink'," Finn leaned up against one of the flaking pillars, his shoulders hunched, long fingers thoughtfully stroking the stem of his glass, "'for tomorrow we die.'"

"Oh, don't Finn, please," Bettina put her hand on his shoulder, "don't tempt fate."

"Oh, you'll be all right. You'll always be all right at Santa Luz." Abstractedly, Finn tore a blossom from the bougainvillaea growing up the pillar behind him, crushing it against his palm. "Did I tell you I'd let the quetzal go?" he said casually.

"No, you didn't."

"It was the best thing, I thought, under the circumstances."

"Yes, you're probably right." Bettina's mind was on other things and Finn, wisely, chose not to dwell on the subject.

"Jack tells me you're taking Layla to England."

"Yes. We've been thinking about it for some time. She's never been, you know. It's about time she saw something of her own country. And this seems like a good time to be out of here. For a while, anyway."

Finn stroked his long chin thoughtfully. "I can't somehow imagine Layla in England."

"No. It's funny, isn't it?" Bettina said. "I can't really imagine her there either. But then I can hardly imagine myself there any more. It's been a long time. I worked it out the other day. More than twenty years; nearly half my lifetime. It must be pretty much the same for you."

"Yes, but you know it's funny how time plays tricks on you. It still seems like yesterday."

Lupita came back with another bottle of wine. Bettina took it from her and poured them both another glass.

"Come on, let's get drunk together, Finn. We haven't done that for ages."

"I've got a better idea," Finn reached into his pocket

and brought out an enamelled box. "I've got some nice grass here. Let's be flower children again for the night. Just you and me."

"Flower children, is that what we were?" Bettina laughed. "Finn, didn't I always say you were my best friend?"

They sat down side by side on the steps.

"England," Finn lit the joint, inhaled delicately, and handed it to Bettina, "do you think it really still exists? Or do you think it's just a figment of our imaginations?"

"A figment, definitely," Bettina said. "Just think: the Tower of London, double decker buses, the Houses of Parliament. Absurd! How can they possibly exist?"

"Never mind all that. What about real English food. Crumpets, for instance."

"Kellogg's cornflakes."

"No, you can't have them. They're American, they don't count."

"All right then, porridge."

"With Golden Syrup."

"And Marmite toast."

"Marmite toast!" Finn groaned. "Hey, and what about English television. Remember 'Hancock's Half Hour'?"

"And 'That Was the Week that Was'."

"Z-Cars."

"Z-Cars!"

"Do you know something," Bettina reflected, "for more than twenty years I have longed for this moment. The moment when I could go back to England, I mean. And yet now it's here," she turned to Finn, her hair a halo in the light of the flames, "and I'm absolutely terrified."

"Why?"

"It's like we were just saying, supposing it's not *there* any more." Staring into the fire, Bettina inhaled again on the joint. "Supposing I find it changed so much that I don't belong any more, that I'm no longer wanted there. I don't think I could bear that." Bettina put her arms around her knees and hugged them to her. "It was always my

182

let-out, you see. If things got too bad here, I would always have a place to go back to. I can't bear the idea that I might break the illusion."

"I've always wondered why you've never been back to England before. Twenty years is a long time."

Bettina did not reply straight away. She looked out, down into the courtyard, towards the rusting iron gateway.

"I remember the first time I ever set eyes on this place."

In her mind's eye she saw the avenue of trees flashing past, their shadows impaling themselves on her retina; the white dust kicking up behind them. Could hear Jack's voice, charged with excitement, "Wait for it! Just round this corner . . . look, look . . . now!" and the vast, shimmering white house rising up, phoenix-like, from the lap of the mountain.

"I was very young, just twenty-two, and I hardly knew Jack at all. He was much older than me – nearly fifteen years older – and I adored him. And yet as soon as I set eyes on this house I knew that it had a hold on him that I could never have. It was his dream, his darling, his pot of gold at the end of the rainbow. Some people are like that you know, they love places more than people. Jack is one of them: he can't help it, he's just made that way."

"That still doesn't explain why you never went back to England."

"Now there's a question," Bettina's eyes glittered, "I've often wondered myself. Partly, I suppose, it was the money. I was rather rich, you know, when I was first married. I often used to wonder if that wasn't the real reason Jack married me." She laughed, a tiny brittle laugh. "Most of my money went into this house. Jack didn't want to take it, not at first anyway. But I insisted. I thought I would be able to keep him that way. It sounds ridiculous now, but we spent so much money on Santa Luz that there was hardly ever anything left over, certainly not for things like travelling. Jack never wanted to go anywhere else anyway."

She turned to Finn. "My God, what was in that joint, a truth drug or something?"

183

"You can tell me anything, sweetie. Your secrets are safe with me, you know that."

"Yes, I know." She reached for Finn's packet of cigarettes, and lit one. "Anyway," she went on, "that was one reason. After a few years I also got this idea into my head that if I *did* manage to go to England, I'd never come back. Either that, or I'd find that when I did get back, I really had lost Jack." Bettina paused. "It's funny, isn't it, I don't think I've ever managed to decide which was my greatest fear." She looked away. "And then of course there was Layla. I was never very good with her when she was small, but I could never have left her, not for that length of time."

"Couldn't you have taken her with you?"

"No," Bettina said shortly. "In this country, believe it or not, a woman has to have her husband's permission before she can take her children abroad. Barbaric, isn't it?"

"But Jack could hardly have refused his permission. Could he?"

"Darling," Bettina stubbed her cigarette out on the step, "I wasn't the only one who thought I wouldn't come back."

Beneath them in the courtyard some of the young children had already fallen asleep, oblivious to the noise around them, bedded down by their mothers in shawls and old blankets. The music, plaintive, monotonous, rang out across the stones.

"Where is Layla, anyway? I haven't seen her all evening," Finn asked.

"Down there," Bettina nodded in the direction of the chapel, "can't you see? Talking to Baltazar."

Finn looked and saw Layla and Baltazar standing together. Two little Indian girls, miniature versions of their mother in stiff woven skirts and plaits, hung off each of Layla's arms. In one hand they held a piece of corn-on-the-cob which they chewed at silently, looking up at her from time to time with solemn eyes.

"You know," Finn said, after contemplating them for a while, "I sometimes used to think that you and Baltazar – perhaps?"

"One of the aunts who brought me up, my aunt Connie, always used to say that the women in my family only ever fall in love once." Bettina laughed. "Besides, I'm into older men, not babysnatching – or haven't you noticed?"

Finn put his arm around her. "He doesn't deserve you."

She put her hand to his face. "I'm not exactly easy myself, you know. Don't worry, I can keep my end up."

"Yes. I know."

They were silent again, looking down at the dying fire.

"Is she in love, do you think?"

"I should be asking you," Bettina said sadly. "I always seem to be the last to know what goes on inside Layla's mind, you know that." She leant forward, resting her chin between her hands. "Things have not been easy recently. I don't know why, but I seem to have lost the knack with her –" she hesitated, "– on the other hand, perhaps I've never had it. I've always hoped that if we could go away somewhere together – away from here, away from Santa Luz – like this trip to England, for instance, it would be different."

"You must give her time, that's all," Finn said. "Layla has always been secretive. It's in her nature."

"Like Jack, you mean."

"No, I've never thought she was particularly like Jack," Finn said. "When she was younger I always used to tease her that she was a fairy child. She was always so quiet, so self-contained."

"But she'll grow out of that, surely? She gets prettier every day."

"Prettiness has got nothing to do with. There's an air of mystery about her, it's hard to explain." Finn looked across at Layla and Baltazar, still standing together at the foot of the chapel steps "If I had to make a prediction, I would say that men will always fall in love with Layla because she will always keep them guessing."

Fourteen

The next day Baltazar called in at Santa Luz to say that he was going to visit Mauricio Hidalgo. Hidalgo was a gunsmith who lived in San Pedro de Cotani, a small village high up on the windswept plateau beyond Cotacotani and the mountains overlooking Santa Luz. It was a day's drive there and back. If Layla had nothing better to do, Baltazar said, then he would be glad of her company on the trip.

It was very early, before dawn, when he arrived to pick her up. In the darkness beneath the stars the house was transformed, a still, silent world of shadows and moon-blue walls. She was waiting for him as he drove his jeep in through the gates of the Stable Court at the back of the house. He was wearing a woollen poncho and a trilby hat on his head.

"Here," he said to Layla, handing her a fold of thick cloth, "I brought you this. The heating system in my jeep's broken down. Until the sun comes up it's going to be a cold drive."

As he spoke his breath condensed on the cold air.

"That's all right," Layla accepted the poncho, catching the scent of the raw wool which smelt familiarly of straw and animal dung, "it makes a change from being so hot all the time."

Baltazar opened the door to the passenger seat. Layla climbed in and looked around her. Although the jeep was old, there was something intimate about its interior. On the back seat was a clutter of tools, a wheel jack and a collection of screwdrivers; a litter of old papers and empty cigarette packets; a paperback novel; an old artist's palette and some tubes of paint. The leather seats were scarred as if they had been slashed open with a knife.

As they drove off the chapel bell struck six, a clean, pure sound. Above them the stars shone in a sky the colour of ink.

"When I was a child I often used to dream about this house," Baltazar said. "For some reason I always saw it like this, at night. I think it has something, when everything else is still in darkness. A kind of purity. As though it's no longer a place for humans at all, but part of the land. An extension of the mountains, almost."

"Yes, I know just what you mean."

Layla was exhilarated by this thought. Looking through the window she saw a finger of light trace the mountains in front of them, until their outline was haloed with the distant dawn. "I often get up at this time, with Magdalena."

"Maria-Magdalena." Baltazar repeated the name. "A formidable woman by all accounts. Not at all unlike my aunt Esmeralda, you remember the one I told you about? Finn says he's scared stiff of her."

"Finn exaggerates," Layla laughed.

"You're very close to her, aren't you?"

"Did Finn tell you that too?"

"No. He didn't have to; I can see it for myself," Baltazar smiled. "You know, she reminds me of someone, although I can't for the life of me remember who," he shook his head. "I keep on thinking that I'm going to remember, but it eludes me every time."

"I know who it is. It's Santa Luz," Layla said. "The figure of the saint in the chapel. That's who she reminds you of."

187

"Ah, so that's who it is," Baltazar said. "Of course."

For a time they drove without speaking, watching the blue and gold dawn break over the horizon. At the roadside two girls emerged from a whitewashed adobe house. The eldest was a child no more than six years old, her body bent forward against the weight of a baby, a tiny brother or sister, slung in a shawl across her back. Layla watched them as they walked towards the fields, the red of their skirts, bright as hibiscus flowers, flitting and dipping like butterflies through the morning mist. In the distance, down through the valley, came the sound of the chapel bells.

By the time they joined the Altamirada road the sun had risen. At the turning Layla caught sight of the road workers. They squatted by the roadside around a meagre fire, pulling their jackets around them, warming their hands against their tin mugs. With their paler skin, Layla recognised them as men from the coastal plains, invaders from another country, hunched and cold in their yellow helmets. Beneath the road, crescent-shaped drifts of cloud hung in the gorge like spirit matter.

Baltazar raised his hand to them in greeting.

"You know, I've never really worked out why your father is so against this road. He is really a puzzling man. Do you know how long it would take to get somewhere like San Pedro if there was a way to get a vehicle across the mountains behind Santa Luz? We could be there in a matter of hours, instead of taking a whole day to go this long way round."

"He does not often talk about it. Finn says he's afraid of change. Afraid that the old ways will be lost, the way they already have in so many other parts of the country, and that the Coca-Cola culture, as he calls it, will leave nothing lasting in their place." Layla thought for a moment. "I think he's afraid that he will lose Santa Luz. Not physically, but – how can I put it? – spiritually, I suppose. Does that make sense?"

"It certainly does." Baltazar threw his hat into the back

188

of the jeep, and ran his hands through his hair, pushing it back from his face. "And you, what do you think?"

"I don't think that change," Layla said slowly, "is necessarily what matters. Look at this new road," she pointed to the scars etched across the mountainside, "we can't stop it being built – although Dad would have liked to – but it's not up to us. What matters is land."

"Yes," Baltazar swerved to avoid a pothole, "go on, I'm listening."

"For the Indians the land is a sacred thing, a living being of which they are a part, indivisible from it like trees, or rocks or plants. Everything in their lives is connected to the land. All their gods and spirits, their *apus*, exist in it. They won't put a plough to the mother earth without asking permission; and often they won't even eat or drink without first giving *Pachamama* her share."

"You're right," Baltazar nodded in agreement.

"My father has this idea that the Indians have a great, great passion for their land. Their reverence for it is like a love affair, that's how he describes it. That's what he's always loved in them, and I suppose is what he's always tried to protect."

"But you don't agree with him?"

"Well, yes –" Layla sounded doubtful, "only sometimes –" she floundered. "Actually, no; no, I don't."

"Why not?"

"It's hard to describe."

"Try me."

"Well, if you have a great passion for something, or someone, it isn't you, is it? I mean you love something when it's on the outside . . . I can't describe it . . . when it's something other than yourself."

"Yes, I know exactly what you mean."

"I've always had this idea that the land was like breathing air. It is so much a part of you that you are hardly even aware of it most of the time. You certainly don't love it, or hate it, not in the way that people usually mean anyway. It doesn't even make you particularly happy, or unhappy.

It's only when you don't have it that you really notice; and then you die." Layla paused, "They don't love the land because it *is* them . . . or rather *they* are *it*. Oh, I don't know," she threw her hands up, "I'm not very good at explaining it, I'm afraid."

"On the contrary," Baltazar smiled at her, "you explained quite beautifully."

All morning they drove west along the Altamirada road, jack-knifing up the gorge away from the town, higher and higher into the mountains. They stopped occasionally to buy fruit, oranges and the fists of diminutive golden bananas known as 'doritos', from wayside stalls. Sometimes they talked; the rest of the time Layla looked out of the window, or dozed. From time to time, when she woke from her sleep, she found herself watching Baltazar as he drove. His hands were very sure on the wheel. He had beautiful hands, she thought, noticing the fine black hairs, still flecked with paint in places, which grew along his long fingers and up his arms.

At midday they reached a pass in the mountains. The pass was marked by a crude plaster crucifix to one side of the road.

Baltazar stopped the jeep and they got out of the car, hugging their ponchos around them against the cold. Layla felt the wind whipping her hair across her face, and when she breathed the thin air was frosty. It caught against her throat like vaporous ice.

On one side they could see the road beginning its long descent westwards, striking out across the high mountain plateau towards the coastal plains; while on either side of them, for as far as the eye could see, stretched the immense, spiky white backbone of the Andes.

"Look over there!" Baltazar shouted to Layla over the wind. "See that little cloud? Well, see the peak immediately underneath it, the very pointed one? That's our mountain, Cotacotani."

Layla nodded, her eyes smarting.

"Whenever I used to drive this way with my father he

190

always used to stop at this same place," she shouted back. "We used to bring binoculars with us sometimes. On a clear day you can just see Magdalena's village. I could never believe that it was possible to see so far."

"You're shivering." Baltazar put out his hand and touched her shoulder.

"Come on, let's go."

As they walked back towards the jeep Layla reached down and picked up a pebble which she placed on top of a pile of stones at the base of the crucifix. Baltazar followed suit.

"Who taught you to do that?"

"Magdalena did, the first time she took me up the mountain."

Baltazar started the jeep and pulled out into the road.

"Up the mountain?"

"Yes, to her village. I was only about seven," Layla smiled at the recollection. "For months and months I begged her to take me there, and so eventually she did. We went to visit Tio and Tia, her parents. Tio's dead now. It was terrible," Layla remembered, "I spent the whole time trying not to cry."

"Why was that?"

"I never dreamed that something I wanted so much could be so very difficult," she reflected. "I'd always seen these little shepherd girls, Indian children the same age as me, running up and down the mountainside. It never occurred to me that I hadn't been born with springs in my legs too. I wanted to be like them, I suppose."

"A difficult thing for the *patrón*'s daughter to be."

"Yes." Layla nodded. "I can see that now. But it didn't feel that way then. That day especially," Layla hesitated, realising what she was about to tell Baltazar, "you see, that was the day they cut my hair off," she said quickly, "at Tia's house. They cut off all my hair."

"A First Haircutting?" Baltazar laughed in astonishment. "On you?"

191

"Yes." Layla was laughing too. "Can you imagine how cross my mother was?"

"Furious, I should think. So would anyone have been."

"Oh no, Dad wasn't."

"No?"

"Oh, no. He was never cross about things like that."

About two miles from the pass they reached the turning for San Pedro. Baltazar swung the jeep off the road on to a dirt track.

"So who was behind the First Haircutting then?" Baltazar said, "Magdalena, I suppose?"

"Yes. At least I've always presumed it was."

"You really love her, don't you?" Baltazar asked.

"Magdalena brought me up, you see," Layla said. "She even nursed me, when my mother could not."

She paused, aware of the intimacy of what she was saying, but Baltazar, his eyes fixed on the dusty track ahead, seemed quite unperturbed by it.

"She was your wet nurse, you mean?"

"Yes. She lost a child, you see," Layla explained. "A little girl. If she had lived she would have been exactly the same age as me, almost my twin. I often wonder what she would have been like."

*   *   *

The mountain plateau near San Pedro was a desolate place. A strip of brown land, as flat and brittle as a dried-out tortilla, straddling the *cordillera*. Nothing grew here. The hard earth always gave Layla the impression of having been burnt out millennia ago by altitude and the mountain winds, great gusts of which buffeted the jeep as Baltazar drove along, turning the dirt kicked up by the wheels of the jeep into tornadoes of dust.

Despite the extraordinary mountain light, which at Santa

Luz could transfigure most things into a semblance of beauty, the villages they passed had a barren look to them. They would appear from nowhere, shimmering on the horizon like mirages; but close to they were desert places, each one the same as the last, with their decaying houses of breezeblock and corrugated iron strung out along the road. The people gazed after Baltazar's jeep with beleaguered eyes.

Except for the church, an ugly modern building pitted with black marks like bullet holes, there was nothing to distinguish San Pedro from the other places they had passed through. They stopped for lunch in a cheap *comedor* in the main street. A sluttish *mestizo* woman in a tight green dress and a crocheted shawl served them. At first she was sulky and unco-operative, as though she resented the intrusion, but she brightened up when Baltazar came in, and cleared away the beer bottles and cigarette ends from the table nearest the brazier where they would be warm.

The interior of the *comedor* was dark and gritty. The woman served them with watery soup, bread and *queso de campo*. As they ate she loitered in the doorway, leaning up against the fly-screen, torn between eyeing Baltazar and watching for any signs of life in the street outside.

There was not much life to see. Opposite them Layla could see a drunk slumped against a wall. Graffiti, in paint the colour of dried blood, emblazoned the peeling plaster: *Viva la Revolución; Tierra y Pan; Revolucionarios a la Lucha.* Two yellow-eyed dogs, their thin shanks quivering with mange and cold, sniffed the drunk cautiously.

"Has San Pedro always been like this?" Layla asked.

"It's much poorer than I remember." Baltazar looked out into the shabby street. "I only came here a few times before and that was with my father, when I was a boy. The drought has affected everyone; even here where it hardly ever rains anyway."

"What is a man like Hidalgo doing in a place like this?"

Baltazar cut himself a piece of cheese, paring off the rind with his knife.

"This is his home, I guess," he shrugged. "Don't forget, the old railway used to pass through here. That's probably why San Pedro was built in the first place. It must have been quite prosperous once." He looked at his watch. "I should go and find Hidalgo now. I said I'd meet him at his house. Can I leave you here for a few minutes? His workshop is on the other side of the village, so we'll come back this way and pick you up. You finish your lunch. You'll be all right with her," he nodded towards the woman still standing in the doorway, "she won't let anything happen to you until I get back to pay the bill."

When he had gone, the woman came over and sat down opposite Layla.

"*Casados?*" she asked conversationally. "Are you married?"

Her voice had the distinctive thick lilt of the *paramo*. Layla shook her head.

"*Que lastima,*" the woman sighed, "what a shame."

She stared at the empty doorway, as if hoping to conjure Baltazar back into the room. She was still young, in her mid-thirties Layla guessed. The thin straps of her dress bit into plump brown arms.

"He's a fine man, that one." She lifted Layla's face up by the chin. "You are young and pretty, *hijita*. You should get him while you can. He'll give you lots of children, that one," she laughed, a coarse good-natured laugh. "You can tell, you know," she winked, "it's in their eyes."

Layla could not help smiling. After the oppressiveness of the village, there was an enormous vitality about this plump vulgar woman.

"And you, *señora*, do you have children?"

"You're asking me?" the woman opened her eyes wide. "Everyone knows that there are only old men and children left in San Pedro these days. And they're no good to anyone," she made a crude gesture with her hand, "certainly not for that. You look around, you won't see a single pregnant married woman in the whole place. Not even the

194

young ones – not even the unmarried ones! It's not right, I tell you."

"Have the men gone to find work?" Layla was puzzled by this outburst.

"Bless you, no," the woman shrugged. "The *banditos* took most of them. Either that or they've gone into hiding to avoid them. My husband's been gone six months now, and I still don't know where he is, the *desgraciado*. It was a good excuse to get out, I guess. I should have left at the same time. San Pedro has always been a dump."

The woman spoke without rancour, adjusting the strap of her dress. She looked out into the empty street. "This place is dead now. Look at it: only old men and drunks."

Layla waited for over half an hour but still Baltazar did not return. The woman, whose name was Dolores, lapsed into silence again. She took out a lipstick and an ancient, almost empty powder compact and started to dab in a desultory way at her face.

Another ten minutes went by. Another customer, the only one apart from Layla and Baltazar, came into the *comedor*, and sat down at the far side of the room by the door. Reluctantly Dolores got up to serve him. Layla looked out into the deserted street but still there was no sign of Baltazar. The next thing she knew Dolores was at her shoulder.

"Not still here, are you," she snapped at her. "Look, I've got better things to do than to be sitting here waiting for you all day."

"But we haven't paid you yet," Layla said, "he won't be long now –"

"Can't you see," Dolores hissed under her breath. "I've got other customers, d'you hear. Just go, will you.'

"I'm sorry, but if you could just wait another five minutes I'm sure –"

"Forget it," Dolores led her to the door and almost pushed her out into the street. "It's on the house. Just go."

She turned and went inside, slamming the fly-screen shut behind her.

195

Layla walked down the road, following the direction Baltazar had taken. The houses clustered along it like flies around the eyes of a broken horse. Despite the cold brilliance of the air, a powerful stench of stale urine came from the doorways and the dark alleys leading off the road. Soon Layla came to the end of the line of houses and found herself in a disused railway siding. Two old carriages, their windows smashed, stood together a little way off. Layla walked towards them, balancing her way along the tracks. The carriages looked strangely vulnerable; tiny black silhouettes against the vast, golden-brown expanse of the *paramo*.

When she reached the carriages she sat down on the steps and looked up into the dome of sky overhead. It was very quiet. Cupping her hands around her eyes it was possible to cut out the houses, the carriages, the mountains, even the *paramo* itself, until all she could see was the perfect, bewitching blue void above.

Layla turned and walked back towards the village. This time, instead of heading along the main road, she decided to take a short cut down one of the alleyways. As she reached the top of the alleyway she saw two men come out of one of the houses. The first had a brown trilby on his head and a dirty aertex singlet beneath a tracksuit top. The other wore a baseball cap bearing the logo of a well-known brand of gasoline. Despite their *mestizo* dress, both had the aspect of Indians. When they saw Layla they stopped: the man in the trilby hat whistled under his breath and nudged his companion in the ribs.

Keeping her eyes to the ground Layla picked her way over the refuse-strewn ground. The walls, from one length of the alleyway to the other, were scored over with graffiti. Although she tried to avoid looking directly at either of them, she could feel the man in brown watching her greedily. His eyes darted to and fro, bright as a little rat's.

'I must not look at them,' she thought, 'I must not let them see I am frightened.' Instinctively Layla kept walking. Overhead she could hear the sound of the wind singing in the telegraph wires. 'I must keep calm,' she repeated to herself. 'In broad daylight, what can they possibly do to me? I must keep calm.'

She had nearly drawn level with them now, could almost feel the rank smell of their breath. Above them on the wall, in large red lettering, was scored the legend, **PNRPI**, *Partido Nacional Revolucionario para el Poder Indígena. Viva la Revolucion.*

"*De-li-ciosa.*" The insulting words were exhaled softly, no more than a murmur. "*Mira la negra. Mm-m, deliciosa.*"

The man in the baseball cap giggled, staggered forward as though to grab Layla by the arm. But he missed his footing and stumbled against a stone. Her whole body taut with nerves, Layla swerved to avoid him.

She was past them at last. The man in the baseball cap lay sprawled on the ground where he had fallen. But the other man, the one in brown, was not to be got rid of so easily. Although he was the smaller of the two men, in height scarcely taller than Layla herself, something told her that it was this one she should be most afraid of; that this was not just the usual, insouciant insult of a man against a solitary woman. There was an intensity about him, in the line of his mouth and in the hard brightness of his eyes, which made Layla really afraid.

She could hear the sound of his footsteps keeping pace with hers, following her down the alleyway; could hear him still murmuring those obscene endearments, uttering words she had not even heard before. In her mind she could almost see the slow oozing of hairs escaping from the holes in his string vest; smell the sourness of his mouth, and the stale sweat on his body. Her body felt exhausted, as though the air had become viscous, like treacle. It was an effort to move at all. Her legs felt weak; her arms heavy, useless, as if they had been turned to lead. Tiny droplets of sweat broke out on her forehead. All around her the red graffiti on the walls crowded in on her. PNRPI. PNRPI.

At the far end of the alleyway she could see the street at last, and the drunk lying against the wall. A familiar form appeared, standing over him. Baltazar. Layla could feel a great sob, relief mixed with terror, rising in her throat. She could feel the rat man behind her, closer now, his eyes burning into her; she could almost feel his hand stretched out to catch her by the throat. He was so close that she could feel his breath on the back of her neck.

Then, from the corner of her eye, she caught sight of him. He had drawn level with her. Layla felt faint with the nausea of fear. For several long seconds they walked together in tandem down the dark, urinous tunnel. Then, just as suddenly, he strode past her, turned, and was gone down the street, disappearing out of sight. Alone, Layla stumbled out into the painful sunlight.

"Layla, are you all right?" Baltazar was at her side. He took her arm. "Where have you been? I have been looking for you everywhere."

Before Layla could recover her breath he was leading her, none too gently, down the road to where they had left the jeep.

"What's the matter? I'm all right, nothing happened."

"Stay close to me," Baltazar urged her on. "Don't run, just keep walking as fast as you can."

As soon as they were in the jeep, he started the engine and headed out of town. They swept down the road, past the *comedor*.

"Oh no, Dolores!" Layla remembered with dismay. "I completely forgot. We never paid her for lunch."

She turned, caught a last glimpse of the solitary customer still sitting at the table by the door. He looked up as they sped past: a single, utterly vivid moment, freeze-framed against her retina. There was a dusty, travel-stained look about him, but otherwise he was an unexceptional little man. Layla would have been hard pressed to have guessed his height, or weight, or even his age. And yet there was a quality about him – not in his face, which was obscured beneath his hat – but in something less tangible. The set of his shoulders, perhaps; a certain air of watchfulness in his manner, and in the hooded eyes beneath the rim of his trilby.

For a fraction of an instant a shock of recognition passed

between them, and then she was gone, the wheels of the jeep screaming, kicking up the fine brown dust of the *paramo*.

It was only when they reached the pass and were safely on their way back down to Altamirada that Baltazar told Layla what had happened. A few minutes before he had arrived at the gunsmith's, a group of Quintero's men had burst into his house. They had then taken Hidalgo out into the road outside, in full view of his wife and children, and cut his throat.

"But why Hidalgo? What has he ever done to them?"

"I think it was more what he hadn't done." Baltazar was pale. "He was a gunsmith, remember. Apparently a man came to him a few days ago and asked if he would consider working for his organisation – he didn't specify what it was called, although Hidalgo had a pretty good idea. All he had to do was to service and mend all their equipment, as and when they brought it to him, and not ask too many questions. The man was very polite about it, according to Hidalgo's wife. No bully boy tactics, nothing like that. They even offered to pay him. But of course, Hidalgo refused, the poor old fool," Baltazar said bitterly. "The waste of it! The man was an artist, a genius. One of the last real craftsmen of his kind in this country. What a mindless, senseless waste."

"Quintero," Layla said hesitantly after a while, ". . .was he with those men just now?"

"I don't know. No one knows, that's just it, we know nothing about this man at all. We don't know if he is a killer himself, or just a kind of demonic intellect behind it all. We don't even know what he looks like, for God's sake." Baltazar's knuckles were white against the steering wheel. "There must be a clue in all this somewhere, there has to be." He shook his head. "First Tumbez, and now this."

"And Santiago Menchu."

"And Santiago Menchu. No one can prove it, but yes, I'd say that was Quintero."

"I know it was."

Baltazar looked at her.

199

"What do you mean?"

"I mean I saw it happen, or rather I heard it. I was there. There is a place I go to sometimes" – Layla could feel the colour rising to her face, and hoped that he would not notice – "Martin the Eye showed it to me years ago. It's just beneath the El Indio rock. I was there when it happened." She turned to Baltazar, feeling a little sick. "Quintero's hallmark, or his men's, is to use a knife, right?"

"Up until now, yes," Baltazar nodded.

"Santiago was already wounded when my father arrived. I saw that, although I didn't realise it at the time because I was too far away. But there was only ever one shot. I would have heard if there had been any more. They had first used a knife on Santiago, not a gun, as we were all led to believe." Layla looked straight ahead, unblinking. "Those men were not thieves, and my father knew it. He's known it all along."

By the time Baltazar and Layla returned to Santa Luz it was nearly dusk. A few miles from the house he drew up by the side of the road. To their left stood the little graveyard, surrounded by rusting railings.

"Are you in a hurry to get back?" he asked.

"Not especially, why?"

"Then I would like to show you something. Will you come with me?" Baltazar led Layla into the graveyard.

In among the simple tombs of the Indians were the sepulchres of the Imbaburra y Perons, some of them as big as chapels, most now crumbling and ravaged with age. On the far side of the graveyard over one of the most recent tombs knelt an angel of death, spreading its feathered wings. The marble walls were still warm to the touch; but when Layla pressed her face to the bars she could almost taste the dank, dark smell of death within.

"Both my grandfather and my great aunt Esmeralda are buried in here." Baltazar said. "All my family except for my father, in fact."

On the steps just beneath the bars, on a drift of flower

petals, a single candle burnt, its shadows beating against the walls like the wings of a moth.

"And your mother?" Layla asked, watching the flame. "Where is your mother buried?"

"I never knew my mother," Baltazar said. "She died quite soon after I was born. My aunt Esmeralda brought me up, I told you. I never wanted any other mother."

"Why?" Layla turned on him, "Were you ashamed of her, because she was an Indian?"

"Ashamed? No, not ashamed. Rather the opposite. I have always been proud of my Indian blood," Baltazar said.

He leant back against the marble. She was very aware of him, and of how close he was standing to her.

"It was a fact of life," he went on. "Besides, there were many in my family born to Indian mothers, you must have known that."

"Tell me about it."

Layla stood very still. Inside the sepulchre the candle spat and fluttered.

"It was the custom here at Santa Luz," she could feel Baltazar's eyes on her, "in the old days. Surely you have heard of it?"

"Yes. I once heard something like that, when I was young." Layla looked at him. "But I'd like you to tell me. Would you, please?"

"All right." Baltazar picked at the crumbling plaster with his fingernail. Although neither of them had moved, he seemed even closer to her than before.

"In my family every few generations at least one of the *patrón*'s children – a son was preferable, I regret to say – was conceived with an Indian woman from the hacienda. They used to say that on the feast of San Juan, the same day that the summer solstice was celebrated in the old days, the most beautiful woman was sent to bewitch the *patrón*, to make magic on him, so that he would lie with her and conceive a child."

"But why?" Layla said. "Why did they do it?"

201

"Why?" Baltazar looked down at her. She could see a tiny scar on his cheek bone, and a single grey hair – or was it paint? – in his black hair. In the graveyard the evening air was very still and warm.

"To keep control, of course. There was never any stigma attached to illegitimacy here. Rather the opposite: it came to be considered a great honour, to be the chosen *patrón*. It was an ingenious, brilliant idea. The Indian mind is nothing if not pragmatic. They could not use force; they are not a warring people."

"So they used love instead."

"Yes, you could put it like that," he nodded. "At Santa Luz the two worlds meet. Indian and Spanish. It has always been more difficult here than anywhere else to separate the two." Their eyes met. "It's not what you are born, my grandfather used to say, but who you choose to be that matters."

"But supposing there is no choice?" Layla's voice was anguished.

"There is always a choice." Gently he put his hand to her face. "Always. I promise you."

They stood facing one another; neither of them moved.

"I did not bring you here to talk about myself," Baltazar said, breaking the silence at last. "I came here to show you something." He took her by the hand and led her to the far side of the graveyard. Here, with difficulty, he found a small unmarked grave all but obliterated beneath the vegetation.

"Do you remember what I was saying back in San Pedro, that there had to be some clue to Quintero?"

"Yes."

"Well, I think I might have thought of one, although I'm not exactly sure where it will get us." He tapped the stone with his foot. "It's been here all along; I had completely forgotten about it."

"In this grave?"

"It belongs to a boy I once knew." Baltazar squatted down beside it, pulling away the grass. "When I was growing up here we had a priest called Father Ignatius. He was a Jesuit, very strict. He hated all the Indian ways and tried his best to obliterate them, even though my grandfather said they should be tolerated. Anyway, one day he found out that this boy had taken part in some ceremony – I forget exactly what it was – so after mass he called all of us together, and then took the boy out into the Great Court and flogged him."

"My God," Layla looked at him with horror, "what did your grandfather do?"

"He was sent away the next day."

"And what happened to the boy?"

"He died." Baltazar stood up again. "His name was Aureliano Quintero."

"Quintero." Layla felt her skin go cold. "What are you saying? You don't think they were related, surely?"

Baltazar shrugged.

"I don't know, but there's a good chance. It's not a common name around here. And Quintero certainly seems to know the area."

Layla stared at Baltazar mutely.

"The PNRPI, Quintero's organisation, is about one very simple thing," he went on, "it's about land. About power, through the ownership of land. As far as Quintero is concerned big landowners, like Jack, are out. And foreigners – it doesn't matter if they're Spanish, English or Outer Mongolian – anything which is not purely Indian is out too."

"What are you trying to tell me?"

"I'm telling you that sooner or later you're going to have to leave Santa Luz," Baltazar said. "If Quintero really is a local man, with local knowledge, then it is not going to be safe for any of us for very much longer."

"But we are going, hasn't my father told you? We're going to England in just six weeks."

"Six weeks could be too late," Baltazar said. "This latest visit to Hidalgo looks as if they might be about to step up their operation. Look, I don't know why, but for some reason your father has never admitted the real seriousness of all of this, you've said so yourself. I don't even think he's admitted it to himself. I have tried to persuade him, on several occasions. So has Finn. But he's like a man in a dream. Someone has got to get through to him."

"What do you think we should do?"

"Leave Santa Luz."

"But when?"

"Within the week. Sooner, if possible."

"A week! But I have to arrange my papers, my passport –" Layla tried to keep the note of desperation out of her voice, "nothing is ready yet."

"Then go to Veracruz and arrange them."

Layla shook her head.

"My father will never leave. You don't know him like I do."

"Then go with your mother. The two of you is better than nothing. Will she go with you?"

"Yes, I think so."

"Then go, Layla," Baltazar's voice was gentle, "go soon."

FIFTEEN

That night I lay awake watching the moon rise outside my window. My body felt restless. My skin was hot, almost feverish to the touch. I could not sleep.

At last I got up and stepped to the window. My room faces westwards, out towards the mountain and the track which leads to El Indio. I remember pressing my face up against the bars, feeling the cool air against my cheeks.

I don't know why, but that night had a particular quality to it, an edge. Whether it was from fear, or whether from love, I shall never know. It was quite unlike any other night I have ever lived through.

Outside the world was absolutely still. On the air I could trace the night scents of the garden – jasmine and rose – and the damp smell of the earth where the gardens had been watered that evening. In the darkness, the outline of the mountain was softened until it looked like the outline of a woman's shoulder, cupped like a protective muse around the house. Beyond the walls, where the eucalyptus whispered, I remember seeing two lights moving together, a group of Indians walking through the night, lighting their way with torches.

As I stood there looking out I realised that, for the first time, I had been forced to see things as they really were. It was not so much the death of Mauricio Hidalgo, or even the man in the alleyway, although I think that was the first time I had felt personally threatened. It was not even the things Baltazar had revealed at Aureliano's grave. In San Pedro it was more the hopelessness of it all, and of the people, and of the way they had submitted to their fate. It was as if I had witnessed a kind of sickness of the soul. Not only of the people but of the land itself; as though with the dying of the land, the people had died too. Not externally, but deep within themselves.

As Baltazar said, it was as though we had all been asleep, or dreaming. It was as though Santa Luz had bewitched us all. All my life I had clung to the idea that the house was a refuge, in some way impregnable, immune. Inside its walls nothing could touch or hurt us. The outside world was silenced. Now I realised that all around us the world was slipping into chaos and would subsume us, and we had not seen it coming.

That night I realised many things, not only about Quintero. Through Baltazar's eyes, I saw myself more clearly than I had ever done. And I remember that at this moment, this moment of revelation, the way forward became simple suddenly. Instead of feeling frightened, I looked out towards the mountain and felt quite calm again. I remember thinking, 'Out there somewhere, quite probably, is Quintero', but even this no longer had power over me. That night I knew I would be safe. Santa Luz would keep her spell. My body felt light, as if a great weight had been lifted from me, and I realised that I was no longer afraid.

As I stepped back from the window I caught sight of myself in the mirror: a slender naked body, dark hair, grown long over the last few months to below my shoulders. In the mirror my skin was marbled in the moonlight, like a pale statue in a garden. The shadows from the bars across the window fell over my breasts, and across the tops of my thighs. I put my hands to my head and piled my hair on top of my head. I saw the curve of my arms, the arched line of my neck. I stared at the reflection in the glass, at this other, cool-limbed, moon-blue self. I thought of Baltazar, and how his hand had felt that afternoon when he touched my face.

'If he came now,' I thought, 'he would see me like this.' In my mind's eye I saw him behind me, watching as I stood before the mirror. I thought of his eyes on me, in the half-light. I turned my head, and from my shoulders I could smell the sweetness of my skin, faint, earthy, like the night-scented garden. I imagined Baltazar rising from the bed. He was standing behind me now, looking at me in the mirror. I could feel his hands, dry and warm, circling my waist. I saw him stoop to kiss my neck, and the soft skin of my shoulders. I could feel his body, barely touching me, his skin burning into my skin.

It is strange how love and death are connected in my life. That night I dreamt strange dreams. Once I woke and thought I saw a dark figure enter my room, and stand watching me from the foot of my bed. After that I slept again, a dreamless sleep this time. But when I woke the next morning, my whole body was still soft with desire.

SIXTEEN

It was Luke's idea that we should go to the seaside for the day, he and Debbie and I, just the three of us. Three was company, he said, rejecting the idea that he should find a friend to come with us; four a crowd.

We took the train from King's Cross and then, at huge expense, a taxi from Ipswich to Aldeburgh on the coast, which Luke paid for with handfuls of crumpled and dirty five pound notes which he seemed to be able to pull out, haphazardly but apparently at will, from the pocket linings of his greatcoat.

Despite my protests, he had paid for all our train tickets too.

"Why can't you get a wallet, like everyone else," Debbie said as we waited by the ticket office while Luke fumbled about inside his coat. "He always has to do things differently," she complained, taking my arm and walking off down the platform ahead of him. "Pure affectation half the time."

At that time in the morning the train was half empty. The only other people in our carriage were an elderly couple and a peaky-looking young woman with three children. The children, a boy, a girl and a sleeping toddler, were heavy-boned with large, chubby round faces and rosy cheeks. Their mother – although she looked far too slight and lank to have produced three such lumpen offspring – issued the two elder children with a stream of admonitions. Her voice was tired and slightly whining. "Sit still Darren, stop fidgeting like that, will you?" And then, "Drink up, Kylie, you haven't got all day, you know."

The little girl, who had been drinking from an oblong box full of orange juice, obediently put the straw back in her mouth and sucked on it energetically. Both she and her brother regarded their mother unblinkingly with baleful eyes.

Were English children always so silent and well behaved? Where I come from, I remember thinking, they would be rushing, unchecked and exuberant, up and down the passageway to a chorus of approval and admiration. Complete strangers would compete to entice them over to their seats. I could see them – '*Mira, que lindos*', '*que dul-ce*', '*preciosos*' – patting their flaxen curls, pinching and caressing their chubby cheeks, which the children would submit to with a mixture of grace and guile, knowing it their due.

Across the aisle the elderly couple regarded the children neutrally. After a while the woman leaned over, proffering a box, "Would your little ones like a sweet?"

The girl shrank back, shaking her head. Her mother dug her in the arm,

"'*No thank you*', Kylie, where's your manners?" She gave the woman a ghost of a smile.

"No thank you," the child muttered.

Her brother shook his head equally vehemently, and turned away to look out of the window.

"Poor little souls," I heard the elderly woman remark to her husband.

"Poor little souls nothing," Debbie whispered unexpectedly in my ear, "they've eaten so many sweets they're probably wishing never to see another one in their whole lives," she pointed to a débris of paper and silver foil littering the floor under their table, "greedy little pigs."

209

"So that's why they're so well behaved," I said, "I was wondering."

"Sick as dogs," Luke grinned.

The suburbs of London flashed past. The sidings were thick with blackberry bushes, their fruit hung lustrously and black. The gardens backing on to the railway tracks were neat little oblong parcels. In one I saw a woman hanging up her washing on the line to dry. Her laundry was meticulously sorted: large items, sheets and shirts at one end, graduating to the tiniest of babies' booties at the other. Next door, behind a potting shed, a bonfire of autumn leaves smouldered.

I wondered: 'Is this how we might have lived? In some London suburb, with a neat house, and a neat pocket-handkerchief garden. Dad would have tried to grow plumbago and eucalyptus to remind him of home. And lived out his days, his old age, watching them burgeon amongst the staked dahlias and the runner beans.'

In Aldeburgh we went down to look at the sea. It was difficult to walk on the beach. Our feet sank into the shingle which crunched and whispered under us. Debbie and Luke walked in front of me; they moved slowly, tilted slightly forwards, like men walking on the moon.

After London I could not believe how huge the Suffolk skies were, or how fresh the air, tinged with salt and the faint marine smell of old boats. There was no wind that day and the sea was very flat. The water was grey, reflecting the sky, so that at certain times when you looked out you had the odd impression that there was no horizon, only an infinite, soft grey transparency. I felt, briefly, exhilarated; intoxicated by so much light and space.

Debbie and Luke sat down together a little way off. I saw Debbie lie back on the shingle, her hands over her head. Her skirt rode up above her knees, and her thin legs encased in their black tights and black shoes stuck out, strangely angular and childish. Luke leaned over her. I heard them talking together, a murmuring of low voices.

Later, Luke went off to buy us some coffee. Debbie came

over and stood beside me looking out to sea. The tide was going out; a bar of sand had emerged, deep yellow, almost bronze in colour, between the shingle and the breaking of small waves.

"The English seaside," she said. "Well, what do you think of it?"

"I think it's wonderful." I breathed in the smell of the sea.

"That's because you haven't been brought up here." Debbie picked up a stone and threw it into the water. "I hate it. When we were children we were always taken by an au pair, in the summer, while my parents went off to France or Greece on their holiday. We used to go to Devon mostly. That's where my father's family come from." Debbie stepped on to the sand. She lifted her arms above her head and then, with one foot on tiptoe, like a ballerina, slowly raised her other leg behind her. "It always rained; and I was always cold." She held her position, quite steadily. "That's how I remember the English seaside. Being dried off with a scratchy wet towel which stung you all over because there was so much sand impregnated in it. Gritty sand inside my bathing costume, always gathering like a weight in that little fold in the gusset. Sand in my shoes and in my hair. Damp jerseys and goose pimples. And prunes for breakfast at the boarding house – that part wasn't too bad; I used to quite like prunes," she grimaced, "until I discovered why people eat them. You know, it's to make you *go*. Can you imagine anything more disgusting? All the old people used to eat them." She lowered one arm down to her waist height, brought her pointed toe swiftly to her knee and then raised it again to her side.

"We used to have to spend the weekends with my Bowyer grandparents. They liked Charles because he was a boy and played cricket and things; but I don't think they could ever really think what to do with me. They weren't used to girls."

Debbie was possessed, suddenly, of a manic energy. She moved down the beach, pirouetting and spinning on her

211

thin black legs. She was wearing a full-skirted short red coat, and her fair hair was tied back from her face with a roll of scarlet silk.

I watched her: a bright, glittering thing against the greyness of the sea and sky. I sat down on the shingle.

"Where did you learn to do that?"

"Do what?"

"To dance."

Debbie came to a stop in front of me. "I surprise you, don't I?"

I met her gaze steadily. "Yes."

We smiled at one another. Gracefully, like an insect folding its wings, she sat down beside me and put her head on her knees. We stared out to sea.

"Has it ever occurred to you, Layla, if you had been brought up here instead of South America we might even have gone on those seaside holidays together?" Debbie said. "Actually, I think you've had a lucky escape."

"You still haven't told me."

"What?"

"Where you learnt to dance."

"Oh, I always loved to dance. Even when I was very small. Miss Vacani's. That's another thing you missed: Miss Vacani's dancing classes. But that was when we were all very young. Even Charles came to those. Later, at school, I took ballet classes and it all went on from there."

"You're very good, aren't you?"

"Oh, Layla," Debbie laughed at me, "you haven't seen *anything*; those are just bar exercises."

"No," I was insistent, "I could see. The way you hold yourself. You're good."

Debbie hugged her knees. "I could have been. Perhaps."

"But?"

"I don't know. My mother didn't approve – not really. It's all very well to be a good dancer, but to do it professionally – you know what she's like, I don't think it ever occurred to her that *one* could." She emphasised the 'one'. "So I gave it up. No point."

"Couldn't you go back to it again?"

"No, I don't think so. Not classical stuff anyway. You have to start your training very young or else you never get taken seriously. It's far too late now – thanks to my dear mother."

"What about non-classical stuff then?"

"Maybe." Debbie shrugged. She seemed suddenly bored by my questioning. "It's not the same. Look, here comes Luke."

Luke walked slowly carrying two paper cups with plastic lids on; two others were wedged precariously into each of his coat pockets. I guessed that the fourth cup was for him. Luke always drinks cups of coffee in twos, it is one of his peculiarities. Or affectations, as Debbie would call them.

"Look at this place," warming her hands against the sides of the paper cup she gazed down the beach, "dead as a dodo. I can't think what possessed you to suggest coming here, Luke."

"I've always liked places like this out of season."

On the front, the houses with their painted bay windows stared with blind eyes out across the sea. A grey-haired woman in a striped blue and white fisherman's jersey walked along the shingle. Apart from her there was no one else about. I followed Debbie's gaze: a handful of fishing boats pulled up on to the beach, the fisherman's hut selling fresh fish; the genteel, potted-palm-fringed windows of the Wentworth Hotel; a lookout tower, for a lifeguard perhaps, with a wrought-iron spiral staircase. There was something clean and wholesome about it; a little lonely, I decided, but perhaps that was its charm.

"We used to come here every holidays," Luke said. "My parents lived in Suffolk for a long time, quite near here. In the summer, when it's hazy, this beach is like a Seurat painting. The shingle has a kind of pointillist effect, don't you think? You keep expecting those bottle-shaped women with parasols to appear and start gliding up and down the sands."

"I think I prefer it like this. Sort of blustery and pewter-grey. This is how I have always imagined England to be. At home there's this myth that England is always grey. When you tell people that you're coming to London they say, very seriously, ah yes, the smog. They have this notion that it's always like that. Something to do with reading Sherlock Holmes, my father says. I'm sure they think that we still drive around in horse-drawn carriages."

"We do, practically. Or hadn't you noticed," Luke said. "I can see we're going to have to take your education in hand."

"You'll be making poor Layla eat fish and chips next," Debbie said.

"But of course. What else could you possibly want to eat here? They have the best fish and chips in *England*, I promise you. Don't tell me you've never had them?"

"No," I laughed, "never."

"And how about jellied eels?" Debbie mocked, but underneath I could see that she was smiling. "English cuisine, you know, Layla. You'll *love* it."

"I think I'll stick to fish and chips."

"Cod and chips."

"Plaice and chips."

"Sausage and chips."

"Chicken and chips."

"Egg'n'chips."

They chorused, "And on special occasions: gammon *with a pineapple ring*."

"Prunes!" Debbie shrieked.

"Custard!"

"Prunes AND custard!"

Later I sat on the beach with Luke. Debbie, more restless than the two of us, walked off on her own.

"How's it going?" I nodded in her direction.

"Oh. You know," Luke said inconclusively. We watched her disappearing, an exotic silhouette walking along the sea front.

"She's very – how shall I put it? –" he thought for a moment, "I think mercurial is probably the word. Likes to

214

keep me on my toes." He grinned self-deprecatingly. "It works. Sometimes too well, I fear."

I remembered the sight of her dancing on the sand, a scarlet dervish, a thing possessed.

"I saw her dancing," I said. "I had no idea."

"No, not many people do. She's a mystery girl, I told you. Actually I think she likes it that way. She's like you, sweet coz, likes to keep people guessing," he smiled. "With Debbie, it's all very fascinating – I adore it – but remember your Henry IV,

> . . . being daily swallowed by men's eyes,
> They surfeited with honey and began
> To loathe the taste of sweetness, whereof a little
> More than a little is by much too much.

I'm not sure I don't sometimes feel like those children on the train: as if I've eaten too many chocolates."

I felt a twinge of loyalty towards Debbie.

"You know I'm not sure I should be talking like this about my cousin."

"I'm not sure I should be talking like this about my girlfriend." Luke smiled again, irrepressibly.

"I'm beginning to like her," I said. "I didn't at first."

"I know. She's not easy. But then I don't think she's had a particularly easy time." He looked at me. "I'm sorry, that's a stupid thing to say."

"Please, Luke, don't keep apologising."

"OK." He patted my arm. "You know – and don't say I shouldn't talk like this, because I'm going to anyway –" he ruffled his hair impatiently, "but I feel as if I know you far better than I know her. And I don't *mean* anything by that – you know what I mean – it's just, that's how I feel, that's all."

"Yes," I looked at him. "I know what you mean."

We stared out to sea, thinking.

"Perhaps it's the connection between Connie and your grandfather. I've sometimes thought – it's odd, like you

215

said the other day – it's almost as if we are related after all."

"I told my grandfather about you. He wants to meet you." Luke scratched in the sand. "You know, I think he still carries the flag for your great aunt. Even after all these years."

"Have you ever thought what they were like when they were young. I mean, we see them as old people now, but to them they are just the same underneath. It's only their bodies which have got worn out, the externals. I can't imagine what it's like, can you? To be old."

"No. I've always thought that the worst part must be to see everyone around you dying off – your contemporaries, I mean. Not only your husband or wife. But friends. Brothers and sisters. Knowing that you could be the next one to go."

"Are you a big family?" I asked.

"Yes, quite big. There are five of us. Four brothers and a sister. But I'm the youngest by quite a way. An afterthought, I guess. How about you?"

"Very small. My mother and my father and me. Just me." I pulled my coat more closely around me. "Although I sometimes dream –" I hesitated.

"You dream? About having other brothers and sisters?"

"Yes," I hugged the coat closer still, "that sort of thing."

*   *   *

It is a dream I have not had for some time. I have been wondering about the significance of this. Is it that I have been released at last? And if so, then from what? From some last residue of doubt. Or finally perhaps, in some obscure way, from the house, from Santa Luz itself.

In my dream we're sitting together on the verandah, the two of us, I in my best dress. We are waiting. I feel happy

216

and excited, full of importance, even though I am not sure what it is that is going to happen. There is a table laid out before us set with beautiful cups and saucers, dark blue and pink and gold, the ones you brought with you from England when you were first married. There is no one there except ourselves: we wait patiently long into the afternoon. The sun begins to dip, filtering through the eucalyptus trees at the edges of the garden, but still no one comes. At last I look up at you, and I realise that all this time you have been sitting with your back to me. I realise too, that you are not alone; you are holding another child in your arms, a tiny baby. I feel a great desire to look more closely at the child. I walk slowly up behind you. Very quietly. I do not want you to see that I am going to look at it. I draw close. Closer still. Until finally I am looking over your shoulder. It is only then that I realise that the child is dead.

*　　*　　*

Later we ate our fish and chips, as Luke had promised. We walked along the high street, visited an exhibition of watercolours. Had tea and cakes, I think, in some hotel. Luke and Debbie sparred at each other in that private language which lovers use, thinking that no one else will understand them. But I am used to that: used to the hidden ripples, the unsung songs, a practised interpreter of all the unspoken breezes and the squalls. It was, I realise now, their swansong.

These days I see them both, but not together. I have not yet been back to the sea, but there will be other days, I know.

To my surprise, I find I can talk to Debbie now. Ours is not yet a friendship exactly, more a kind of solidarity. A feeling of kinship, you could call it. She is independent-

217

minded, unsentimental, and I value that. She listens, and does not judge.

I wonder sometimes if it is as Luke says, and that we are alike in some strange way. I think it is more that I see myself in her, my English self. I see in her, in her memories and her desire, what might have been. I see my *other*, so long denied. I see you. I'd like you to meet her, one day.

Of the two, however, it is Luke whom I see the most. He comes to visit us at Connie's house and sits at her feet, adoring her – as who would not? I sometimes think that he is half in love with me; but then again, perhaps not. After all it was he, perhaps more than anyone, who first showed me – how shall I describe it? – the possibilities of this England. And for the time being I am content with that.

Love, in all its guises, has too much of a cutting edge just now. Wouldn't you agree?

SEVENTEEN

In the end it was not Bettina who drove Layla down to Veracruz after all. The next morning she went into her mother's room to find her still in bed, lying, pale and still, amongst her piles of white lace pillows. Magdalena was moving silently around the room, smoothing the coverlets, clearing away the breakfast tray which lay untouched on the bedside table.

"You look terrible." Layla sat down on the bed. Bettina's face was drained of colour.

"I feel about twice as terrible as I look," she managed a small smile, "if that's possible."

"What's wrong?"

"Must have been something I ate. I was up all night, chucking up like you wouldn't believe. How are you feeling"

"Fine."

"Thank goodness for that. Dad seems to be OK too."

In the half-shuttered room Bettina's skin had a sickly, yellowish cast to it like old, handmade paper. Her hand, when Layla held it between hers, was cold and clammy.

"I'm not going to make it down to Veracruz today, I'm afraid."

"You mustn't worry about that." Layla stroked away a strand of hair from Bettina's forehead. "Should we get a doctor for you?"

"No, really. I've asked Magdalena to make me one of her herbal teas. *Lo cierto, Magdalena?* Magdalena?"

"*Sí, señora?*" The Indian woman looked up. Her eyes were enormous, shadowed with black, as if she too had not slept. "*Sí, en seguida.*" She picked up the breakfast tray and left the room, stumbling and nearly falling over a pile of Jack's shirts which she had left by the doorway. Layla looked after her.

"What's wrong with her?"

"God knows." Bettina closed her eyes. "She seems completely distracted. She nearly emptied the entire contents of my tray into the bed this morning. But whatever it is, right now frankly I really couldn't care less," she groaned. "Oh yes, she's been insisting to me that you must still go to Veracruz today to sort out your papers, even if it's without me. She says she's sent Martin the Eye to ask Baltazar to take you."

"*What?*"

"She's being very insistent about it, I warn you."

"I'd better go and talk to her." Layla bent down and kissed her forehead. "Sleep now, you'll feel better after you've slept for a bit."

"Where's your father?"

"I don't know, I haven't seen him today." Layla pulled the shutters back across the windows. "I expect he'll look in later, don't worry."

She looked down at Bettina. Without the usual careful makeup her face had a colourless, withered look. For the first time, Layla saw with something like shock, Bettina looked old. 'She really is ill; he should be here,' she thought. 'Why is he never here?'

"Mum," Layla began, impetuous suddenly.

"Yes, darling?"

"Oh, no, nothing." *Not now*, she reconsidered, *not like this*. "Look, I tell you what, why don't I stay with you until you're asleep."

"Sweet of you, darling," Bettina murmured opening one eye, "be sure to tell me if I start raving in my sleep."

"Go on, close your eyes."

220

"Bully."

"I thought you said you were ill," Layla smiled down at her. "Just go to sleep, will you?"

"All right, I'm asleep, I'm asleep."

Outside the sun beat down in the little courtyard. In the darkened room it was cool and silent. Light slanted through the shutters, slashing across the white coverlet on the bed, the pale lace cushions, the reddish strands of hair laid out across them.

Layla looked around her. There was nothing of Jack's here; nothing of the decaying grandeur, the ravaged lunacy of the rest of Santa Luz. This was Bettina's room entirely. Even as a child Layla had been aware of the different quality of this space, this small oasis of England which Bettina had constructed round her like a carapace.

In a cabinet by the bed were the enamel boxes, the ivory elephants. On her dressing table were photographs: of Layla, of Jack, of the English aunts. Objects and images so well known that she rarely stopped to look at them. Now, when she examined them again, it was with a strange sense of dislocation, as if she was seeing them for the first time.

Towards the back of the dressing table there was an old black and white photograph of Bettina in a silver frame. Layla picked it up, turning it over in her hands. In the picture Bettina was kneeling on the ground, leaning over something on the floor, a large box or a trunk, looking up towards the photographer, Jack presumably. Her eyes were open wide, smiling, a little startled. Her body was tilted forwards, one hand extended towards him, as if to catch him by the arm.

'This is how he must once have seen her,' Layla thought, 'young, rapturous, tender. Sometimes, even now, when she looks at him you can still see that face. But there is no record of his face, of how he looked at her. Nothing with which to compare the then and the now. What does she see, I wonder, when she looks into his eyes?'

*   *   *

In the end, at Magdalena's insistence, it was Baltazar who drove Layla down to Veracruz. The feeling of calm which had been hers the night before had now left her utterly. There was none of the ease which had existed between them previously. To Baltazar she seemed nervous, jittery almost, a state which she hid behind a more than usually silent façade.

"You are very quiet today." It was Baltazar who broke the silence between them.

"Am I?" Layla glanced at him and then looked quickly away.

"Yes, you are."

The jeep switchbacked along the road. Ahead of them the mountains rose steeply. Overhead the sky was dull and leaden. Behind them, to the east, Layla could just make out the outline of El Fin del Mundo poised, like a white bird, as though ready to plummet into the bottomless green throat beneath.

Baltazar saw her look.

"Did Finn tell you that they are leaving?"

"Yes," Layla said sadly. "The other day, when we had the *fogata*."

"Finn," Baltazar shook his head. "Finn *y la Meredith*. I wonder what will happen to them. You will miss them, no?"

"Terribly. It won't be the same without them. El Fin del Mundo, the end of the world," she mused. "Finn always said it was too strong a diet for most palates." Layla looked away. "You know, it's funny, I always thought Finn was like me. I could never imagine him anywhere else other than here. Now I am not so sure."

"Finn will be the same wherever he goes," Baltazar smiled, "and the sister, too. Like all English people."

"And you?" Layla asked. "Will you go, or stay?"

The question rippled the silence between them, a shining stone into a pool.

"I never stay long in one place," he said at last. Turning

222

to look at her, he saw her dark, tender face turned towards him, "but I will stay this time, as long as I have
to."

They drove on upwards: past the crucifix on the pass,
past the turning to San Pedro, and across the golden *paramo*.
As they started to descend on the other side, Layla could
feel the cool air of the mountains turning gradually into the
soft, humid kiss of the coastal plains. The heat made her
restless. She had yearned to be with Baltazar again, to be
close to him, but the sensation, sitting beside him now, was
bittersweet. There was a feeling between them, a restraint,
which she could not quite put her finger on.

She opened the window, watching the austerity of the
golden mountain plateau turn slowly to green.

"What will happen?" she asked.

"To Santa Luz?"

He was with her again, inside her mind, guessing her
out.

"Yes."

"I used to think she would go on for ever. Now . . . who
can say?"

"She?"

"The house has a female spirit, don't you think so? I
don't know why. Perhaps it is because of Santa Luz herself.
Maybe because the house has always been dominated by
strong women. My grandmother, my aunt, and now –"

"And now my mother?"

Layla interrupted him, a little too quickly. She had
turned towards him, was watching him intently.

'She keeps pushing me,' he thought. 'First at the graveyard, and now this. She wants me to ask her. Is it possible
that she really believes what I think she's trying to tell me?'
Baltazar considered carefully before he answered her.

"No," he said at last, "not so much your mother,
although in her own way she is very strong. I feel that your
mother has always resisted Santa Luz, and you have to be
very strong to do that."

223

As he spoke he could feel a watchfulness come over Layla. But she said nothing, so he went on.

"She once said to me that you can do battle with people, but it is much harder, impossible perhaps, with bricks and mortar." Baltazar smiled at the thought. "They don't play by the same rules, is the way she put it. But Santa Luz is more than that, and she has always known it. Santa Luz is – what?" Baltazar shrugged his shoulders, searching for the words. "Light, and air, and spirit matter. A state of mind. A passion. Everything and nothing."

"She has talked to you about it?"

"Yes, many times. She is more sensitive to the place than perhaps any of you realise." Baltazar glanced sideways at her. "She loves you very much, Layla."

To her horror Layla felt tears start in her eyes. She turned her face away, so that Baltazar would not see.

*   *   *

Towards afternoon they emerged like hunters from the mountains on to a parched green and brown plain. Brittle scrub replaced the luxuriant growth of the foothills. This was a landscape of surprises. In places the colour of the trees was acid green. In others the branches were naked, hung instead with arcane pods and gourds; withered fruits; a nimbus of startling scarlet or yellow blooms.

Now that they were away from the mountains, Layla felt her spirits lift. Excitement rose in her throat like a shining fish. As they drove on across the plain, heat enclosed the jeep like a snakeskin glove, contracting steadily in the sun.

Where the plains opened up there were signs of settlement for the first time. The people here were a race apart from the Indians of the sierra, a chocolate-skinned *mestizo* race, in whose blood the swarthiness of the Spanish and Indian was mixed with the blood of Negro slaves once

224

bound for the cotton fields of the northern Americas, and shipwrecked off the coast. These were a beautiful, sensual, lazy people, famous for their thievery and their charm. When they laughed, they laughed a little too much, showing their strong, dentrifice-white teeth.

Traditionally the *mestizo* despised the Indians, calling them primitives; too melancholic, too superstitious to escape from the earthbound round of their lives.

Traditionally the Indians did not think about the *mestizos* at all. If they had, they would have considered them apostates. Men and women who had abandoned the world of mountains and gods for the pagan and swampy heat of the plains.

Zulay, a small town sitting on a flat pampa-like expanse of acacia bushes, cacti and singing telegraph wires, was the first petrol stop after the mountains. They found the petrol station, a single pump outside a tumbledown shack, on the road on the outskirts of town. The proprietor, a fat man in a string vest, did not come out when he saw them pull up, but called out from the shade of his porch, "*No tenemos gasolina.*"

"What does he mean? How can they *not have* petrol?" Baltazar stuck his head out of the window, '*Qué pasa?*"

"*No llegó el camion,*" the man made a vague motion with his hand as though he were swatting away a fly, "the truck hasn't come in."

Above the house, the Codeco sign blew rustily in the afternoon breeze.

"When do you expect it?"

"Tomorrow maybe," the man shrugged, lay back in his chair and started to excavate his chest with a toothpick through the string vest, "maybe not. Until then, no petrol."

"No petrol until tomorrow," Baltazar drummed his fingers against the side of the truck. "We'll just have to try in the town. Someone must have a supply."

The afternoon pressed down from a hot, white sky. The plaza was deserted. In the desiccated square of grass at its centre a man lay sleeping under a dusty hibiscus. Its flowers thrust out their proboscis like vast, scarlet insects.

Overhead a pair of vultures circled, too lazy, too hot, it seemed to Layla, even to flap their wings.

On one side of the plaza was a raised arcade and a small stall selling fruit juice drinks. The stall consisted of a trestle table laden with fruit – papaya, melons, oranges – and an ancient Moulinex juice extractor. Lying behind it, in a hammock under the arcade, was a girl combing her hair. Baltazar went over to talk to her.

The girl was wearing a tight orange miniskirt and a white broderie anglaise bodice. Her hair was dark, with the fierce ringlets of a mulatta. Layla watched as she put some fruit in the Moulinex. When she leant forward her breasts fell, brown as toast against the white lace of her bodice. Baltazar made some remark, making the girl laugh. She looked down coyly through long eyelashes, pushing her heavy hair away from her face. As she watched them together, Layla felt a stab of jealousy towards this girl, so deep, so terrible, she felt faint.

But Baltazar had turned away and was coming back towards the jeep. "Here, try this," he handed her a glass of pale green juice, "I'm going to see if there is somewhere else around here where we can get petrol. Why don't you stay here," he put his hand out and brushed away a damp strand of hair from her face. "You can sit with Romana," he said, indicating the fruit girl, and making Layla wonder with unease how it was that he knew her name, "she'll look after you."

Layla sat in the jeep drinking the melon juice. It was curious, she thought, that in all the journeys she had made from Santa Luz to the capital she had never once stopped in Zulay for any longer than it took to buy petrol from the Codeco man in the string vest.

With Jack they had always carried spare petrol with them in the jeep, since shortages were not unusual in this part of the country; with Jack the drive was undertaken so that as little time as possible should be spent in the wilderness.

With Baltazar, she reflected, the wilderness held no fears. He had the wanderer's instinct, a certain detachment. He could be happy anywhere; had no need of the familiar, no need of a known place to lie down in at the end of the day. Layla tried to address herself to their predicament, but the question of whether they would or would not find petrol, whether they would or would not get to Veracruz that day, or even the next, was out of her control. After her initial dismay, she found that she was strangely exhilarated by the thought. No one knew her, nor she anyone. Santa Luz, Bettina, Jack, Magdalena, none of them existed here. She was herself only. She was absolved, free.

At first Layla stayed sitting in the jeep, but after a while she got down and, avoiding the fruit girl, walked slowly round the plaza. The bandstand, an ornate white birdcage, was overgrown and rusting, covered in thick creepers of bougainvillaea. On the far side of the plaza was the church, and on the other three sides buildings fronted by a raised wooden arcade. Apart from Romana's fruit juice stall, the shops were shut against the afternoon heat. The arches had once been painted, but the paint was now peeling off in dingy green flakes; the walls beyond plastered with a thick humus of posters and notices.

A poster advertising a circus caught her eye, and another announcing a forthcoming sale of farm implements. Partly concealed beneath them was a third, an old police notice with the headline "'Chico' Gonzales Tupac: Wanted . . ." The crude artist's sketch beneath it was already discoloured, the paper yellowing and bubbled with age.

Layla was now back at the jeep. From the corner of her eye she could see that the girl, Romana, was still there swinging in the hammock. Layla could feel the girl's eyes following her, languid eyes narrowed like a cat's. Now, seeing Layla approach, she sat up and motioned her to come over.

"It's so hot, would you like another juice?" she said. "Have one, please."

Layla accepted. She took the glass which the girl offered her and looked out into the plaza, but there was still no sign of Baltazar. The girl went through a curtain nailed up over the door behind her and came out with a chair.

"He's not back yet then," she said conversationally.

"No, he went to find petrol. There was none at the pump on the main road."

"I know, the lorry never turned up," the girl shrugged her shoulders as if this were a common occurrence, "don't look so worried, he'll be back soon." With her wild mulatta's hair and her pale green cat's eyes, the fruit girl was striking rather than obviously pretty. Her nose was a little too big, and her teeth were crooked, but her lips were full. Her upper lip protruded slightly over the lower, a sensuous asymmetry.

Even in the shade of the arcade, Layla could feel the skin of her whole body singing with the afternoon heat. The glass the girl had given her was cool, and the melon juice was sweet.

"It's terrible, this heat, no?" the girl said.

"Is it always this hot?"

"At the beginning of the season, often. But now it is the time of rains, or it should be. They are a month late this year." She shrugged again. "It has been the same everywhere."

In the silence of the afternoon, the plaza swam before Layla's eyes in an erotic haze of heat. Little whirlpools of dust danced up the street beneath them. Idly, Layla toyed with the brush with which the girl had been doing her hair.

"Your hair is all knotted at the back," Romana said, "here, let me do it for you."

She took the brush from Layla and started to comb her hair. At first Layla tried to stop her, but the girl simply laughed and pushed Layla's protesting hands back down by her sides. She brushed slowly but quite hard, so that the bristles bit luxuriously into her scalp.

Layla closed her eyes. Behind her the girl's skin gave off a faint but troubling scent, the smell of fruit mixed with another deeper, more disturbing odour which Layla could not identify. From time to time, when Layla's neck was pulled back, she could feel the top of her head brushing against the girl's breasts.

After a while Layla started to relax. As she lay back in her chair she could feel her whole body pulsating with the heat. Her thin blouse stuck to her back, her arms, her narrow waist.

"Tell me about Baltazar," Romana said as she stroked Layla's hair away from her face, "is he your man?"

Again Layla was filled with vague disquiet: how did the girl know Baltazar's name? But Romana was so sweet, so tender with her that she found she no longer cared all that much.

"No," she said simply.

"Ay, but he likes you. I know, I can tell." From behind her Romana's cool voice smiled into her ear. "He wants you, I can tell that too."

When she laughed her voice broke huskily in the middle, "You'd better watch out. He's bad that one, know what I'm saying?"

With deft hands Romana swept her hair on top of her head. Layla felt the sudden relief of air cooling the back of her neck.

"You have such beautiful hair," Romana said, "beautiful hair and a beautiful neck."

Layla could feel her running her finger slowly down the downy part of her neck, until her skin pricked all the way down her back. She laughed as Layla shivered. She could feel the girl drawing nearer to her. Could feel her breath, fruit scented, as she bent her head towards Layla's naked neck, and then her kiss, delicate as a butterfly's wing, against her skin.

*　　*　　*

"Nothing. I've tried everywhere." Baltazar lowered himself into Romana's hammock. "Not a single drop of petrol to be had in the whole town."

He looked hot and travel-stained. His hair, pushed back from his face, hung down in rat's-tail strands.

229

"What shall we do?"

Layla felt quite unmoved by this development.

"We'll just have to stay here until the next supply truck comes in. There's a delivery due in first thing tomorrow morning, so we should be all right."

Lying back in the hammock, Baltazar closed his eyes.

"Is there somewhere we can stay?" Layla turned to Romana.

"You can stay here, of course."

She had been watching Baltazar in silence, through her sleepy cat's eyes.

"Are you sure?"

"*No te preocupes, linda*," Romana rose with a graceful, jointless movement, "it will be my pleasure."

Layla watched her shimmy through the curtain into the house behind. When she looked round, she saw that Baltazar had also been watching her with admiration.

"So, you have met Romana."

"Yes." Layla looked at him. "I have met Romana."

"She likes you." Baltazar's eyes glittered.

"She likes you too, I think," Layla countered.

Baltazar laughed, and shook his head.

Later they ate *bistec* and *papas fritas* in the *comedor* on the far side of the plaza. Although they asked her to go with them, Romana stayed behind to look after her fruit stall. Business was best, she said, at that enchanted hour when all the town came out for their evening promenade.

As the sun set and dusk fell, the shops and market stalls opened up again and the town, which had seemed terminally sunk in the stupor of afternoon, came to life.

Sitting like this with Baltazar in the warm evening, Layla was filled with inexplicable happiness. She felt liberated, freed from something, although she could not say exactly what or how. All her perceptions were heightened, as though a veil had been lifted inside her head.

Overhead the sky was the colour of dirty indigo. Cheap Cuban dance music throbbed from an open window. Across the plaza, on the church roof, the vultures sat shaking their wings. Layla imagined the sound as a dry rattling, like dead men's bones.

Men and women appeared from the shuttered eyes of the houses to take the air, walking slowly round the bandstand and the hibiscus bushes; the women in bright skirts, the men with watered hair, smelling rapaciously of eau de cologne.

"I never realised Zulay was so beautiful," Layla said, watching them.

"Zulay?" Baltazar looked around him at the plaza, "I have always thought it was so ordinary." He turned to her, "But I suppose even ordinary places can be transfigured, if you catch them at the right time," he smiled, "it depends who is looking at it, and why."

Although she could not say how, the constraint she had felt towards him earlier in the day had now vanished. In its place was a new intimacy. His manner towards her was light-hearted, almost tender. He did not look at any of the other girls who passed by them, the dark beauties in their bright dresses, but only at her.

I wonder if they think we are lovers, Layla smiled inwardly to herself, noticing the way his eyes narrowed as he talked to her, the way Romana's had done.

In the plaza a small girl was selling gardenias. Baltazar called her over and bought two bunches. He sent the girl over to Romana with one bunch, and gave the other to Layla.

"Here," he took one of the flowers and placed it behind her ear, "now you look as you did down at Tumbez that day, like a jungle princess."

Layla fingered the flowers, the bruised petals smelling like honey.

It grew late, but neither of them made a move to leave. Layla found that she was watching him; no longer hesitantly, with sideways glances as she had done in the past, but straight on, almost playfully, matching him gesture for gesture, as if in a dance.

He had showered before they came out and had put on

231

a white shirt over his jeans, clean but crumpled, the long sleeves rolled up to his elbows. When he turned away from her she could see his profile, the unmistakable slant of his cheekbones, his nose. His hair and skin looked very dark against the whiteness of his shirt.

By some unspoken agreement they did not talk about Santa Luz. Instead he told her about his student days in Paris and in Lima; about his travels; his new paintings, and the exhibition he was preparing for in Veracruz.

Layla listened, laughed at his stories, was astonished to find how little she had really ever known about him before. But soon she became aware that she was only half-listening, half-laughing; noticed how much more aware she was, in fact, of the lines just beginning at the corners of his eyes, and of the dark hairs at the base of his throat; of the way he looked at her and his ability to hold her gaze, disconcertingly, just a little too long.

She could not tell what he was thinking. At times she had the feeling that he was seeing right into her; at other times she knew that she was still closed and mysterious to him, that he was somehow trying to find her out, discovering her like a new and secret country. It occurred to her that here, tonight, she could be anyone she chose to be, one woman, or a thousand rolled into one.

She was seized with the sudden, absurd idea that the whole town was colluding to push them together. As the people walked by their table in the tropical night they seemed to smile their approval.

The bedroom which Romana and Layla shared together was a small room with a single window which gave out over the fruit stall and the hot little plaza beneath it. Inside the floor was bare, the naked floorboards scrubbed and smooth. On the wall over the bed was an old framed picture, faded to sepia by the sun, of the Virgin of Guadalupe.

In the tiny space, darkness brought small relief from the heat of day. Romana had removed all the covers from the bed leaving only one thin sheet, but still Layla could not sleep. She lay awake listening to the night, to the cicadas

232

calling, and the sound of the men's voices coming from the *comedor* across the plaza, and thought how different this was to the cold lunar silence of Santa Luz. These people were so different, so full of energy. Did they never sleep?

Sometime later, she did not know how much later, she was aware of being awake again, staring up into darkness. Outside the window, apart from the hum of the cicadas, there was silence. The neon glow from the *comedor* had been extinguished. Romana's warm body lay next to her in the bed, one arm heavy with sleep thrown across her shoulder. Layla thought how long it was, not since childhood, that she had shared a bed with another. In those days she had often slept with Maria-Magdalena: her presence had been like a talisman against the spirits of the night. Gently she disengaged Romana's arm, got up and made her way down stairs.

In the kitchen she filled a glass with water, and then stepped outside on to the porch. After the oppressiveness of Romana's bedroom, the air was cool out there. In the distance a truck went past on the road to Veracruz.

"Layla?" A voice came out of the darkness, making her jump and her heart rise painfully into her throat. She looked, saw the glowing tip of a cigarette in the darkness. "Baltazar?" His form appeared beside her out of the shadows. A few feet away from her he stopped.

"Couldn't you sleep?"

"It is too hot to sleep."

"For me too."

All around them was silence, a great, humming, cicada-filled silence.

"You look like a ghost."

She could hear the smile in his voice as he drew closer.

"It's something Romana lent me," she became conscious of the thin white material around her, so soft, so insubstantial, "a kind of petticoat."

Through the darkness her voice sounded hollow. Some-how, in the hot night, the ease which had existed between them earlier that evening was gone. All she could think of

233

was the glow of his skin and hair. His hands. The careful distance which they had placed between each other.

"Do you want to have a walk around the plaza?" he said at last. "That's what I was going to do. It might help you sleep."

Layla stared absently across at the darkened square.

'I should not be here,' she thought. 'I should leave, go back inside before it is too late.' Too late. A feeling of panic, almost of fear, rose up in her throat. The silence between them was unbearable.

"I don't think so," she said, with effort. "I should go back." She took a step towards the door but found, some-how, that she had only moved closer to him. Another step, and another. She felt Baltazar's hand against her cheek. He was not touching her, but was holding his hand so close that she could feel the warmth of his fingers against the outline of her face, her lips, her throat.

She felt faint, vulnerable, an insect pinned against a card. All thought was gone. All strength. She was aware only of the softness of her own body, and of Baltazar's standing so close now that she was looking up at him, into his eyes.

He bent down and she felt his lips touch her forehead. She closed her eyes. When she opened them again he had moved away. For a few moments Baltazar stood with his back to her looking out across the square; when he turned around again she was gone.

EIGHTEEN

Years later Layla often wondered what would have happened if she and Baltazar had become lovers that night. She never could be quite certain what it was which had made her so sure that they should turn back to Santa Luz: a sixth sense, an intuition, unbearably heightened, as all her perceptions had been, by that long, hot evening in Zulay.

The next morning Baltazar was very tender with her.

"Layla, about last night."

"Yes?"

At first she would not look at him.

"You went away."

"Yes."

"I wish you had not gone. Not like that." He picked up her hand and held it. "I don't know how to explain –" he searched for the words, but she interrupted him quickly.

"You don't have to explain."

"But I want to."

Layla could not look at him, hardly heard his excuses.

The whole of her ached, body and soul. All night she had lain awake, as if in a delirium, willing him to come to her. For hour after hour, in her mind's eye, she had traced the outline of his body with her fingers, marvelled at the smooth skin of his shoulders, his back, the inner sides of his arms.

She had imagined the two of them lying there, dark on dark, their limbs entwined so that it was impossible to tell where his body ended and hers began. It would be, she told herself, like climbing into each other's skins. And in the morning she would smell the sweet smell of him, his sweat and her own sex, on his skin and hair.

"Have you ever thought that perhaps it is not me you are in love with," he was saying, "I think perhaps you associate me too much with . . . who knows? With other things. You do not really know me at all."

She looked at him at last. "Does it matter," was all she said.

Layla stared down at her hands; their fingers were entwined like lovers' hands. 'My lover,' she thought, turning the word over and over in her mind, tasting it, feeling its texture. 'My lover – just for one night he could have been my lover. Now he never will be, never again.'

"No, I know," she looked up at him, "you never could be mine."

He had eluded her, as somehow she had always known he would, and now it would never be the same between them.

"That's not it." Her simplicity disarmed him. "It's not that I don't like you. It's not that I don't want you. Last night, I wanted you too. I came so close, you'll never know . . ."

"And then?"

She seemed perfectly composed, a quality of hers which had always had the power to disconcert him. If she had been a Latin woman, he reflected, there would have been tears, recriminations. Drama.

"It's just . . . you are so young." She regarded him steadily with her dark eyes. "You are going to England. I am going back to Veracruz." The excuses sounded so predictable, even as he said them they made him wince. "I don't want to hurt you."

What else could he say? How could he tell her that almost anyone else he knew, any other man of his acquaintance,

236

would have taken her willingly, without a second thought. Not knowing that intensity in her, which he had recognised, and the frightening power he held to mould her life in his own image, to make or break her at his will.

"You are too young," he said again. "I don't know how to explain it any better than that. I would end up hurting you. I would never want to hurt you, but I know I would, eventually."

To Baltazar's relief, Layla showed no sign of wanting to talk about it further. A kind of lassitude, an outward dreaminess came over her, with which she covered up her sickness, the empty hole in the pit of her belly. She moved about Romana's house collecting her things together, very slowly, as though she was moving through water.

Later, when they were loading up the jeep, Baltazar saw her stand still, staring at the row of posters under the arcade. He cast his eye over the thick papier mâché crust to see what it was that had caught her attention, and saw the circus poster, with its crude tinsel-town illustrations of plumed horses, and a girl in a sequined body stocking with feathers in her hair.

Layla stepped towards the wall, as if to inspect the poster more closely.

"What's this, do you want me to take you to the circus, niña," Baltazar called over, trying to reach her again, to dispel her solitariness.

"No, it's not that," she said, curious despite herself. "It's the other one, the one underneath. Look, here, the man's face." Baltazar stepped up behind her. "I didn't think . . . I really didn't look at it before. But how *strange*."

" 'Chico' Gonzales Tupac," Baltazar read over her shoulder. " 'Wanted' – Wanted for what, I wonder? Have you seen this man somewhere?"

"The quetzal," Layla said, "this is the man who sold Finn the quetzal. I'm sure of it. Look at this." She ran her finger down the side of the man's face. "At first I thought it was a discoloration in the paper, but it isn't. This is what he looked like. There was something strange in the skin pigmentation down one side of his face, like a white blemish. And those albino eyelashes. Yes, I'm sure of it."

"And you met this man?"

"Only once. He sold Finn many of his birds, but after the quetzal he never came back. Finn always thought there was something not quite right about him." Layla stood staring at the poster, concentrating on it. Inside her head it was as though someone had snapped their fingers. She was wide awake again. "But there was another man with him, I remember now," she turned to Baltazar, "and I did see him again, quite recently in fact. In San Pedro."

"San Pedro? Are you sure?"

"Yes. I thought I recognised him from somewhere. I remember now, he was with the quetzal man."

"Are you sure it was him?" Baltazar took her arm.

"I don't know, I don't know. Wait, let me think." Layla felt her heart racing.

"Layla, the man you saw was almost certainly one of Quintero's men, you realise that, don't you?"

"Yes, yes." She put her hand to her head.

"You must think very carefully."

"You see, there was always something very strange about that whole transaction. The man was very nervous, very jumpy about it. In the end, he practically gave the bird away, as though he was desperate that Finn should have it. I remember Finn saying that he could have sold the bird for ten times the amount in Veracruz. We decided he must have stolen it and was frightened of being caught out. But I was curious about him. When he left, I watched him walk down the road. I saw that instead of pocketing the money, he gave it to this other man – the man I saw in San Pedro."

"Did you ever tell anyone about this?"

"No. It never occurred to me that it might be important."

"From what you say, it sounds as if the quetzal was deliberately planted on Finn."

"But why?" Layla was stupefied. "What could anyone possibly gain from it?"

"I don't know." Baltazar sat down with his back against

one of the pillars. "Let's work this one out. What do we really know about quetzals? We know that they are fabulously beautiful and rare. We know that some Indians, most notably the Santa Luz Indians, consider them to be sacred birds, and that their appearance is thought of in the light of a miraculous or supernatural sign."

Baltazar counted these points off on his fingers.

"We know that they die in captivity."

"And that the penalty for killing a quetzal, in ancient times, was always death."

They looked at each other.

"You think someone wanted to kill Finn?" Layla said, incredulous still.

"Or in some way to stage-manage his death," Baltazar said.

"No," she shook her head, "it's not that, I'm sure of it. It feels all wrong. We must think again."

Despite the events of the previous evening, now instinctively they drew together. Side by side, they sat in silence.

"There is one other thing," Layla said at last. "In the end it was not Finn who let his bird go free. The quetzal was stolen. Did you know that?"

"No," Baltazar said, "I didn't. When did he tell you that?"

"It wasn't Finn who told me," Layla turned to him, very serious suddenly, "it was Magdalena."

"How could she possibly have known?"

"It was Magdalena who stole it."

"What?"

"Magdalena took Finn's quetzal."

"When?"

"After Tumbez."

Baltazar stared at her. "Did she have any idea how dangerous that could have been for him?"

"Yes. It was very wrong of her. But after Tumbez, after that terrible day, she said it was the only thing which was powerful enough to withstand Quintero. According to her Quetzalcoatl, the Plumed Serpent, is only one side of the equation. She has some theory that he has another side, an evil counterpart. According to one version of the legend, Quetzalcoatl had a brother, Tezcatlipoca, 'Smoking Mirror', whose devotees believed in human sacrifice – oh my God," Layla put her hand to her mouth, "that's it! How can she use the quetzal against Quintero, when it was one of his men who planted it on us in the first place? Surely he would have known that someone, one of the Indians, would try to take it, for that very reason."

"Hold on, hold on," Baltazar put his hand on her arm, "not so fast."

"But don't you see," Layla thought of Magdalena, of how nervous and distracted she had been that morning, "it was not necessarily Finn the quetzal was intended for at all."

To put Layla's mind at rest Baltazar said he would call Santa Luz on the RT, to make sure that all was well. Layla went back to Romana's to wait for him, and when he came back again she knew, without turning her head when he came into the room, that something was wrong.

"Is something the matter?"

"I couldn't get through."

"You couldn't get through last night either," Layla put down her coffee cup.

"There seems to be some kind of fault on the line." Baltazar's expression was neutral. "I rang the operator, to see if she could find out what the problem was. Apparently they've been having trouble with quite a number of telephone lines in the Altamirada area." He took her hand and held it. "She seemed to think that there had been some kind of disturbance up there."

*　　*　　*

On the journey back Layla was very calm. She stared ahead of her at the road, looking neither to the left or to the right.

Baltazar marvelled at her composure, at the stillness she seemed to be able to draw on at will. Once, on impulse, he stopped the jeep and drew her to him, wanting to reassure her, to protect her from what was ahead. Wordlessly he kissed her hands, her hair, as if he was trying to breathe his own strength into her. She did not resist him, but her body no longer responded to his. He had the feeling that he had somehow lost her; that her spirit was no longer his for the taking in the way it had been for that one night in Zulay and, with a sadness which surprised him, that he would never possess her in that way again.

This stillness left her only once. In the late afternoon, just after they passed the turning to San Pedro, she turned to him and asked, quite matter-of-factly, "What do you think we will find there?"

"I don't know," Baltazar tried to keep his own dread from his voice, "perhaps nothing at all. We have only guess-work to go by, no positive proof of anything. And as far as I know, no one has ever managed to out-guess Quintero."

He drove on in silence, expecting that she would lapse back into her own reverie again, but a few minutes later she spoke up again.

"How much longer will it take us?"

"It is about four hours to Santa Luz from the San Pedro turning."

"Four hours! So long?"

Her tone was different this time, agitated, as if something in her had given way, as though the still centre could no longer hold. "It didn't seem so long before."

After they had driven on a little way, she reached out and grasped his arm. He felt her fingers gripping at his skin.

"She was really ill, you know. I had almost forgotten. How could I have forgotten her? We should never have left her behind." She sounded desolated. "What do you think they'll do to her? They won't hurt her, will they?"

"No, they won't hurt her," Baltazar tried to reassure her. When he turned towards her, he saw that tears were rolling

241

down her cheeks. She was not crying the way that most women cry. Her eyes were not red, nor her face swollen, and she made no sound at all. Neither did she make any attempt to check the flow of tears. Baltazar had the odd notion that she was hardly aware that she was crying.

"You see," Layla went on, "if anything happens, I know that Magdalena will be all right, and my father. But she will be so *alone*. I – I can't explain it," she dashed at her face with one hand, "I don't mean physically alone. I mean . . . inside. Inside alone." She turned to Baltazar as if to gauge whether he understood her.

"Your mother is a very brave woman. And she is strong too," Baltazar said, "stronger than you think, perhaps."

"My *mother* –" Layla hid her face in her hands. Her voice was anguished, "You don't understand, you couldn't possibly. Oh God, how could I?"

"Perhaps I understand more than you think."

The question, so long unasked, lay on his tongue like a ripe fruit ready to burst its skin. She must tell me, he thought. If she does not tell me now, she will never tell anyone, and this will be her undoing.

"How long have you known?"

"How long have I known what?"

"That your father and Magdalena are lovers?"

"How long have I known?" she repeated, almost dreamily. "I don't think I can remember a time when I have not known." She looked at Baltazar without bitterness. "And you, how long have you known?"

"I didn't. Or not for sure, anyway. I guessed."

"I see." Her voice took on the same strangely impersonal inflection as before. "I always wondered about that. If anyone else knew, I mean."

She sat with her hands clasped in her lap, composed again. Baltazar kept silent, willing her to go on talking, but for a long while she just sat without moving, looking straight ahead of her down into the long green slash of the Altamirada gorge which revealed itself gradually beneath them.

242

"What I've always wondered," Layla said at last, "is how she found out."

"She knows?"

"Oh yes." She nodded.

"You have talked to her about it?"

"No. But I've always wondered how she found out."

Layla reached for Baltazar's cigarettes on the dashboard and lit one with care.

"I hope it was not in any . . . vulgar way." She stared ahead of them, into the middle distance. "I don't know how I found out. If there was one particular occasion, I might have just blocked it from my mind, but I don't think there was. There are other ways of discovering these things. Childhood is an honoured state: people are at once so careful in front of you, and yet so much more careless. Things slip through the net; a certain mood, a look, a name whispered into the night. People seem to forget that children, already living in their own fantasy world, are more perceptive of all these things. And that they can *feel*, even if they do not understand. Even Magdalena made that mistake. It is surprising, thinking about it now: she who was always so careful not to be found out. It was a sign, I think, of her absolute certainty of her control."

"Over your father?"

"Over all of us. Over Santa Luz. Sometimes I think she bewitched us all."

"You seem to be so sure of all these things," Baltazar was amazed by her certainty.

"Oh no," Layla turned to him with a small smile, "you have no idea how unsure I have been, about so many things."

"But now?"

"Over the last few days I have been thinking, thinking. I have thought so much that nothing seemed to make sense any more. And then suddenly the other night, after we came back from San Pedro, everything seemed to come clear, I can't explain it. At San Pedro, Quintero became a real threat to me; and in the wake of that, all sorts of other

243

things became real too. It was as though I had been jolted out of myself, forced to see things for what they really were."

She put her hand on Baltazar's arm, "Do you remember what you said to me at Aureliano's grave? You said, 'It's not what or who you are born, but who you choose to become that really matters.' For the first time I realised that I did not only have to see myself as part of Santa Luz. That I did have a choice, and that if I wanted to I could choose to be free." She kissed her fingers and put them delicately to his face.

"Don't you blame Magdalena for what she did?" Baltazar was shocked by her apparent acceptance.

"No, I don't blame her," Layla considered, "how could I? It was the custom, as you yourself have explained to me. Besides, I think they were probably lovers long before my father was married. No," she shook her head, "I don't blame her. It has always been that way at Santa Luz, you said so yourself."

"Who do you blame then?" Baltazar pulled the jeep over to the side of the road. "Who do you blame?"

"Why are you stopping?" she said in alarm. "We can't stop now."

"I'm stopping because I want you to tell me what you *really* feel about all this."

"What do you mean?" she looked at him, astonished.

"Stop pretending to yourself, Layla. All this crap about Santa Luz, Santa Luz, always Santa Luz, as if anything and everything that happens there, however terrible, however hurtful, is somehow above criticism. You are beginning to sound like Jack, for God's sake. You say that you have been forced to see things as they really are, so why can't you say them?"

Layla got out of the jeep. She stood with her back to him, looking up at the mountains. Baltazar got out to join her. They stood together, but a little apart, not quite touching.

"The truth can't hurt you," he said, "and if anyone can understand it is me. Isn't that why you have been telling me things, dropping hints? It's as though you wanted me

244

to find out," his hand brushed her face, "I was brought up at Santa Luz; the land, the house, the spirit of the place run in my veins too. I have Indian blood. Layla, my mother was an Indian."

"I feel as if you are trying to ask me something."

Layla's voice was far away, as though she was barely listening to him, thinking her own unreachable thoughts.

"Yes," Baltazar heard himself say, "yes, I am trying to ask you, has it ever occurred to you that Magdalena might be your mother?"

"Has it ever *occurred* to me?" Layla turned to face him. "Look at me, look! Do I look like Bettina's daughter? I am dark, dark. My eyes, my hair, my, oh, my everything. How could it not have occurred to me?" She was out of breath, panting with anger. "Magdalena and my father are lovers. Magdalena even had a child – almost certainly by him – at almost exactly the same time that I was born. Did I ever tell you that my own 'mother' would have nothing to do with me when I was a baby? Magdalena did everything, everything. She carried me around with her on her back, she even breast-fed me . . . Yes, almost all my life it has been occurring to me that Magdalena might be my mother." She covered her face with her arms.

He took her hand, "Look," he held her palm up to his face, "it's me, feel me, yes, that's right." He felt her fingers, so soft against his face and across his mouth. "It's all right now, it's all right."

With her body lying against him, he was amazed, appalled, by the sudden strength of his feeling. He could think of nothing, not even of the horror ahead: only of her, standing against him, her face wet, shining like pearls in the dying evening light.

*   *   *

245

It was after dark when they finally reached Altamirada. They found the police station already shut for the night. Eventually, after some investigation, they discovered a back entrance down a narrow alleyway, and after a good deal of knocking a young man's face appeared behind the metal grille in the doorway. His face shone greasily, like the globules of fat on cooked milk, and his hair had a dishevelled look, as if he had been sleeping. The light from the wall above it shone down on his face, illuminating him like an exhibit in a museum.

He replied with sulky brevity to their enquiries. No, Captain Buenaventura was not available, and, no, he did not know when he would be back on duty. Tomorrow morning, perhaps. Yes, there had been some kind of disturbance reported that day but no, he did not know if it involved the hacienda Santa Luz. As he spoke his eyes darted nervously across their faces. Behind him a television screen flickered silently into the bare, neon-lit room.

The moon had not yet risen as they drove on up the mountain road to Santa Luz. At the turn-off they passed the road workers' camp. There was no one about. No lights came from it, not even the smallest glow from a cooking fire. Around each corner, between two shoulders of mountainside, Layla caught a glimpse of the snow-flecked peak of Cotacotani, dark against a dark sky.

At the sight of it a kind of calm descended on her again. 'This is my territory, these are my people; no harm can come to us here,' she repeated to herself. 'Santa Luz has been a place of safety, for all of us, for so long now. What harm can come to us?' Further on they reached the gateway which marked the beginning of the Santa Luz estate. Baltazar stopped the jeep.

"What is it?"

"I'm not sure."

He got out to look. Layla peered out after him into the night. A small tree trunk lay across the road like a barricade, although whether it had fallen or had been deliberately pushed there was impossible to tell. Between the two of them they rolled it easily to one side. Layla sniffed the night air, so cool after the sweet, rotting-fruit odour of the coastal plains, and shivered. She thought back to Zulay and to the long night she had spent in the little room above Romana's fruit stall, a hundred years ago.

Baltazar came and stood beside her. "Let me take you back," he said. "It's not too late you know, no one will blame you. I can take you back to Altamirada and you can stay with Finn."

"I can't do that, you know I can't. Please." Layla put her hand on his shoulder. She seemed very distant still, but calm; far calmer, he realised, than he felt himself. "Besides we may find nothing, nothing at all, you said so yourself."

An arc of light came from the great courtyard, a deep orange burst, brighter than moonlight.

At first Layla feared that they might have set fire to the house, but when they grew closer they could see that a great crowd of people had congregated in front of the house, and that the light came from the glow of their torches.

Leaving the jeep parked out of sight behind the trees, Baltazar went on foot to have a closer look.

"There's no question of taking the jeep in there," he said when he came back, "not until we know exactly what's going on."

"How many of them are there, would you say?"

"About four or five hundred, maybe more."

"Four or five hundred," Layla was astounded. "Are they all from Santa Luz?"

"I don't know, I doubt it."

"What are they all doing here?"

"I don't know that either. We'll have to wait until we get a closer look. Is there still a way to get into the Great Court other than through the main gates, from the other side of the chapel?"

"Yes. There's a place where the wall has partly fallen in. We can climb over quite easily I should think."

"Let's go then."

Even in the darkness, without torches of their own,

Baltazar and Layla found their way easily. As they grew closer the light from the courtyard seemed to grow in intensity. Once they were through the gap in the wall they saw that most of the light was not coming from the torches at all, but from the chapel.

Although there appeared to be no one inside the building or anywhere near it, the whole place was alight. A ritual fire had been lit just outside the entrance. Not only the interior, but each of the steps leading up to the entrance way was solid with wax candles: shining, capricious sheets of them, their flames sending an unearthly brightness into the night sky. In between the candles the steps were strewn with petals, with the blossom of roses and lilies, a voluptuous, pagan river of flowers which dripped from the steps like blood.

"My God," Layla stared, clutching Baltazar's arm, "have you ever seen anything like it?"

"No, never." Feeling a wave of nausea, he put his arm up to shield the lower half of his face. "And the smell from the fire, it's overpowering."

"Incense. They must have been burning it all day."

"But not just the ordinary incense. It's mixed with something else, some kind of herb. The day they buried Aureliano Quintero, that's what it smelt like." Baltazar took his handkerchief out of his pocket and held it over his nose. The smell of death. "Come on, we must find a way to get into the house."

Near to the stone crucifix at the centre of the courtyard, facing towards the house, stood the crowd of Indians. Some of the women had covered their heads, as if they were in church. They stood closely together as though guarding some object, still concealed from view, which lay between them on the ground. From where Baltazar and Layla stood, hidden in the shadows at the very furthest perimeters of the courtyard, it was impossible to tell whether they were shielding it, or imprisoning it, or both.

"It's as though they are waiting for something," Baltazar

whispered. He was watching them closely. "Any idea what it could be?"

"I've no idea," she shook her head, as much at a loss as he. "This is ridiculous," she turned to him, "why are we hiding from them like this? Why can't we just go out there and ask them? I've known these people all my life, they're not going to hurt me . . ."

"No!" Baltazar pulled her back. "Don't let them see you. Not yet. Not until we find out exactly what's going on. Just have a look first, see what you can gauge from here."

Layla looked into the crowd. At first she thought she could recognise most of the faces from the farm, but when she looked more closely she also saw a group of strange men among them, *mestizos* in western clothes, whom she did not recognise. The men's faces were contemptuous or angry. The Santa Luz Indians were more bewildered than angry. She could hear them whispering among themselves in low voices.

Some of the men were dispensing bottles of alcohol, the colourless, potent homebrew of the mountains normally reserved for the biggest feast days. Layla watched as they passed the bottles round, urging the people to drink. "Here, *chico*, drink," she could hear one man saying to a young boy on the outskirts of the crowd.

The boy could have been no more than twelve. Layla watched as the man tipped the liquid down the child's throat, watched the blood rise to his face. Finally, when the boy could stand it no more, the man let go of him, watching in amusement as he came up, gasping and retching, as if he had been held underwater and left to drown.

'*Maricon, ma-ri-con*," the man taunted him, "you drink like a woman, little gay-boy." Calculated, insulting words.

He held the bottle to his own lips, and then shook it impatiently in the boy's direction again.

"Here, drink, gay-boy. You'll need all the balls you can get tonight. Drink!"

But the boy could take no more; he broke away from the man's hold, tears of humiliation shining in his eyes.

Laughing, the man watched him run off, then pushed his way contemptuously back into the crowd. As he turned Baltazar saw that he had a gun strapped to his belt.

There was a movement at the doors of the house. The crowd stirred, a murmuring sound like wind through a field of maize. As Layla and Baltazar watched, the doors opened and a man stepped out. Dazed, he held his hand up to shield his eyes from the sudden light, and then made his way to the base of the steps where the group of strangers had gathered together a little apart from the rest of the crowd. Propped up against the wall behind them, Baltazar noticed, were more guns, rifles this time. The Indian stood talking to the group of men. He then turned and made his way rapidly back into the house. As he ran, the firelight caught the side of his face. Over one eye he wore a leather patch.

"Martin! Martin the Eye!" Layla was nearly in tears. "What is he doing?" She turned to Baltazar. "We must find a way to get inside the house. I've got to know what's going on. What do they all want, for God's sake?"

Almost as if they had heard her question, the crowd stirred again. Layla could see the women's gold beads glittering in the torchlight. Their faces were bowed. A man's voice, cracked with drink, shouted, "*El patrón*, where is he? Why is he hiding from us?"

"Whose *patrón*?" jeered one of the strangers in reply. "What do we want with some white man, some foreigner and his red whore."

There was more shouting, and the crowd surged forwards towards the doors of the house. The strangers, who until now had been waiting nonchalantly, picked up their guns and made their way to the front of the throng.

"Now's our chance, run!" Pulling Layla behind him, Baltazar ran silently, keeping to the shadowline along the walls of the courtyard until they reached the dark recess of the verandah. They climbed the steps; threw themselves, crouched and breathless, against the floor.

"Whatever you do, keep your head down," Baltazar warned. "Don't let them see you."

Lying on the ground, Layla could feel the wood of the floorboards against her cheek, its sweet decaying smell in her nostrils, pungent as smelling salts. She had torn her dress on a nail. The material hung down, flapping against her leg. Her knee was wet; when she put her hand down to feel it, her fingers came away smeared with blood.

Layla watched as Baltazar crawled on his belly, out of sight along the length of the balustrading. When he was within reach of the entrance way to the house he stopped and beckoned her to follow him.

"Look." Baltazar dared do no more than breathe into Layla's ear. He pointed ahead of them into the jostling red and gold throng to where the women stood. "I can't believe it. The Saint. They've brought her out of the chapel."

And there beneath them, in full view now, was Santa Luz herself enthroned in her palanquin, stiff as a virgin bride in her petticoats and gold thread, her black face impassive as she gazed towards the house.

Next, it would always seem to Layla, two things happened at once, in one very slow, all-emcompassing moment. The women picked up the palanquin with the effigy of Santa Luz inside it and began to move towards the steps. The crowd parted to let her pass, and as they did so the doors of the house opened silently to receive her. The next thing Layla was aware of was Jack standing at the top of the steps. As he looked down into the crowd, even in the unnatural, fiery light of the torches, she was shocked by how drawn his face was, as pale as death.

Standing there, at the top of the steps, he seemed uncertain what to do. Uncertain whether to stay or go. Uncertain who to turn to. The crowd in the courtyard fell silent, watching him. At first some of the men started to heckle him, calling out in their insulting voices, but gradually the noise died away as though, for a moment, they too were uncertain of which way the tide would turn. For a few

251

seconds the two sides, *patron* and people, were suspended, facing one another across the burning courtyard.

From her hidden vantage point Layla looked down into the crowd. Apart from the group of strangers, she could recognise all the Santa Luz people, could even call them by name. She found herself reciting their names in a litany: Sebastian Menchu, Santiago's brother, with his sons Octavio and Antonio; Herminia Hualpa and Filomina Quilcana from the dairy; Conchita and Maria-Jesus Amaru; Pablo Yuopanqui; Javier Topa; Clemente Titu; Herman Quispe . . .

'I have known these people all my life,' she thought. 'I speak their language. I know their ways and customs, their feast days and their superstitions. I love them.' And yet, as she watched them looking up at Jack, she had the notion that she no longer knew them at all. It was as if, almost overnight, they had become strange to her. She could not tell if they were hostile or sorrowful or afraid. In the courtyard, through the fire and the smoke, their faces were like bronze masks, faces from another age.

The outcome hung in the balance. Jack looked at the people of Santa Luz below him, and they at him, both sides waiting for the other to make some move. It was, Layla would remember, a moment of surprising delicacy.

"Talk to them," Baltazar willed Jack under his breath, "bring them back to your side. You can still do it."

Go on: Layla willed him too, her heart in her mouth.

But Jack, his gaunt frame casting a long shadow down the steps, stood uncomprehendingly, made no sign. Santa Luz, the black and gold goddess, surrounded by her people, faced him from her candlelit palanquin.

There was a disturbance, only half seen, from the men on the far side of the courtyard. The stillness, and with it that strange hypnotic link, was broken. Layla looked up. The men were gesturing angrily in Jack's direction, and then at the crowd. They were calling things which she could not clearly hear, although even from her hiding place she could see that their movements were threatening. The crowd whispered, hesitated. When they saw this, the men became louder and more threatening than ever. Some of them picked up their guns.

"My God, what has happened?" Layla breathed to Baltazar. The moment was over. Imperceptibly, the balance had been tipped.

"For God's sake, we must do something," she whispered to him. "We must think of something. They'll burn the house down."

"All right," Baltazar pulled her to him, "I don't know if this will work, but I can't see any other way to do it. When I say go, follow me. Don't run, and stay as calm as you can."

"Wait! What are we going to do?"

"We're going to get Jack, and then walk back in with him through the gates."

"What, just like that? You must be mad."

"Is there a way to bolt the gates once we're inside?"

"Yes, I know a way."

"Good; now just follow what I do, OK?" He put his hand to her face. "Trust me. Now!"

Layla watched Baltazar as he stood up and walked calmly along the verandah to the front of the house. She saw Jack turn to face him. Saw his uncomprehending stare as Baltazar put a hand under his arm and led him back through the doors of the house. She saw, too, the way his empty gaze turned to something like shock as, seconds later, she and Baltazar closed the gates, bolting them against the crowd.

"What are you doing?" She heard his cry, saw his shock turn to horror. "Layla, no! Open those doors. You don't know what you're doing." She heard the rich, well-oiled click of a revolver cocked: then the sound of a man's voice behind them, "Good evening. *Señorita. Señor.*"

He spoke softly. She turned. Saw the familiar, half-expected form in the shadows behind them, the watchful, unseen face beneath the brim of a dark hat. "We were not expecting you so soon."

NINETEEN

It is strange how love and death have always been connected in my life. Love and death connected us all as we sat
in the *sala mayor* that evening: you and me, my father, Baltazar, and of course, Quintero.

As I sit here writing this, I can see the room now: that
long echoing chamber weeping cobwebs like widows'
weeds; the death mask of Don Pedro over the doorway;
the damask hangings shredded by the mice. Years ago I
remember you saying that the Peron y Imbaburras must
have been a family of giants, and that the furniture in the
sala mayor was so big that each time you went in there it
made you feel, like Alice in Wonderland, as if you had
shrunk in size. It was curious that he of all people, who
after all was unused to the house's strange symmetries,
should have chosen that room.

I remember being surprised by how small he was, how
insignificant. He wore a stained blue suit, and a shirt,
open-necked. His hands were immaculately clean. Plump
and soft; pale-skinned. They did not look like a killer's
hands. I don't think anyone ever said his name the whole
time he was there. We knew who he was. It was enough.

You were already waiting there when they ushered us
into the *sala*, sitting very upright in one of the high-backed

254

chairs. We all sat down. He placed himself opposite you in the other cardinal's chair, next to the fireplace. You were still pale from your sickness and the skin around your eyes was strained, tinged with blue, as if you had not slept. Two of his men stood behind you, but you looked composed. Your hands lay quietly along the carved arms of the chair. I remember that you smiled at me as I came in, and I knew you smiled to give me courage.

At first, although I am not sure why, I remember feeling absurdly grateful. At that moment there was something almost protective about him, as though he was the only thing which stood between us and the crowd outside. But then what else had I expected? Violence, I suppose. I always had a dread of that. That his men would threaten us, would lay hands on us. On you.

But that was not always his way. He was, in a manner of speaking, a man of subtleties. He knew, for instance, that what frightens us the most is not what is known, but what is not known. Concealment was his art. That is why he had always taken such pains to cover up everything about himself. Why even now, perhaps, he could still walk the streets of Veracruz, or even Altamirada, with impunity. We had all been fed on rumours, on a myth, so much more potent than any single, flesh and blood, fallible man.

"You have been to Veracruz, I believe?" he began. An absurd social question.

"Yes." I think it was Baltazar who answered him.

"And you are soon going abroad, *señorita*, back to your own country?"

"Yes."

My voice sounded so small in the vast room that I hardly recognised it. It was like hearing the voice of a stranger.

"Ah, yes, it is good to travel." He spoke sadly, in his soft accentless voice, as though the thought was something that he regretted. "Travel broadens the mind, they say."

As he spoke, his hands moved along the massive carved arms of the cardinal's chair as if he was stroking an animal. I was fascinated, hypnotised by those spotless, cityman's hands. I could not stop looking at them. Nothing else in the room moved. It was as though he was the only thing in the room that was really, fully alive.

"And you, Don Baltazar, so recently returned from yours." It was a statement, requiring no answer. And then, "You are a Peron y Imbaburra?"

"My father was Patricio Peron."

"Yes, yes," he held up one hand, as though it was not necessary for Baltazar to answer him, as though he already knew everything there was to know about us, every last and most intimate detail of our lives, "and your mother was Filomina Quipu. I knew her."

His eyes seemed to bore into Baltazar, examining him, finding him out. This time Baltazar kept silent.

"We have something in common then. My mother also was an Indian," he said in his soft, dry voice, a voice like dust. "I would like to talk to you, you could be useful to our cause. The liberation of our country depends on the strength of its Indian blood."

"Spilled Indian blood," Baltazar said dryly. "You seem to kill off quite as many of us as you recruit, *señor*."

Quintero digested these words slowly. He had a way of holding his head to one side when anyone spoke to him, so that it was impossible to tell whether he was pleased or angered by their words, but was merely registering them in the vast, dark labyrinth of his mind.

"A pity, a pity," he murmured, "Indian blood, Indian strength is what we need." He turned towards me, "And you, *señorita*?"

And for the first time I found myself looking straight at him, looking straight into his eyes. They were cold, passionless eyes, the eyes of an underwater predator. It was then that I realised that there was no defence against a man like this. He was a vacuum, and because of this men would project anything they liked on to him, hatred, fear, or even love.

"And you, *señorita*?" he repeated when I did not answer him. "What about you, I wonder?"

There was silence in the room as he looked from me to you, and then to my father.

"There are those who claim that you too have – how shall I put it? – the blood of our land in your veins. Although not everyone is in agreement. There seems to be some confusion. *Señorita?*"

I could not look at him. I could not answer. I wanted to comfort you. To say, 'Don't listen to them, don't listen to their lies', but I could not speak. You looked so pale sitting opposite him: this man who had come here, unasked, to play our god and our tormentor.

When they brought Magdalena in, she saw me and cried out as if in pain. They had not harmed her, but I knew she would be in anguish to see me there.

"So," he said as the guard brought her before him, "Maria-Magdalena, the witch of Santa Luz."

Magdalena spat at him. He did not move, but the guard hit her hard across the face. The blow sent her staggering back against the wall. My father made a move to go to her but one of the other guards held him back. I saw a trickle of blood seep from the corner of her mouth. Quintero turned to me again.

"It was a clever move, sending you away to Veracruz."

"She did not send me –" I began.

"She had hoped to keep you away from all this. A most maternal thought."

"Bastard!" My father was struggling with the guard. I could see the veins standing out in his neck. But he looked so old, so weak, that it did not take much for them to hold him back.

"Jack, no. He's just trying to provoke us," Baltazar was studiedly calm. "Don't listen to him," he looked round at all of us, "he's playing games with us, that's all."

"I am sorry you should think so."

It was the only time I ever saw him smile. A brief shadow passed over his lips but did not reach his eyes. He was still absurdly courteous. Apart from the soft, colourless hands caressing the arms of the chair, his body was motionless.

I remembered how they said that this man never slept; that his energy was phenomenal. It occurred to me then that this was not the stillness of tranquillity, but the result of an extraordinary, terrifying control. Behind this semblance of calm was a psychotic tension. He was like an animal, crouched and ready to spring.

"These people are superstitious, of course; they believe all sorts of fantastic nonsense," he went on. "For instance, they believe that there are women among them who can perform rituals, for the crops, for protection against evil spirits, for relief from certain illnesses, and so on. They even believe that these women can bewitch a man to love them, and to give them a child. Isn't that so, *señor?*" he turned his gaze towards my father. "You see, the mothers of children, especially girl children, are thought to have a special power over the land. It's an absurd belief, of course; a belief which gradually will be eliminated. But until then I find that these women are revered to a quite . . . dangerous . . . extent." He paused, flexed his fingers; looked down at his hands as though examining them.

"Of course, if these women are shown to be not quite what they have always appeared, they would begin to have, how shall I put it, less influence."

In the room there was not a sound. Quintero got to his feet and came over to where I was sitting. He took me by the hand, and led me into the centre of the room. Then he turned me round until I was facing Magdalena.

"Is this woman your mother?" he stated the words baldly, without preliminary, in his soft, expressionless voice.

I felt a singing sound in my ears. I could see Magdalena looking at me, her eyes pleading with me, imploring. I tried to answer him, I wanted to, but the words would not come.

"Magdalena," he turned to her, "is this your child, your daughter?"

I could feel my heart beating as though it would break.

"*Yes.*" Magdalena's voice was filled with longing.

"*Señor?*" He turned to face my father.

258

He looked so pale still. I willed him to look at me so that, for once, I would be able to see the truth in his eyes. But he did not look at me. Quintero indicated Magdalena again.

"Is this the mother of your child, *señor?*" he repeated.

"She has always – " his voice quavered, the voice of an uncertain old man, "I believe she has always loved Layla like her own child."

"That is not an answer."

"I . . . it is difficult . . . there was some confusion at the birth. There were two children, you see . . ."

Quintero turned from him contemptuously.

"And you, *señora?*" he turned to you at last, where you sat in the high-backed cardinal's chair, saying nothing, outnumbered, outmanoeuvred, your most private and most painful humiliations uncovered, stripped naked for all of us to see. "What do you believe?" He turned me round to face you. "Do you believe that this is your daughter?"

"No. I don't believe it," you said to him, your voice was very low, very steady, "I don't have to *believe* it. I know it. Of course Layla is my daughter."

"*No!*" Magdalena called out, her face distorted. "It isn't true! Look at her, look at her colouring. She is black, black as I am. How could she be the daughter of the *gringa?* It isn't possible."

"That is not true. Genetically there is no reason why Layla should not be my daughter. I have red hair, you see," you put your hand to your head, pulled out a red gold strand, "red hair carries every kind of gene. My own mother was very dark. Layla takes after her, it's as simple as that."

"No! *Niña, niña* Layla!" Crying, Magdalena held her arms out to me. "*Mi hija*, my daughter . . ."

But by then she must have known that it was too late, that the pretence would not hold any more, even in dreams. I looked towards Baltazar, but he could no longer help me. I was on my own now.

"No," I shook my head, "I'm sorry, Magda, no."

All those years of doubting. But had I ever really doubted? Magdalena tried so hard to make me believe it was true. I don't think she ever dared say so, not in so many words, but there were always hints, innuendoes, stories. Of course it was her hold over Santa Luz, and over all of us. It was her ultimate hold over my father; her surest and cruellest defence against you. They say she went a little crazy after her own baby died. I believe that in her desire to bring it back to life, she told herself so often, and so passionately, that I was her child, that she really began to believe it was true. And there were times, I don't mind admitting, when I wanted it to be.

But there was no time to think of these things now. My denial meant that he was already halfway to breaking Magdalena's power, and with it our hold over Santa Luz. Quintero seated himself in the cardinal's chair once again.

"As I have said," he went on, "these beliefs will be eliminated, but it is a slow process. Have you ever wondered why governments in this country have never tried to do so before?" He looked around at us. "Well, I will tell you. It is because all our governments, since Independence and even before, since the time of the conquest, have been in the power of the Catholic Church. The Catholic Church claims that it has civilised the natives of this continent, that without it they would still be floundering in the mud of barbarism. But what has it really done?" Again he looked around at us, but of course we were not meant to reply. "All that the Catholic Church has done," he went on, "is to replace one set of superstitions with another. 'Blessed are the meek, for they shall inherit the earth.' The Church glorifies the weak and the helpless, but why? So that they can keep power for themselves. Is it any wonder that our people have never progressed? They have been kept in bondage, denied their rights, denied their lands." He turned to my father. "So you will see, *señor*," he nodded, still courteous, "why we must begin by redistributing the land, by giving it back to the rightful owners, to the people."

"You don't really believe that you can do that, do you? Just walk in here and take what you want, just like that? It's not that easy."

260

"Oh?"

"There are people who will stop you; the government, the police –" my father leant forward, but I could hear the hope running from his voice, like sand from an hourglass.

"Of course. The forces of law and order." Quintero's voice was melting butter. "The police." A shadow of a smile passed over his lips. "I met Captain . . ." he thought for a moment, his head held slightly to one side, ". . . Captain Buenaventura the other day. A nice man, I liked him. I think you will find him . . . reluctant . . . to interfere." He looked round with the air of a man dealing with a class of small and wilfully stupid children. "And besides, what makes you think that I will need to do anything by force?" He held out his hands, with their bloodless white skin, palms upwards; a gesture of innocence. "Do not believe all the stories you hear about me, *señor*."

"I don't have to rely on anyone's stories any more, I've seen for myself what you're capable of, God help you," my father passed his hands over his eyes as if to shut out the memory.

"We are not in England now, Señor Hallett. This is a violent land," Quintero said softly. "I use violence against those who understand the currency of violence. But there are other means at my disposal."

But my father was at the end of his tether.

"So what do you intend to do with all my land, once you have robbed it from me? Give it to these people?" he shouted, stabbing the air in the direction of the crowd in the Great Court.

"Jack, please."

You tried to go to him, but it was no use. The guard pulled you back.

"Well, I don't believe you," he went on, oblivious to anyone except the torturer in the chair before him. "Your sort never does. You feed them lies, corrupt them with your false philosophies, and do they ever end up any better than they were before? Of course not. The land will be in your hands, under your control, instead of mine, that's all. In

261

fact, they'll be worse off, because they'll be living with the daily fear that if they resist you in any way, even by the most trivial thought, you will destroy them and their families. At least they have some say now in the running of the land; I give them fifty per cent of all the profits I make. I defy anyone to do more –" he stood up. His whole body was shaking with impotent rage. "You don't understand, how could you: I have given the best part of my life to Santa Luz."

"You are a reactionary. We cannot have reactionaries."

"What?" My father stared at him, stupefied.

"You are like the Catholic Church, Señor Hallett. You resist all forms of change. You know that change will only lessen your power. It is much more comfortable, is it not, to keep things the way they are?"

"That's not true –"

"Why were you so opposed to the building of the road to Santa Luz, Señor Hallett?"

"What kind of question is that?"

Quintero sighed. "Were you, or were you not, opposed to the building of the road?"

"Yes, but that's different, surely you can see that. I want to preserve what is here, the road would only destroy it. If only you'll let me explain –"

The rest of us could do nothing but listen in silence. I remember thinking that this man must have had pity once, pity and compassion, along with this adamantine belief in the rightness of what he was doing. Perhaps, once, he was even a humble man. I tried to imagine what it would be like to live in a world of his creation. A world bereft of the spirit, in which places like Santa Luz would have no meaning; in which land was only a commodity, its ancient resonances lost. A bankrupt world in which quetzals were only birds, and there was no more magic.

Fanatics, bigots, crazymen, call them what you will, they are the stuff of newspaper print, divorced from the lives of real people. But then again, perhaps that was how he saw us too, clinging to this ravaged house, here at the end of the world. For you, and you alone, the prospect of leaving

Santa Luz must have seemed like a release. So why was it then that when you looked at me I saw that your eyes were full of tears?

"What are you going to do with us?"

It was Baltazar who asked the question.

"What makes you imagine that *I* will do anything," Quintero looked down at his hands again, turning them over with a kind of detached interest, "when I have Magdalena to do it for me." Magdalena was still crouching on the floor where she had fallen when the guard had hit her. Her back was against the wall. She was calm again now; like Quintero, her body had taken on an unnatural stillness.

"Don't you think you've done enough to her already?" Baltazar said.

"You really think I should worry about that? She would stop at nothing to destroy me. We are two of a kind." Quintero looked down at her impassively. "She even took the risk of stealing the sacred bird, the quetzal. Didn't you, Magdalena?"

Magdalena said nothing, but she was watching him closely now, her eyes fixed on him, huge, unblinking, like a snake about to strike. He looked round at the rest of us.

"There is another superstition in these parts, which holds that the quetzal is the spiritual protector of Indian chiefs and priests." Quintero turned to Magdalena. "The bird is supposed to accompany them wherever they go, guiding them in their battles. Dying when they die. There is a legend from the time of the conquest about the chief Tecun Uman who fought in single combat with the conquistador Pedro de Alvarado. During the fight a quetzal miraculously appeared over the battlefield, crying out and tearing at the conquistador with its beak. At the exact moment when Alvarado pierced Tecun Uman with his sword, the bird fell dead from the sky, covering the chieftain with its feathers.

"The bird lay like this all night, so the legend goes, but in the morning it rose up, transformed. Instead of having pure green plumage as before, its breast was stained crimson, the same colour as the chieftain's blood."

263

He shrugged his shoulders lightly. "Children's stories, of course, like all the rest, but what can you do?"

"But you'll use these children's stories, as you call them, for all they're worth if they suit you," Baltazar said bitterly. "We know it was you who planted that quetzal on Finn. You knew the legends, and you knew exactly what effect this 'miraculous' appearance of a quetzal would have on the people here."

"Of course." Quintero was unmoved.

He leant his head against the back of the chair and closed his eyes, as though all this talking, all this thinking, had wearied him. When he spoke again his voice was so low we could hardly hear his next words. "And I have especially imagined what the effect will be when they find out that the quetzal has been killed."

"What?"

Quintero did not move, did not open his eyes, "Ask Magdalena."

Magdalena was still crouched against the wall, not moving, as if she had been turned to marble.

"With the quetzal in her possession Magdalena stood a chance of keeping me out of Santa Luz. The bird, even I will admit, has proved an exceptionally powerful symbol. But the quetzal died, isn't that so? Magdalena?"

"No!"

"Yes. Two nights ago."

"No." Magdalena's voice was no more than a whisper.

"But yes. It is well known that you cannot keep a quetzal in captivity. It is miraculous that it lived as long as it did. I was becoming quite concerned." He turned to Jack again. "Before – in her, how shall I put it?, special position here – there was always a chance that she might be able to plead against the penalty, since in theory it only applies to commoners. But in the light of what we have just heard here this evening, I doubt that it will be possible."

"My God, you've really thought of everything, haven't you."

"Which is why, you see," Quintero carried on seamlessly,

264

"Magdalena will now do exactly as I say. And why she will tell the people of Santa Luz to do likewise."

He stood up with the air of someone who had just conducted a long and wearying interview. He had his back to me and, briefly, now that I could no longer see his face, it was as though the spell had been broken. With a strange sense of dislocation, what I saw was nothing more than a small, insignificant man in a dusty suit. And for a moment, for one wild moment, I thought that we might, after all, go free.

But he had crossed the room, and came to stand in front of you. "This is a violent land, Madam. I regret –"

Ever courteous, he held out his hand and led you from the room.

TWENTY

Luke's grandfather's house: a low, grey stone cottage at the foot of hills. From the front of the house, at a little distance, you look out on to a small lake. Waterbirds, duck and snipe and moorhen, feed on it; and each year in the summer, they say, a pair of swans come here to nest.

I never realised how beautiful the winters can be in the English countryside. The light is silver, the skies the colour of gentians. I even enjoy the cold. Luke laughs when I tell him this, and says that secretly I am an Englishwoman at heart. Everything is so pure, so uncomplicated: the earth sleeps, life is pared to its essentials.

On the far side of the lake is a folly, a tiny domed gazebo, raised up a little on the side of the hill. On our first day, even before we had been to see his grandfather, Luke took me there. From the folly you can look down over the lake to the cottage, the woods, and the sweep of hills beyond.

"Coming up here is always the first thing I do," Luke said. "I've always done it, ever since I was a boy. It's a kind of ritual, I suppose."

"I'm not surprised," I breathed in the cold air, "it's beautiful up here."

"I've always thought so." Luke sat down on the steps and looked down over the lake towards the cottage. "My parents never managed to settle for long in one place but this has always been here, for as long as I can remember. I don't come here all that often any more, but it is the one place in my life which has always remained the same. There's a kind of permanence about it. If ever I've been sad, or in trouble, this is always the first place I think of coming back to."

"Houses do that, don't they? They have a way of focusing people's minds, people's energies, I've always believed it."

"Did Santa Luz do that?"

"Oh yes," I looked around me, "but this is a very different kind of place; there is something so simple about it. Santa Luz is many things, but it is not simple."

"I'd like to go there one day."

"Yes." I smiled at him, "I'd like to see you there. One day."

Luke got up, walked a few paces down the slope, stood with his back to me.

"Layla, can I ask you something?"

"Yes, of course."

"You said to me once that you had come here to find answers, but that the difficulty was to know which questions to ask." He picked up a stone and lobbed it into the air where it caught the sun, flashing briefly, white against a cerulean sky, before falling into the water below. "Have you found your questions yet?"

"Some of them; yes, I think I have."

"They were about your mother, weren't they?"

"About my mother, yes. And about me, too. About the two of us, I suppose. Mother and daughter."

"What happened to her, in the end?"

Luke still had his back to me, hunched against the cold in one of his grandfather's old overcoats, the collar turned up. He did not turn round.

"They shot her." My breath was like silver mist on the cold air. "In the Great Court at Santa Luz."

"I'm sorry."

"It's all right. It doesn't shock me to say it nearly as much as it used to."

I sat down on the steps of the gazebo, following Luke's gaze over the dark waters of the lake.

"I think Quintero was intending to kill all of us in the end. All of us except Magdalena, that is, she was still too useful to him. But the police got us out before he could get round to it. They killed Quintero, and most of his men. The captain, Buenaventura he was called, has become something of a hero. Apparently Quintero had tried to bribe him. Buenaventura had been playing him along for weeks, just waiting for the right time to hit back. He's in Veracruz now, in some smart city job."

"And your father?"

"He's still at Santa Luz. He'll never leave, not now. I had a letter from him just the other day. He is not very well, but Magdalena looks after him. He has never forgiven himself for what happened, I don't think. I doubt if he ever will. I think he knew, you know, before any of us that something was happening, he just couldn't bring himself to admit it."

Luke turned round and came and sat next to me on the steps.

"And Baltazar?"

"Baltazar?" I said. "Baltazar was so good to me, to all of us. He took care of everything. Without him I sometimes think I would have gone mad. It was he who persuaded me that I should leave Santa Luz for a while. It wasn't good for me, he said; when I was there I retreated too much into myself. It was he who persuaded my father to write to Connie; he fixed my papers, booked my flight, everything."

"Do you still love him?"

"I think I was in love with him before I even set eyes on him," I said. "I was in love with the *idea* of him, does that make sense? And part of me will always love him. But I think I always knew that whatever happened between us would be finite. Baltazar would never be happy in one place for any length of time. And, despite everything, I am like my father," I smiled at Luke, "I like to stick to one place. Besides, for a long time after my mother's death I found it hard to feel anything much, except her loss."

"You must have loved her very much."

"I loved her, yes. But I felt many other things too. I have begun to think that perhaps these feelings are the questions I have been looking for." I stood up, tucking my hands into the sleeves of my coat to keep them warm. "Baltazar said that if I was going to learn how to love my mother, perhaps I had to learn how to hate her first."

"That's a sick idea."

"Yes, that's what I thought, at first."

"But you didn't hate her, surely?"

"Oh, but I did."

"But why?"

"For all sort of reasons. Because she made me feel guilty, for a start."

"Guilty?"

"I felt guilt for her loneliness, for all her years of isolation at Santa Luz. Because I knew I did not love her enough, none of us did. Because I loved Magdalena more.

"I think that is probably the hardest part." I sat down on the steps again. "My mother was not interested in small children, so when I was little I spent most of my time with Magdalena. I always adored Magdalena. She brought me up as if I were her own. It was she who taught me everything I know about Santa Luz. About the *apus* in the mountains, about Pachamama the mother earth, about the Indians' relationship with the land. Her father, Tio, was what we call a *brujo*, or a *curandero*, a kind of witch-doctor; and she inherited her knowledge, and many of her ritual powers through him. As I grew older there were times when I think she really began to believe that I was her child. If I had not been born so dark, perhaps none of it would have been possible, but as it was –"

"You started to believe it too?"

"Yes; at least part of me *wanted* to believe her. I know it sounds incredible, doesn't it? Unbelievable."

269

"What I don't understand is *why* should you have wanted it to be true?"

"When I think back to it now, I can't fully understand it myself. I think I always had a terror of being the *gringa*; a fear that however much I felt I was a part of Santa Luz, in the eyes of others I would always be the outsider, the one who didn't belong."

I hesitated, feeling a little foolish.

"Go on."

"You won't laugh? I know how bizarre this must all sound."

"I won't laugh." Luke was serious. "I am used to bizarre things."

"It started as a sort of fantasy for me, like the games of make-believe that children play. I used to pretend that I really was Magdalena's child, that I had somehow been stolen away from her when I was a baby, that they had swapped me around with the other dead child, my mother's child, when I was born: Oh, I used to dream about that dead baby, almost as if it was my other self –" I put my hand to my eyes. "Of course, the more I played this game, the more real it started to become. In the end it had such a grip on me that even when I grew older, even when I *knew* it wasn't true, the idea refused to fade completely. I was stuck with this possibility, this half-truth, for ever."

"Didn't your parents ever realise, didn't you ever talk to anyone about it?"

"Never. I would rather have died than admit to it."

As we sat together on the steps, the bright afternoon sky faded to dusk. Around the lake, at the water's edge, the branches of the trees stood out like black paper cutouts. I could hear the sound of the waterbirds coming in to roost.

"You know, the most curious thing I realised recently, is that a part of me always longed for her, for my mother, to claim me back, to make me hers again." I pulled my coat more tightly around me against the chill air. "There was one time when things might have changed. After my First Haircutting. That time I really thought Magdalena had gone too far. My mother was furious. I had never seen her like that before. I can remember her face to this day, white with rage, when she saw what they had done. I remember her insisting to my father that Magdalena would have to go. They had a huge row about it. In the end he agreed. I was appalled, but part of me was glad, too, almost proud. I felt as though she had claimed me back as her own."

"And so what happened?"

"Oh, Magdalena talked him out of it, of course. She could always make him do anything. And after that my mother never mentioned it again. She was beaten. The whole incident was just forgotten, dropped, as if it had never happened." There was an ache in my throat. "I think that's when I began to hate her. I hated her for not fighting harder for me. For not fighting harder against Santa Luz. I hated her because, as I saw it, she was prepared to sacrifice everything to keep my father. Even me."

"Do you still believe that?"

"I don't know." I shrugged. "I have to learn to accept that people do things for many reasons, and that we may not always know what is in their hearts."

*   *   *

The other day I found some letters which you had written to Connie, many years ago. In one of them you wrote saying that Santa Luz was a haunted place, haunted not by ghosts, but by the weight of the past behind it. A past that had no relevance to us, but belonged to other people, other lives. There have been times when even I have thought that there was something about it which was too strong, too highly flavoured, for any of us to bear.

Santa Luz. Capricious, like a god of the old order. Venge-

271

ful and benevolent by turns. Stones and mortar? Or a trick of the light?

My question remains: can a house be held responsible?

*   *   *

Luke stood up. Over the lake the sky was the colour of lilac, tinged with gold.

"It is a shame you couldn't persuade Connie to come with us. I don't know what my grandfather's going to say. Mrs Rogers says she's never seen him like it, he's been in a twit all week," Luke said.

"She was going to come, she really was. I found her sitting on her bed, her suitcase packed; she even had on her hat and coat."

"What made her change her mind?"

I looked down at my hand and at the ring Connie had given me of the two gold dolphins with emerald eyes.

"I don't know. She said something about being too old for this kind of thing; and your grandfather too. She said that they had had their chance," I looked up at Luke, "and now it was ours. She said: 'I will live on in you. Bettina and me, both.'"

Luke took my hand and together we walked down the hill, towards the waiting house.